Praise for

NIKKI TURNER

#1 *Essence* bestselling author

"Few writers working in the field today bring
the drama quite as dramatically as Nikki Turner. . . .
[She's] a master at weaving juicy, 'hood-rich sagas
of revenge, regret, and redemption."

—Vibe.com

"Turner [takes] street literature to the next level,
further proving that she is indeed 'The Queen
of Hip-Hop Fiction.' "

—UrbanPublicity.com

"USDA hood certified."

—Teri Woods, author of *True to the Game*
and *The Dutch Trilogy*

Also by Nikki Turner

NOVELS

Black Widow

Forever a Hustler's Wife

Death Before Dishonor
(with 50 Cent)

Riding Dirty on I-95

The Glamorous Life

A Project Chick

A Hustler's Wife

EDITOR

Street Chronicles: Christmas in the Hood

Street Chronicles: Girls in the Game

Street Chronicles: Tales from da Hood
(contributing author)

CONTRIBUTING AUTHOR

Girls from da Hood

Girls from da Hood 2

The Game: Short Stories About the Life

GHETTO SUPERSTAR

Nikki Turner

GHETTO SUPERSTAR

A NOVEL

One World · Ballantine Books | New York

A One World Books Trade

Copyright © 2009 by Nikki Turner

Published in the United States by One
World Books, an imprint of The Random
House Publishing Group, a division of
Random House, Inc., New York.

ONE WORLD is a registered trademark
and the One World colophon is a
trademark of Random House, Inc.

ISBN: 978-1-60751-868-6

Printed in the United States of America

Book design by Laurie Jewell

This book is dedicated in loving memory
to a man who was indeed a superstar
in his own right . . . my grandfather,
James "Buddy" Lewis

and

To every ghetto superstar worldwide, but
especially those who have crossed my path,
touched, or impacted my life in some way.
There are too many of you to name
BUT you know who you are!

GHETTO SUPERSTAR

Hot Soundz

Fabiola Mays stood under the hot lights as she grasped the sweaty hands of two of the finalists in the talent show. She and her family had traveled a long way—from Richmond to New York City—and winning this competition could make all their dreams come true.

Wearing a curve-hugging silk tiger-print dress with a high side split and low back that fit her to perfection, compliments of her sister, Adora, Fabiola surveyed the crowd for her support team. There they were: Adora and her mother, Viola, were sitting in the middle row. Mom gave Fabiola *the nod,* and a smile. Adora just kept screaming, "You gave it to 'em, sis! You did yo thang guurrl!"

Hot Soundz, the fastest up-and-coming record label in

the industry, had sponsored the contest, and first prize was $50,000, plus a recording contract worth another $150,000. Hot Soundz was slowly taking over the hip-hop and R & B industries, flooding the radio and the music charts with number-one hits and giving The Wizard, a legendary label that dominated the Billboard charts and was run by one of the biggest music moguls, Johnny Wiz, a run for its money.

"And now . . . the moment you've been waiting for." The commentator's voice echoed from the speakers, causing the final five contestants to hold their breath. The host pretended to have a hard time opening the envelope that held the name of the winner. The anticipation was killing Fabiola, and just when she thought she couldn't wait another second, the MC then removed a handkerchief from his pocket and mopped some invisible perspiration from his brow. The crowd and the contestants were in total silence.

Finally he opened the envelope. "And the winner is . . . hailing from Richmond, V-A . . . Fabiiiiioooolllla Maaayys."

Fabiola screamed and leaped into the air, completely forgetting that she was wearing four-inch stilettos and almost breaking an ankle. She hugged and thanked all the other finalists, then, after regaining her composure, she flashed a radiant smile to the stunned crowd. Had the winner hailed from the Big Apple, the New York crowd would have gone crazy with applause, but that wasn't the case.

It didn't matter, though. Viola and Adora more than made up for the crowd's lack of enthusiasm and were screaming and carrying on as if they had just won the competition themselves. As if they had just sung "Fallen" by Alicia Keys in a version all their own. And in a way, they had. They had both sacrificed to make sure that Fabiola achieved this goal. This wasn't her win alone.

Slowly but surely, the tough New York crowd started to come

around. One at a time they began to come to their feet, clap, and cheer. The girl from down South with the songbird voice had won top prize fair and square. And boy, after hearing her sing, they couldn't deny that whatsoever.

Fabiola always knew in her heart that she was destined to be a star. Now, thanks to the prize money and contract, all her family's worries were about to be over. No more robbing Peter to pay Paul, no more shuffling and scraping to get by, no more waiting and anticipating when opportunity would come a-knocking; this time Ms. Opportunity had kicked the damn door down.

As Fabiola walked up to the host she imagined she was at the Grammys. The host placed a platinum chain with a diamond-encrusted Hot Soundz pendant around her neck, and handed her a bottle of Dom Pérignon and a giant check for fifty thousand dollars. She smiled as she stepped up to the microphone. "I just want to thank Hot Soundz for this opportunity and New York for showing a small-town girl some big-city love!" The crowd continued to applaud as flashbulbs popped in her face. She felt that the smile on her face would never go away.

Viola and Adora joined her backstage as Fabiola changed her clothes for the after-party. Her mother hugged her. "We did it, chile!" She turned to her other daughter and said, "Flag down one of those cute attendants with the champagne; we're celebrating tonight!"

The party was all that and a slice of cheesecake: Well-known music artists, actors, and actresses were in attendance. The old-school players mingled with the new school, and the filthy rich touched elbows with the not-quite-so-filthy rich. Everybody that was anybody was there. An endless supply of champagne flowed as the latest music bounced off the walls and both male and female groupies were in full chase.

When Fabiola entered the room, she was called over to De-

Mond Walker, the president of Hot Soundz Records, who was surrounded by some of the upper management of his label. "Fabiola"—DeMond placed his hand on her shoulder—"I don't know if you are aware of it or not, but Hot Soundz is the fastest-growing label in the industry, and we want you to grow right along with us. The prize money and the recording deal is only the beginning. My people were very pleased with the way you performed."

Fabiola couldn't contain her enthusiasm. "I'll do anything you need me to do, Mr. Walker. I'll move my bedroom suite into the studio if I have to, so that the last thing I do before I go to bed, and the first thing I do when I wake up, is record."

"That's not going to be necessary," DeMond assured her, "but it's damn good to hear. So many young artists these days think it's all about the parties and the money; they forget what it took to get here. Speaking of money, you can pick up the real check for the fifty grand from our Manhattan office first thing Monday morning."

Fabiola fingered the platinum pendant they had given her. "I'll never forget what it took, Mr. Walker."

"Oh, and there's one other thing," DeMond said.

"Anything."

"Call me DeMond." Then the president of Hot Soundz walked away.

"Okay, Mr. Walker." She smiled and covered her mouth. "I mean, DeMond."

After learning that she could pick up her $50,000 check on Monday, Fabiola, Viola, and Adora traded in their tiny hotel room for a three-bedroom suite at the luxurious Peninsula Hotel. They shopped during the day, and at night they ate at some of the finest restaurants and even managed to attend a couple of the hottest Broadway shows. They splurged and spent all the money they'd scraped and struggled to save up for the trip, and maxed out a couple of credit cards they had no business with in the first place, because they figured the fifty thousand they were to receive on Monday was only the appetizer—something to keep them satisfied until the main course, when Fabiola inked a deal and big money would come flooding in.

Monday morning bright and early, Viola had the gospel music playing as everyone primped and groomed before heading uptown to Hot Soundz to pick up the check.

"God is good," Viola said as she glided around the room. "See, he's got favor on us that is something way beyond our control. Who would've thought that we would be blessed like this? See what God can do, if you believe? You will achieve," Viola shouted as Adora counted out loose change and put together the few dollars they had left.

"A-men," Fabiola agreed.

"I'll second and third that there," Adora chimed in.

It didn't bother them one bit that they had to scrape together money for the cab fare. Not only were they broke, they were in debt to everybody and their grandkids, but it didn't dampen their spirits, because they could see the pot of gold waiting at the end of the rainbow.

"We got enough to make it over there," Adora informed her mother.

"I told you God had our backs, didn't I?" Viola began singing Kirk Franklin's song "Our God is an Awesome God." She sung that song from the depths of her belly.

"Mommy, we gone get you a deal next."

"Chile, my day is over."

"At least a duet, mother and daughter—picture that." Adora cheered them on, and Fabiola joined her mother in singing the song.

In the highest of spirits as they left the hotel room, Viola continued to sing God's praises in the hotel halls, the lobby, the streets, and all the way over to Hot Soundz. People couldn't help but smile at her, because Viola could carry a hell of a tune and in New York City it was not unusual at all to hear a songbird on the streets. At a street corner while they waited to cross the street a couple of people even gave them a dollar or two because they thought she was singing for money.

Once they arrived at the record company, they noticed that most of the building was surrounded by double-parked vans. They hopped out of the taxi with Viola leading the pack. As they approached the building, a huge man whose name tag read "Jake" stopped them at the entrance. "Hello, ladies. Where are you headed to this morning?"

"We're going to the offices of Hot Soundz Records." Viola flashed a smile.

"Ma'am, there's been a problem upstairs at Hot Soundz Records," Jake informed them.

"Well, what type of problem, young man?" Viola asked. "My daughter here"—she glowed as she looked at Fabiola—"just won first prize in their national singing contest, and right now we're here just to pick up the check as well as sign our contract."

"Well, ma'am," Jake started, "first of all, I would like to congratulate your daughter on winning the contest. I heard her sing and I think it would have been an injustice if anyone besides her would have taken the prize."

"Of course." Viola smiled at him in agreement. "You got that right, young man."

"But . . ." He paused for a moment. "I'm afraid you can't collect your winnings right now."

"Why?" Fabiola asked.

"There is no money to pick up."

"What?" Adora screeched. "No money? What you mean, 'no money'?"

"I got this, Adora," Viola said.

"Young man, if you have something to tell us, you need to just go ahead and spit it out. We have a plane to catch in a few hours," Viola demanded.

"Well, the IRS has shut down the company and frozen all of its assets," he blurted out. "My uncle DeMond owns the company, and I may not even get my paycheck."

"Get your supervisor down here right away," Viola ordered as she placed her hand on her hip, "because we damn sure ain't going to take the word of some fucking doorman. Man, you gonna make me lose my damn religion up in here."

"Ma'am, we don't want you to lose your religion, but he can't come down here, because he might be going to jail his daggone self," Jake said.

"You get someone right here, right now, or else. I'ma tell you, you people do not want to fuck with me. You really don't."

"Ma'am, please calm down."

"Not when it comes to my fucking kids, I won't. Don't fuck with me, okay?"

"It's really not a good idea," Adora advised Jake.

"I don't want to have to call the police to have you removed, but I will," he added. "I do understand your frustrations, but there's no need to take it out on me."

"That's why I asked you to get someone else down here to shed some light on the bogus-ass situation," Viola demanded through clenched teeth.

Jake picked up the phone and called upstairs, only to be told that someone would call him back with more information.

Two hours later they were still waiting, and Viola was pacing the floor and raising hell while Adora tried to comfort her sister and calm down her mother, failing at both. Someone finally came downstairs and told them the same thing that Jake had.

"No, I am not just taking that!" Viola said. "The IRS needs to make good on any deals that were made before they brought their asses in on this here shit. They're saying they had an investigation going on for a while now. Then why in the hell did they let the showcase go on then? Tell the IRS to get down here and face us. Tell them to explain to my daughter"—Viola pointed to Fabiola, who was sitting in a chair in tears—"who has worked her ass off since she was three years old to get to this point that she's not going to be a star because of them. Have them come down here and face me."

Jake and the supervisor still weren't able to offer any new information, and after several minutes of Viola cussing out anyone within earshot, Adora reminded her mother that they couldn't afford to stay any longer. Their nonrefundable discount airplane tickets couldn't be switched to a later flight, and they had to leave in time for the subway ride to the airport. So, with broken hearts and broken dreams, Fabiola, Viola, and Adora exited the building and headed to the airport in silence.

I Shot the Sheriff

The big bird touched down at Richmond International Airport after ten PM. By the time Fabiola and her family got their luggage and found a ride home, the ladies were mentally and physically exhausted.

Fabiola was sitting on her bed soothing her tired legs with lotion when her mother walked in. "Fab, I know this has been a huge disappointment, but don't let it get you down. I'm going to get right on top of this in the morning. There's got to be some kind of a logical explanation."

"Ma, maybe this isn't what I am supposed to do. I mean, this is the second deal that I've gotten and nothing has come of it . . . Why?"

"Baby, this is the entertainment world, and a lot of folks

had deals that didn't pan out before they got their big break. Don't think one monkey can stop a show, or one clown stops the circus. You know your momma: While you were singing your butt off"—Viola gave her daughter a reassuring look—"I was making contacts. I have lots of business cards from people that I met on Friday who were interested in you, and I'll start contacting them tomorrow, too. In the meantime, we'll just continue booking you everywhere we can to get you more exposure."

Fabiola knew it was no use trying to argue with her mother when it came to anything concerning her career. Her mother knew best, and Fabiola would follow her lead. Dropping her head, she softly conceded, "Okay, Ma."

Viola headed to the door. "Now get you some beauty rest. We'll talk in the morning."

"Thanks, Mommy. I know you are disappointed, too, but things will work out for us." Fabiola knew that her mother was more disappointed than she was letting on.

"I know, baby. I am going to sleep now. We'll start fresh tomorrow."

Fabiola fell into an exhausted deep sleep, only to be awakened the next morning by loud knocking at the door. Still half asleep, she snatched the covers from her head and sat up in bed. Maybe she was dreaming.

BANG . . . BANGGG . . . BANGGG!!!

There it was again. The pounding on the door continued. Fabiola was definitely awake now. Who could sleep through that racket?

Fabiola lifted her eye mask and dragged her feet out of the bed. She slipped on her fuzzy bedroom slippers and headed downstairs to see who was beating on the door. *Maybe it's UPS or FedEx with my Hot Soundz check and contract,* she allowed herself to hope. *Wishful thinking.*

As she walked down the hall, she pulled her Victoria's Secret boxers out of the crack of her butt and fixed the straps on the matching tank top.

Viola beat Fabiola to the door. "Okay, okay. I hear you . . . Who is it?" she called out.

"It's the sheriff's department, ma'am." Viola looked through the peephole.

A sheriff's car was parked in front of the house, and two deputy sheriffs stood on the front porch.

Viola, speechless for a change, turned and looked at her daughter.

"Let me see what's going on, Ma," Fabiola said as she unlocked and then opened the door. "Yes? What seems to be the problem?"

Viola reached for her daughter's arm. "No, I will tend to this; you have to protect your image. We wouldn't want any of this—you dealing with the sheriff's office—to be something that the press could dig up in the years to come."

Viola pushed her daughter out of the way. Although Fabiola stepped aside so she wouldn't get knocked down, she watched and marveled at how her mother was always thinking two steps ahead, regardless of the situation.

"Ma'am, my name is Deputy Wiggins. You were served ten days ago with an eviction notice to vacate the property." Deputy Wiggins, a short white guy who looked as though, if he were taller, he could've been a linebacker for the San Francisco 49ers, stood with his hat in his hands.

"Yes, sir," Viola said, "but I called down to the courts and the clerk told me that the city usually has a heart near Christmastime and doesn't evict people after December tenth. I was assured that we had a few more days to make the rest of the payment to the landlord."

"Well, the landlord enforced the order of eviction, ma'am, and you gots to go. Bottom line," his partner, Deputy Justice, spoke up. "We don't have to do no explaining to these people," she told her partner. "You paid your rent and she didn't. Now she needs to pack her things and get out. She should have paid her rent."

Deputy Justice was new on the job. She was five foot six with walnut-brown-colored skin and weighed about 135 pounds, depending on the time of the month. Her face was scarred from the repercussions of running her mouth back in high school, and evidently she still hadn't learned her lesson.

"Look, lady," Deputy Justice barked at Viola, "this ain't no hospice or even chapel, where we are going to feel any sympathy for you. This is what happens when you don't pay your rent: You get put out. Now, you have ten minutes to get your things, because after that the moving crew will be here to sit your stuff out on the curb."

By now Adora had joined her mother and sister and heard what was going on.

"But we have nowhere to go," Adora chimed in.

"Besides," Viola added, "we talked to the landlord and he said that he would give us until the end of the month to give him the rest of the money we owe."

"No, ma'am. What he meant is that he wouldn't enforce the judgment if you paid the back rent that you owe by next week," Deputy Wiggins calmly said to the family, as Justice walked a few steps away.

"Unit sixty-one to Base," Justice spoke into her walkie-talkie, "we are going to need backup at an eviction on . . ." She read off the address on the notice.

"No, we're not," Deputy Wiggins said to his overzealous partner. "We are going to work this out. Now cancel that call," he demanded.

"I don't trust these people," Justice said to her partner.

"*These people?*" Adora checked. "Who the fuck are *these people?*"

"Listen . . . just calm down," Wiggins said to both his partner and Adora while canceling the call himself.

"Sir, is there any way that you could give us twenty-four hours and come back tomorrow so we could move our stuff out and make this easier for everyone?" Since Deputy Wiggins appeared to be the level-headed one, Fabiola tried appealing to him. "Sir, I know you guys don't want to pack up everything we have between the three of us. None of it's packed."

Deputy Wiggins seemed to be listening, so Fabiola continued.

"Is there any way that you could give us like forty-eight hours to talk to our landlord, because I am sure it must be some kind of mistake. My mother is always on top of these kinds of things and I know for a fact that she was working it all out with him. I think there is some kind of mix-up."

"I am not sure if we could do that."

"Listen, Deputy Wiggins, we honestly didn't know this was going to happen. Please," she begged. "Would you help us this one time? Please, sir, it's Christmastime."

"I'm sorry, but this is out of my hands," Deputy Wiggins said apologetically. "There isn't much I can do to help at this point." He paused for a moment. "Maybe we can go to the other houses and come back to you last. At least that way you can get some of your things out."

"Thank you, sir." Fabiola felt relieved that she was able to buy her family some time. "I appreciate anything you can do for us. And if somehow you could manage to delay this until tomorrow, we'll be forever grateful." Fabiola flashed her puppy-dog eyes.

"That's not going to happen," Justice quickly intervened. "You should have thought about that before you were out there shopping for Christmas gifts instead of paying your rent," Justice said as she rubbernecked a few gifts around the big pine Christmas tree that stood in their living room.

"You would be blessed if you could find it in your heart," Viola said, feeling very humbled.

"Don't try that God stuff with us. You need to pray to him to get you the money to pay your rent."

"Sistah," Viola said to Justice, "why are you being so nasty to us?"

"I ain't your *sistah*," Justice spat with a little roll to her neck. "It's poor examples like you that give a real black woman a bad name."

"Fuck you, bitch." Adora had digested just about all the shit she was going to eat from this wanna-be super bitch in a tailored UPS uniform. "Who the fuck do you think you are anyway?"

"I'm the person that's going to lock your broke ass up, bitch."

Fabiola saw the anger in her sister's eyes and said, "She can't lock nobody up, because she a deputy, not a police," but not before Deputy Justice got a face full of spit courtesy of Adora. Deputy Justice blanked the fuck out, doing the only thing that she had been trained to do. She snatched her nightstick out of her holster and charged toward them. But she didn't get far.

"Bitch, you must be crazy if you think you gonna put your hands on one of mines." Viola dropped her calm Angela Davis sisterhood and blessed demeanor and smacked the stick out of Deputy Justice's hand, pushing her to the side. That was all the edge Adora needed to get at her ass.

Wiggins attempted to break up the squabble without hurting anyone, but his strength was no match against two angry women fighting for everything they owned. As he tried to grab Adora, Viola pushed him, causing him to lose his balance. Deputy Wiggins then reached for his radio to call for backup, but Fabiola was quicker to the draw than the deputy sheriff. All that image stuff was out of the damn window when it came to her family. After grabbing the man's walkie-talkie she threw it to the other side of the street.

Viola reacted like a fierce lioness protecting her baby cubs from the wild hyenas in the jungle. With her last rational thought long gone, she hit Wiggins with a solid right to the jaw with the butt of his own billy club. Blood squirted from his mouth, along with a couple of teeth.

The melee had attracted onlookers, including Casino, an old gangsta holding his own—and then some—in the city since the early seventies. He was coming out of a house across the street when he saw what was going down. *What the fuck?* After he realized that his eyes weren't trying to pull a fast one on his mind, and that two deputy sheriffs were indeed going toe-to-toe with three women in broad daylight, he sent a few of his personal goons over to break it up. The ladies were putting it down so hard for a second, he thought about offering them a job.

Casino's muscle did what the two deputies could not: They got the ruckus under control without any more violence than necessary. Casino then walked across the street to ask what the brawl was all about. His command of the situation seemed to calm everyone down.

"Sir, thank you very much for your assistance," Deputy Wiggins said, "but this is a police matter and we can handle it from here." It was kind of difficult to understand what Wiggins said because of his missing teeth and swollen lip.

Deputy Justice decided to remain silent for a change.

"I think we can handle this in a way that doesn't have to cause any more harm than has already taken place," Casino offered. "What we have is a small misunderstanding that led to a huge overreaction by everyone involved. If you allow me a little more of your time, I think I may be able to come up with an amicable solution."

"And what might this *amicable solution* be?" Deputy Wiggins wanted to know.

Casino's smile made it all the way up to his eyes. "Money. The entire situation was caused in one way or another by the lack of money or the pursuit of money."

Casino looked at each of the Mays women one by one. "If these good people would have had the money to pay their rent, they wouldn't have gotten evicted. Am I right?" Then he looked to Deputies Justice and Wiggins. "And all the two of you were doing was trying to perform your job in order to earn an honest paycheck, which equates to"—he paused for a split second and finished—"money."

"What exactly are you getting at?" Deputy Justice broke her silence. Deputy Wiggins shot her a look.

"It's Christmastime, a time for miracles—that's all." There was that smile again. "I don't want you to take this the wrong way. By no means am I trying to—well, you know—act in any way that is unlawful. But I have a friend who works for your department and I happen to know that the governor isn't giving out any Christmas bonuses this year. I'm willing to give you each one thousand dollars just for doing your job. Nothing more, nothing less. And that's all that has to go in your report; nothing more, nothing less. Insurance can pay for your teeth; you can say that you had an accident on the job." Casino never lost eye contact with Wiggins as he said, "Shit, they may give you some workman's comp."

Deputy Wiggins thought about what this gentleman was offering. If his partner wasn't so gung ho, none of this probably would have ever happened. Besides, if it ever got out that he was manhandled by three ladies, and that his radio and nightstick had been taken from him, he would never hear the last of it. "They still have to be out within three hours," he said to Casino.

"Let's give them until say"—Casino shrugged—"five PM."

"But Mr.—" Viola spoke up.

"Casino . . . just call me Casino," he advised her.

"Mr. Casino," Viola said, "we don't have any money or anywhere to go."

"No family?"

"No, sir"—she shook her head—"it's always been me and my kids. Do you mind?" she asked before lighting a Newport. "Our landlord has basically screwed us," she continued after taking a pull and blowing out the smoke. "I gave him half of the back rent that I owed at the first of the month, and he promised that he would work with me until I could come up with the rest."

One of Casino's workers had dealings with this same landlord before, so Casino knew firsthand that he could be less than fair when he had the upper hand. "Some people's word isn't worth the paper they wipe their asses with."

"Plus, that ain't the half of it," Viola said. She felt comfortable talking to Casino for some reason. "You want to hear something funny? This isn't the worst thing that's happened to us in the last twenty-four hours."

"I'm not doing any laughing, Miss, but what could be worse than getting thrown out of your house right here at Christmastime?" He gazed at her, waiting for an answer.

"Your ever-so-talented daughter winning fifty thousand dollars in a talent contest in New York, and the IRS shutting down the company and freezing their assets before she can pick up the check or the recording contract."

"I think I saw something about that on CNN. The same thing happened to one of those big record companies in New York. Hot Soundz." He looked at Fabiola and Adora, who watched from the door. "That wasn't the company that she had the deal with?"

"Yes, it was. My youngest daughter, Fabiola," she said proudly. "Yep, she beat 'em all out." Viola bragged but thought about reality quick. "If it wasn't for bad luck, we wouldn't have any luck at all." She shook her head. "But we ain't giving up."

Casino was a hustler, as well as a visionary and a shrewd businessman, but at the end of the day somewhere under that metal armor he had a heart that always rooted for the underdog. Hell, as a black man living in this white man's world, most of the time he *was* the underdog.

"I don't blame you. And being that there aren't many entertainers to come out of our capital city, I'm going to help you out," he said. "Tonk"—he looked at one of his goons—"get a couple of moving vans over here, pronto. And get some strong bodies and people to pack up their house."

Tonk said, "I'm on it, boss." He moved quickly and began punching numbers on his phone.

Turning back to Viola, Casino said, "I'm going to put you up in a hotel tonight. I have a place that I usually rent out, but I haven't done anything with it since the last tenants skipped out. You and your family can use it rent free until you get back on your feet. Just make sure you keep it clean and well maintained."

"What?" Viola was stunned as her heart jumped with gratitude. No one, including her children's fathers, had ever done anything this nice for them.

"Are you sure?" Viola said in not only a tone but a look of disbelief, which Adora caught.

When Adora saw the doubt written all over her mother's face, she whispered to Fabiola, "I ain't gonna let Ma mess this one up for us." And Fabiola nodded in agreement.

"Ma, come here for a second," Adora called out to her mother.

"Excuse me, sir," Viola said before walking toward the apartment to see what her eldest daughter wanted.

"Ma, don't mess this up. I heard all about this guy, he's legit." Then Adora quickly schooled her mother on Casino's reputation in the streets. "He's a man that could be ruthless if disrespected, but he's been known to have a soft spot for people who have been wronged."

"Really?"

"Yeah," Adora began to plead with her mother. "Please don't jack this up for us."

"Ma, maybe this is a real blessing. Take him up on his offer." Fabiola grabbed her mother's hand. "Please!"

Viola softened up as she looked at her two daughters in their pajamas and slippers shivering in the brisk December air. Although she was hesitant, she'd die and go to hell with gasoline panties on before she let either of her girls be on the streets. She was almost sure that Casino's offer was better than hell. She walked back over to Casino. "Are you sure, Mr. Casino? I mean—"

"I wouldn't have opened my mouth if I wasn't sure," he cut her off.

"I don't know what to say." Tears were forming in Viola's eyes. "Thank you so much."

"That's plenty. It's not plush but it's a place to call home until your daughter lands that big deal. I'll make a call. I can have it ready in a few days. In the meantime I have a friend that has a moving company; I'll make sure all of your things are put in storage tonight. 'Tis the season to be jolly—right?"

That night, Fabiola vowed to herself that she would one day

buy her mother a house in cash. And the icing on the cake would be the power to help someone in the same situation that she and her family had been in, just as Mr. Casino had helped them. As she drifted off to sleep that night in the hotel bed, her thoughts drifted to the man who came along at the right time: Mr. Casino.

The Chicken Shack

It had been three years since the night Fabiola and her family were almost put out on the street. Fabiola was still determined to make it, and during that time she worked hard to make sure she was at the top of her game mentally, physically, and artistically. Her mother continued to work two and three jobs at a time to invest in Fabiola's career, and any money that Fabiola earned she put into her development as well. She took weekly voice and dance lessons, worked out with a trainer for two hours a day, kept a dermatologist on speed dial, and tried to fit the image of the star she wanted to be, which wasn't hard, since her sister Adora designed all of her clothes and was a fabulous stylist. Fabiola was on her grind and took every opportunity that came her way to perform. One such gig was as a singer with Ricky Chunnaly's band.

"Ricky, it's two PM and you haven't called me with the color yet," Fabiola said in frustration as she walked on the treadmill at the gym.

"I'll call ya back in five minutes, I'm about to decide now." Ricky put Fabiola off to the last minute, like he always did. She may have gotten most of the applause when they performed, but in his mind *he* was the real star.

"A'ight, call me back in five minutes, because I need to get my stuff straight. We are still on to meet at six, right?"

"Yeah, that's right: six sharp. And if you not there at five fifty-nine, I'm leaving without you." Ricky had no intention of letting anyone tell him how to run his band, especially not a nobody dreaming to become somebody like Fabiola. Ricky didn't care that he was just a has-been himself. In his prime he had a number-one hit on Billboard's Top 100 chart for sixteen straight weeks. He had plenty of women, money, and drugs at his fingertips and the world at his feet. He became an overnight success. But then he started chasing the pipe more than he chased his craft. He was good, but not good enough for the record company to keep absorbing the cost of the producers and engineers he kept waiting, wasting expensive studio time. Eventually the label dropped him. His reputation in the industry was so bad that no major or minor record label picked him up.

"Well, give me the damn color then so that I can get my shit together, and you won't have to worry about me not being there on time." Fabiola rolled her eyes and mumbled under her breath, "This doesn't make no sense."

"Five minutes," he said. "I said I'll call you then." He hung up abruptly.

Fabiola sighed. "I don't know why in the hell that mother-fucker needs five minutes to decide on a color for us to wear," she said to Adora, who was on the treadmill right beside her.

"Ricky is so extra," Adora agreed, slightly out of breath. "Why does he make such a big deal about the color scheme anyway?"

"It's simple," Fabiola said as she looked at her sister in the mirror. "Because he's an asshole and that's what assholes do."

"I agree, but wouldn't it be so much easier to tell people the color the day before the gig instead of hours before?"

"I think all those years of getting high wore out his common sense."

"The fucked-up part is that the colors he choose is always some shit none of us have in our closets."

"I know." Fabiola shook her head. "Like the other night—rust and gold."

Adora laughed. "How about that time when he was feeling his inner bumblebee and had all y'all wearing yellow and black?"

"Thank God Mommy had that dress in her closet, even though it was too small for her."

"I know, girl, be grateful that Mommy don't throw shit away."

They both laughed.

Fabiola got to thinking. "You know, when I buy her a house we gotta make sure that her closet is extra huge so she can keep all the dresses she wants to."

"Don't encourage her, girl. Mommy will pull out a dress that we ain't ever seen and be like, 'I had this since '82.' "

"You ain't lying either." They laughed even harder. "But as soon as she pulls it out, you'll come up with an idea to cut that baby up some kind of way—asymmetrical—or add some stones or another fabric to it to make it work out and be some star-quality type of shit."

Adora was touched that Fabiola was so supportive of her talent. Even though there were times that she was a little jealous of all the attention that Fabiola received from their mother and everyone else, she knew that Fabiola was the ticket to taking the whole family to the next level. "You know your big sis can't let you go outta here looking like an antique."

"Ain't that the truth? Not over your dead body anyways. I just hope that clown doesn't come with some whack-ass mess like brown and hunter green and you have to run out to buy something."

"Don't hold your breath, because you know he will. I don't want to have to go out and buy anything and deal with that Halloween crowd. But don't worry, Fab, we'll make it work. I just wish that muthafucka wasn't so unprofessional," Adora said.

"You know what? I just try to soak up his madness and think of it as preparation for the major leagues. Putting up with his bullshit keeps me quick on my feet. It'll only make me a better performer in the end, and it'll be that much easier to work with any choreographer, manager, or producer that comes my way—even if they are crazy."

"You right, sis. I'm glad you can look at it like that," Adora said. "That's what makes you special. Not only are you a remarkable singer, you were born to be in this entertainment industry. Because had it been me, that motherfucker would have long been cussed the hell out."

Fabiola smiled at her sister, as she turned up the speed on the treadmill. "Girl, I am about to take my frustrations out on Ricky and put in these two miles."

Two miles later the phone rang. Fabiola reached for it, hoping it was Ricky.

"Hello?" she said, as she gasped for air.

"I'm going to make it easy for you tonight," Ricky said. "Red and white. No exceptions or you will be fined. And don't forget to be on time. Six o'clock on the dot."

"How could I not?"

"It's not like you've never been tardy before. I'm just giving you fair warning: Anybody not on time gets left."

"I heard you the first couple of times, Ricky," she said to him as she grabbed a small towel to wipe the sweat from her face. But she knew good and well that he wasn't going to leave until she got there. How could he leave the *real* star of the show behind?

Fabiola showed up at the meeting spot with her bags packed at eleven minutes past six. Four hours and forty-five minutes later the band was in the deep sticks of North Carolina. Ricky put the van in park and scratched his head while double-checking his papers, and said, "This is it?"

"What the fuck, Ricky? Damn, maaann." Keys, the keyboard player, shook his head and asked, "This is where we're performing? You couldn't do no better than this here shit?"

"Yeah, this the right spot. They supposed to have the best chicken in all of North Kakilaki, and they say we can eat all the chicken we want." Ricky tried to assure his fellow band members that this place was official.

"I can buy my own guyd-damn chicken," Keys said, "as long as that muthafuckin' paper is right at the end of the night."

The Chicken Shack looked just like the name boasted; a wooden barn that probably should've been torn down a long time ago. But if the parking lot was any indication, the place was jam-packed.

"It looks like they may have a decent-size crowd in the good ole Chicken Shack," Fabiola said, hopping out of the van. She was in a hurry to clear her head of all that stinky cigar smoke she was forced to inhale while Ricky chain-smoked down the highway. The clean country air felt soothing as it worked its way through her lungs, but then she was assaulted by the smell of chicken grease. "Wheeew." Fabiola fanned her nose. "That chicken smell is strong."

"This place sho lives up to its name," Boonie, the drummer, said.

They got all their equipment on the dolly and headed in. The venue wasn't much. The stage was in the front and the kitchen was toward the back. There was a dance floor in the middle of the space, and tables covered with chicken-printed tablecloths were lined up throughout. There was enough seating to handle a crowd of three hundred or more. The barmaids wore all black, except for the aprons tied around their waists, which were the same print as the tablecloths. They hustled back and forth from two fully stocked bars making sure everyone's glasses stayed full to the brim. To the left, on the opposite side of the restrooms, was a set of stairs that led to a balcony. The sign read VIP.

Fabiola laughed and pointed to the sign. "Damn, they got VIP in the Chicken Shack?"

They had a little more than a half hour before they were to perform, so Fabiola sat with the rest of the band for a while in a little sitting room the owner had set up for them. Platters of chicken lined the tables. Fabiola had never in her life seen chicken wings that huge. *These people must be shooting them birds up with steroids,* she thought.

Boonie jumped into a plate of the chicken first thing, sucking bones so hard he could have been doing a commercial for the establishment. "Damn, this barnyard pimp is good as a mug," he squealed.

"Fab?" Jack, the trumpet player, called out with his mouth full. "Fab, you gotta get you some of these wings."

"Hell yeah, Fab. This shit right here is gooder than a mutha," Keys insisted.

"I'm afraid to try it," she said. "The way y'all acting, they might've battered it in crack or something."

Ricky nibbled his lip when she mentioned crack.

"Just give it a try," the drummer said.

"Okay, I'll try it." She picked up one of the wings off of the platter and looked at it. It was damn near the size of a turkey wing. After taking about three bites, Fabiola decided that it was good all right—good and greasy. "Did they bring us any bottled water?"

"Nope, but they sent us plenty of this corn liquor." Tommy, the bass player, held up a plastic gallon jug that was more than three-fourths of the way full.

"I'm going to go and see if I can find a water fountain somewhere around here then."

"I'll go with you, Fab," Greg, the sax player, insisted. "Don't want to let you out in that buy-one-get-one-free-chicken-special crowd by yourself."

Greg and Fabiola made their way through the thick crowd. Hands down, Fabiola was the baddest chick in the club. Maybe it was the liquor, or maybe country boys just got down like that, but dudes were pushing up on Fabiola like meat-starved bears. Jaws dropped and mouths drooled; it didn't matter.

"You wanna dance?" One clown grabbed her hand.

"No thanks," she said with a smile.

"Can I talk to you?" another asked.

"I don't think my man would like that." She smiled at Greg, who gave the guy an intimidating stare. Although Greg was as sweet as a peach, with a voice soft as six-hundred-count thread linen, his 350-something-pound physique was definitely threatening.

"Sorry, man, I wasn't trying to get yo woman."

"I understand," Greg said in his soft voice. "She's fine, ain't she?"

One dude, who wore a purple suit, was checking out Fabiola real hard from across the room. He had two women with him, but they must not have been enough, because the thirst for Fabiola was evident in his eyes. Fabiola gave him a once-over; the purple suit was hideous.

She finally found her bottled water at the bar, where she was greeted by one of the assistant managers.

"We've been so busy tonight that I haven't had a chance to come down, meet you, and say hi, as well as show you to your dressing room." As they walked back, he said, "I know it's not much but it is somewhere you can change in private, away from the men," the assistant manager said.

"Thank you so much," Fabiola said, almost bowing, grateful that the club could accommodate her in this way.

As soon as she opened the door to her "dressing room," she was struck by an overwhelming aroma of lemon Lysol, which camouflaged the odor of the smoke-filled club. No chicken smell. "Thank God," she said out loud. A breath of fresh air, finally—even if it did come out of a bottle.

Fabiola's dressing room was normally the employee's restroom. They had brought in a folding table covered with a white lace cloth. Resting on the table was a mirror, a pitcher of water, and a vase with two yellow roses placed inside. *How sweet*, she thought, smelling the beautiful flowers. On the back of the door was a full-length mirror as well as a hook to hang her clothes on. Ten of the band's promotional flyers were taped to the wall.

Fabiola quickly transformed herself into a performer. Her cocoa-brown skin was set off by a red one-shoulder Tarzan-style minidress. Her sexy red stiletto pumps were fierce and their silver heels gave an extra four inches to her five-foot-three-inch frame.

Ricky knocked on her door on his way to the stage. "Almost ready?"

"Yup, go break a leg, I got ya back," she responded to Ricky.

As she painted her lips, Fabiola could hear the crowd singing along with Ricky as he sang his old hit. She could tell by the vibe that they were dancing along as well. Then Ricky tried to slide in some of the new material he'd been working on. That's where he started to lose the crowd. Matter of fact, that's where he always lost the crowd. Even the people in North Kakilaki weren't feeling Ricky's new shit. It was a crying shame; he couldn't even sway the country folks.

The *boos* were Fabiola's cue to hit the stage. She took one quick final look at herself in the full-length mirror and was ready to take on the crowd at the Chicken Shack. Ricky and the band needed her bad.

The band played her introductory medley in the background. "Introducing to you . . . for the first time ever at the Chicken Shack . . . Fabiolaaaahh . . . Maaayys!"

The crowd didn't know her from an ant on the sidewalk, so Fabiola's name meant nothing to them. The women didn't care how beautiful she was and the men were too drunk to notice. She was going to have to win the crowd over with her voice. She began kicking a few riffs just to warm up. The audience started to pay a little bit more attention. And then she turned it up a notch or two. She broke out a pre–Bobby Brown vintage Whitney Houston note, holding it for what seemed like forever. The whole place went bananas. The crowd didn't sit down until she left the stage, dancing and feeding the tip jar all the while.

After the show was over, the whole band sat in the back of the club shaking hands with the patrons, making small talk, and autographing photos. The lines were pretty long.

A woman walked up to Fabiola and said, "I saw you making eye contact with my man the entire time you was singing, trying to be Aretha. Boo, you ain't Aretha."

"Excuse me?" Fabiola looked up at the lady. She looked like she had piled a bottle of Vaseline on her face and probably had a razor blade hidden somewhere behind those big gold teeth that guarded the inside of her mouth.

"Don't play dumb now. I saw yo ass looking at him," she said.

Before Fabiola could respond, Greg stood up, and then Mr. Purple Suit walked up with a girl on one arm and the other empty.

"Baby, I was looking for you," he said to the gold-teeth-having, Vaseline-smeared woman.

Her tone changed and she looked as if she had been busted. "I'm right here, honey. I was just trying to get this photo autographed for you, that's all—since I know you liked the singer girl so much."

Mr. Purple winked at Fabiola and walked off with both of his arm pieces.

"I thought we were going to have to beat up a bitch." Greg always tried to make Fabiola smile.

"I wasn't afraid of horse teeth. I could've taken her if it came down to it," she said and smiled. "I'm not just another pretty face, ya know?"

"Oh, I know 'bout all that. Shorty looked like she might've grew up sparring with pit bulls, but you sho wasn't backing down from her."

"She was tripping from the get-go. I wasn't looking at no man wearing no bright-ass cheap purple suit." They both laughed.

The band was still working the remainder of the line when Ricky came up from behind and handed Fabiola two envelopes.

One contained her pay for the night, and the other held her cut of the tip money.

"Count that shit, Fab, 'cause you know that motherfucker always got some shit wit 'em," Keys instigated.

"You know I'm on it, Keys." She smiled, then took a deep breath. This was the part of the show that she hated most: dealing with Ricky about the pay. She damn near had to go toe-to-toe with the man to get what was rightfully hers. She wished that Viola were there. Her manager would definitely have taken care of this for her.

After getting to her dressing room so she could count her money, she thought, *this shit never ends.* Pissed off, she rushed back to the band's dressing room and charged in.

"Ricky, what the hell is this?" She held up the envelope. "You shorted me a hundred and sixty dollars."

"I didn't short you anything," he said. "I took out for the gas and your fine."

"Gas is usually twenty-five dollars and I don't owe any goddamn fines, Ricky," she said, up in his face and not giving a damn about the rest of the band that was either undressed or undressing.

"That's right. It's *usually* twenty-five dollars, but since we had to come all this long way I deducted sixty from everyone instead of the usual amount."

"Who the hell told you to book us all the way out here if you were going to act petty about the gas?"

"I'm trying to broaden our horizons," he said, doing everything in his power not to look Fabiola in the eyes. He was dead-ass wrong and he knew it.

" 'Broaden my horizons,' my ass. This is some bullshit, Ricky, and you know it." She pointed to his face. "You can't even look me in my eye. Let me do the math on this here shit. Sixty dollars times six . . . or am I the only one getting taxed like this since I am the only female?"

"Nah, he taxed us, too, believe that," Tommy, the bass player said.

"Tommy, stay out of this, all right? You are always trying to keep the peace." She was tired of Tommy's shit, too. Tommy was so far up Ricky's ass, she was sure that he could smell Ricky's shit. It drove her crazy.

"Look, gas ain't cheap, plus oil changes and the general wear and tear on my van all cost money," Ricky tried to defend himself.

"Well, why not charge these motherfuckers who booked us a traveling fee, instead of charging us?" she said. "Whatever, Ricky, I am going to let you have that little bullshit sixty dollars for the gas. But tell me why in the hell my tip cut is not what it's supposed to be?"

"It was divided up among us all," Ricky insisted.

"I have no problem with the band getting their tips, but I do have an issue with you getting a part of *my* tip money. Shit, we bailed *yo* ass out. I heard the *boos* out there and I came running to your rescue like Flash Gordon and shit."

The rest of the band was in the corner laughing, or trying not to laugh, at the gospel Fabiola was preaching.

"I am a part of this band, therefore I deserve a cut of the tips," Ricky demanded.

"Do you?" Keys asked.

"You want to charge us a twenty percent booking fee plus gas, plus you get some of the tips when all you contribute is your one old-ass song. Everything after that puts the crowd in a sour mood, making us have to work a hundred times harder. This is some bull-fucking-shit, and everyone here knows it." Fabiola continued to try to get her point across.

No one said anything except Boonie, who let out a loud fart that didn't break up the tension in the room. Everyone watched the two in action.

"Y'all know she's right. Dead-ass right," Keys continued to add his two cents.

"And you know what? I am so sick of all you niggas talking the same shit and never standing up for yourself." She looked each of her colleagues in the eye.

"Without me, there is no you. You may have came out and sung but they wouldn't have booked you," Ricky said to Fabiola, "or any of you. Not without me or my name or my connections."

"Whatever." Fabiola shrugged him off. "Back to my motherfucking money." She rolled her neck around and said, "Run me the rest of my paper."

She held out her hand.

Ricky gave her dap and started to laugh. "I don't owe you shit. You got fined one hundred dollars!"

"For what?"

"The colors were red and white, not all red. You can't wear anything you want in *my* band, Ms. Fabiola. This ain't Ms. Fabiola Mays's show. For the last time, this is Ricky Chunnaly's and The Band. That's what the contract says, what I say goes, and I said red-and-motherfucking-white. You decided to wear all red," he said while shaking the ashes off his cigar.

Smoke was coming from Fabiola's head and then Ricky went in for the kill.

"You could have worn white shoes or anything," he giggled. "But you didn't . . . and you got fined for it. And no exceptions when it comes to my fines."

"It's past Labor Day. What would I look like wearing white shoes?"

"You a star, you can do what you want! You set trends! Guys, ain't that what she tells us? She's a star." He looked at the rest of the band for a cosigner. No one said anything but Tommy, who grunted in agreement. Everyone else continued packing up their stuff so they could get out of there.

"You could have put on white bracelets or a red-and-white scarf," Ricky went on.

Bunnnppp. Boonie let out another one.

She was shaking her head at the petty S-curl-wearing joker. She smiled at Ricky, which he interpreted as her acknowledging that he had won the argument.

"I don't know why you smiling. No white, then you fined a hunn'ed bucks."

"You know what," she said, "I got yo red-and-motherfucking-white, Mr. Rick the total dick." Fabiola turned around and bent over at the waist and lifted up her dress quickly, flashing her candy-cane red-and-white thongs. "Now, run me my shit," she said while holding out her hand.

The band was in tears of laughter as Ricky paid her the rest of her money.

Scheming on
the Riches

The night had been too long: the drive, playing in the Chicken Shack, Ricky's bullshit, and then the drama with Mr. Purple's girl. Fabiola was exhausted. And then there was Boonie. He had eaten so much of the greasy chicken that his stomach was bubbling the whole ride home. Ricky stopped the van three times so Boonie wouldn't shit on himself and probably would have given him his sixty dollars back if he could've held that gas he was cutting loose all the way down the highway. By the time she reached home, all she wanted to do was take a long bath, get in bed, and go to sleep.

Fabiola turned on the television. She wanted to catch the news to see what was going on in the capital city. She turned up the volume so she could hear it over the running water of the bath while she got undressed. She tested the water with her hand—*perfect*, she thought, and then the rest of her body followed. After ten minutes of enjoying the soothing water, the news music sounded, so she strained her ears to hear.

I wonder what crazy shit has happened now. Did they find Osama?

"Richmond city detectives are currently on the scene of a shooting that took place during a Halloween Party on the city's North Side. We now go live to the scene, where Taylor Thomas has the very latest. Taylor, what can you tell us?"

A young woman stood outside in front of yellow crime scene tape.

"Yes, Jessica. Only a few hours after the initial 9-1-1 call, I can tell you this is still a very active crime scene. Officers are still questioning some sixty people who were at the party at the time of the shooting. Authorities have cordoned off a section of the street, and while investigators have not officially identified the victim, they did release some preliminary information about him. We're told that the unidentified man is in his fifties and a respected real-estate investor who may have had a checkered past. He has a criminal history and may have served time in prison. He was shot in the torso, neck, and shoulder."

While the reporter talked, the camera panned in back of her, where there were people standing around and police cars with their strobe lights still flashing. The camera focused on the reporter again.

"The victim is in critical condition at Medical College Virginia, where a spokesperson has told us they cannot release any additional information about his condition. That's it from here. Back to you in the studio, Jessica."

The screen split to show the anchor and the reporter.

"Thanks for that report, Taylor, but before you go, two questions: Do police have any suspects in this shooting? And when will they release the name of the victim?"

"Jessica, although the police are not officially releasing a name, some of the people who were at the party are saying that he goes by the name Casino."

That name hit Fabiola harder than any of the hot water ever could. She got up and raced for the television remote, almost losing her balance as she slid across the hardwood floor.

"And as far as suspects, all they're saying at this point is that they are looking for two people of interest. We will, of course, continue to follow this story and bring you the very latest when it becomes available. Reporting live from the city's North Side, I'm Taylor Thomas."

Casino?

Fabiola turned the television to another station to see if she could learn more about what happened, but caught only the tail end of the story, which offered no new information.

Although she hadn't seen Casino since the night he helped her family, she often thought about him. By now, her family had lived rent free in one of his houses for three years. He never even came around for a thank-you. In fact, they didn't even know how to contact the man if they wanted to pay him anything. But now she knew he was at MCV.

Fabiola sat naked on the edge of the bed, totally distraught. She had thought of Casino as her Superman, swooping in to save the day when her world had seemed to be falling apart. She wanted to find out if he was all right or if he needed her to help in any way, as he had done for her family when they were in a crisis. She owed him that much. One favor deserved another. Her heart was racing like Dale Earnhardt in the Indy 500.

"MCV, up, up, and away," she said as she dried off and quickly got dressed.

After parking her car, Fabiola rushed into the hospital's waiting room. She couldn't believe her eyes. MCV had one of the best trauma units in the country, and they took anyone, regardless of insurance, so they were always overcrowded. But that morning it seemed as if there were wall-to-wall people. There were mothers with their sick children; a guy nursing what looked to be a broken arm; a woman who couldn't stop shaking; and a man with stab wounds who looked like he was going to bleed out at any minute. In addition to the patients, there seemed to be a ton of people standing around.

Fabiola walked over to one of the clerk's stations. The woman had her head down and was filling out some paperwork.

Fabiola stood there for about a minute, and when the woman didn't look up she said, "Excuse me."

"Yes?" The clerk looked up from her work, clearly annoyed at the interruption.

"I'm trying to get any information you have on a gunshot victim that came in tonight. His name is Casino."

"He must be one helluva man. Everybody is asking about him. He's real popular in these parts it seems. You're going to have to sit down and wait just like everyone else for the doctor to come out." The clerk went back to her paperwork.

It turned out that most of the crowd was there for the same reason she was: to find out what was going on with Casino. Because she didn't know any of the people in his circle, Fabiola felt alone. She tried to sit and wait, but there were no vacant seats.

Wow, he has a bunch of people who care about him, Fabiola thought as she stood next to the water fountain. She thought about leaving. Coming to the hospital was an impulsive decision, but she thought that maybe Casino would need her help somehow. However, it seemed like he had plenty of friends there to support him.

Then why am I still here? she wondered. *He doesn't need me.* Answering her own question, she said to herself: *Because Casino took the time to help a family in need instead of minding his own business like most people would have done—that's why.*

Fabiola's attention was drawn to a big guy wearing a black denim outfit and black boots who was pacing back and forth across the floor. He had to weigh at least three hundred pounds. And from the look on the tall man's face, he was pissed off. He looked kind of familiar to Fabiola, but whoever he was, she sure was glad that she wasn't the one he was upset with.

After observing the man a little longer, it came to Fabiola: He was one of the goons that were with Casino the morning of the eviction.

"How the hell am I going to pay my rent if Casino dies?" Fabiola overheard a woman say who was sitting across from the water fountain whispering to her friend. "You know he been taking care of me since Mike went to jail."

Fabiola thought she must have heard the chick wrong. There was no way that man was lying in the hospital, possibly about to lose his life, and all this woman cared about was his pockets. But once she heard the friend reply, she knew she had heard the woman right.

"You mean *when* he dies," the woman's friend corrected her. "I heard somebody say he got shot so many times the paramedics almost didn't bother to bring 'im to the hospital. They were 'bout to take 'im straight to Scott's funeral home."

Two people came to drink from the water fountain, causing a little water to splash on Fabiola, which was her cue to move. She decided again to look for a chair, which was hard to find. She scanned the room and found another spot in the corner to stand and then moved there. Two women made eye contact with her, and, after appraising her, paid her no mind.

"I know I should have got pregnant by that nigga when we fucked last month," Fabiola overheard one of the ladies say.

"I thought you said he used a condom?" the other girl replied.

"He always does, but damn, I should have put a hole through it."

"I thought you said he didn't fuck you—that you just gave him head?"

"Yeah, that's how it went, but I should have kept the condom and used a turkey baster or some shit."

"Girl, you are crazy. And besides, why would you want to be pregnant by a man that's shot up and could die?"

"So my baby can have his fortune."

"I agree. If I was you I would have just sucked it so good that he would want to give me the fortune anyway. Put me in the will."

The two chicks snickered a little bit.

Fabiola shook her head. *These scandalous bitches,* Fabiola thought as she made sure to get a good look at them so she could tell Casino about them when he got well.

A lady that was dressed like a pregnant nun approached the big guy that was doing all the pacing. "Hey, Tonk, how're you holding up?"

"I'm stressed the fuck out, that's all, ain't much to it," Tonk admitted.

"Me, too, so truly I understand."

Fabiola continued to look around while she waited and saw a woman sitting in a chair fanning herself. *Who is she?* Fabiola wondered. The woman was so beautiful that she almost looked out of place. She looked to be in her midforties and was dressed to the nines, but conservatively. Her black Gucci pantsuit fit her size-eight body to perfection. Gucci loafers matched the bag that rested on top of her knee. It wasn't last season's bag either. Fabiola had seen one just like it in a fashion magazine. The way her curls in her hair were laid down, it wasn't hard to tell that her short haircut probably cost a small fortune in one of those up-scale salons. Fabiola noticed the Rolex watch and the big ring on her left finger and wondered if she was Casino's wife. Whoever she was, she was a diva all the way.

The woman knew that Fabiola was checking her out but wasn't about to acknowledge it—that was her swagger. She had already sized up Fabiola when she had been standing by the water fountain. Had Fabiola been about fifteen to twenty years older then she would have been worried shitless, but knowing good and well that Casino didn't really keep the company of younger women, she brushed Fabiola off as a groupie to the in-famous hood star.

Fabiola's evaluation of the wifey-looking woman was in-terupted when the trauma surgeon came out. He had operated on Casino for six straight hours. The woman Fabiola suspected was Casino's wife ran to the doctor's side, and everyone else hud-dled around him.

"First, let me say that Mr. Winn is a strong man, a fighter in-deed." The doctor squeezed his hands together, trying to relieve some of the tension from the long hours of delicate surgery, not to mention the colorful crowd before him.

"Right now he's stable." There was relief on a lot of people's faces when he said that. "But he's not out of the water yet. And even if he does live, the reality is that a bullet went through his abdomen and grazed the lumbar region of his spine, which could leave him paralyzed from the waist down."

"Oh my God," a woman screamed. She was as attractive as wifey, and judging from her reaction seemed to be close to Casino.

Who was she? Fabiola wondered. *Maybe his sister.*

"Casino is a warrior," wifey said to the woman. "He'll be fine. And all the theatrics aren't going to make this any better than what it is," she added calmly. Fabiola sensed that wifey was annoyed at the other woman's reaction.

Maybe she's not his sister after all. Maybe she's his baby momma or his girlfriend. Casino seems like the kind of man who could pull off a girlfriend and a wife.

"I'm not certain, but he may have to go through a series of surgeries down the line," the doctor said. "But right now he's stable." He patted wifey's hand, and then looked at the crowd. "I'm limiting his visits to immediate family only. Mr. Winn really needs his rest."

"So, what you are saying? Is he going to live, Doc?" a fella bluntly asked. "Will he be able to walk?" another blurted out. The girl who said she needed her rent paid looked like she was about to pass out. Her friend had a smug look on her face like, *I told you so.*

"I'm saying it's going to be tough, but Mr. Winn is a fighter."

Spade, Casino's son and right-hand man, walked away as he waved off the doctor's news. "This shit is for the birds. My pops is on his deathbed and we can't get a straight answer from the gotdamn doctor."

Fabiola was speechless. All she knew is that she wanted to see Casino. But the doctor had said *immediate family only.* The only person she knew was the big dude that everyone called Tonk—if seeing a man one time for a few minutes counted as knowing him, then maybe she could get a favor from him. *But he wouldn't understand why this is so important to me. Maybe he would. What do I have to lose?*

Fabiola looked around for her only shot. Tonk was talking to a lady that looked almost as glamorous as wifey. But this one was tall and thin. She had light-caramel-colored skin and a Farrah Fawcett feathered hairdo. Fabiola couldn't hear what they were saying, but Tonk reached in his pocket, pulled out a twenty, and shoved it in her hand. It looked like feathered hairdo said, "thank you," before switching down the hall as if she had a million dollars in her hand. Tonk went the other way. Fabiola followed Tonk, trying to work up the nerve to approach him.

Then wifey popped up.

"Tonk, I don't know what to do. I'm so devastated."

Tonk gave her a hug. "Roxy, everything is going to be okay," Tonk assured her.

"I hope so."

"It will." He nodded, trying to convince himself.

"What are you driving?" Roxy shifted the conversation.

"I got the Range Rover outside."

"I'm sure that Casino would want me to get the keys from you and keep the truck at my house."

Tonk looked at Roxy like, *Bitch, no you didn't just say that,* but instead said, "No disrespect, but Casino left the Rover in my care and that's where it's going to stay. I've been his driver for ten years, and never had an accident, a scrap, or scratch. Besides"— Tonk tried to make light of the encounter—"who's going to pick him up when he comes home from the hospital?"

"And until that day comes—and I pray that it isn't that long—it won't be necessary for you to be racking up any additional miles on it," Roxy said.

"Look, Roxy." He put his foot down. "Casino left the damn truck with me, and that's where it will be when he comes home." He didn't want to be disrespectful, but she was not leaving him much of a choice. "And frankly, I am not going to be spending energy on talking about a truck or anything material while my boss is lying in a hospital fighting for his life."

"You are not the only one that loves him, Tonk. That's my man that's lying in that bed."

"Well, hopefully we'll be able to get in to see him."

"We will," she said. "The doctor said 'immediate family' and we're the closest thing to that Casino has. I'll talk to you later. I'm going to run downstairs to the cafeteria and get some coffee." She began to walk off and then she turned around and called out to Tonk. When he turned around, she walked back toward him. "Answer me this one quick question?" She put her finger up.

"If I can, you know I will."

"Why weren't you driving him last night?"

"Because I wasn't aware that he was going anywhere last night. He gave me the night off." Tonk had been Casino's driver for ten years, and his friend for nearly twice that, and he didn't feel like he owed anyone an explanation of his whereabouts. But he wanted Roxy to know this: "If you are insinuating that this would not have happened to Casino if I was with him—you're probably right. I would rather it was me in that street bleeding."

Tonk had been wrestling with that thought ever since he got the call that Casino had been shot. And he continued to beat himself up about it. For the life of him he couldn't figure why Casino had given him the night off and went out by himself. "But Roxy, I'm not going to let you or anyone else question my loyalty to Casino—you hear me?"

Jackie walked up and looked Roxy up and down hoping that she was leaving. "You off somewhere, Ms. Roxy?"

"Indeed I'm not, Jackie." Roxy turned her attention to her competition. "I will be here as long as I need to be for *my* man," Roxy snapped back before walking off.

"We'll see, won't we? Because I intend to be here 'til the dust settles," Jackie said to Roxy's back, loud enough for her to hear, even though Roxy didn't turn around.

"Jackie, if you need to go home and take a shower, you can. I will be here," Tonk said.

"No, I got someone bringing me some clothes. And besides I damn sho ain't gonna let that bitch out-sit me," Jackie stressed to Tonk. "You can bet that."

Tonk smiled a little at Jackie's spunk. She had always tried so hard to get Casino's attention. Although she was never successful, she always remained consistent.

Right as Fabiola was about to approach him, someone called out to her. "Hey Fabiola." The voice came from a fake girl named Toy who had been her arch enemy in high school.

I swear I don't need to run into a hater. Not today, not right now.

"Oh, hi! How are you?" Fabiola jumped right into character.

"I'm good, what are you doing up here?" Before Fabiola could answer, she said, "I guess you up here being nosey, huh? Chasing news, like so many of the other folks, huh?"

"Actually, I came up here to see about a dear friend." Fabiola flashed a fake smile as she saw Spade going over to Tonk.

"Oh, okay. Well, have you got signed to a record label or are you still chasing your dream?"

"Girl, I have meetings with some music execs next week." Fabiola bullshitted and changed the subject. "Oh, and how is Rob? I saw him a few weeks ago and he told me that he got another baby on the way." Fabiola hit Toy with a low blow, just as Toy had tried to do to her. "But whenever I see him, I always ask about the two children that he has with you. How are they, anyway?"

Toy lit up and then went in her jacket and pulled out a photo of the kids and began rambling on. Fabiola didn't care, but she played along. She knew that Toy was practice for when she'd really have to deal with the paparazzi and the haters alike.

"Man, I am about to get the fuck out of here," Spade said to Tonk as they stood in the middle of the hall. "Pretty much my work here now is done since I know Pops is alive. It's time for me to get the fuck out of here so I can try to find out exactly what the fuck happened." He adjusted his New York Yankees baseball cap. "I'm going to check a few traps and the crap house. You know gossip come through that motherfucker like a barbershop or a hair salon, so I'm going to see what people talking about."

They both chuckled in agreement.

"Well, I ain't going nowhere. You know I am fucked up already that I was not by his side and a nigga got him. I damn sho ain't leaving his side and let a nigga tear him off."

"I swear, it ain't no security up in this bitch, and the li'l toy cops they got ain't shit."

"*We*"—Tonk pointed to himself then Spade—"security for that nigga laying in there."

"No doubt. But look, you take the first shift and I'll be next shift until we get a read about what's really going on, and 'til we know that he ain't in no further danger."

"Look young'un, he's a powerful man, he's always in danger. You know that."

"I do, but especially now, we gotta hold this shit down until further notice. So, let's do that shit in twelve-hour hits."

"A'ight, I got the first, and find out what you can."

Spade lowered his voice even more. "Who is that bitch over there with the yellow shirt and ball on top of her head?" He motioned with his neck toward Fabiola. "I ain't never seen her before. As fine as she is, I would remember."

Tonk took a look.

Fabiola saw them both look at her and smiled a little as she pretended to be genuinely interested in what Toy had to say.

"She look familiar but I'm not sure. I think that she's the singer chick that your pops gave her family the house on Twenty-eighth. Maybe she here wondering if they gone get kicked out or something."

Spade looked at her. "I seen her hanging around for a while. She wouldn't have been here that long as pretty as she is if Pops didn't have a vested interest in her."

"She is a pretty young thing, but you know your pops ain't interested in nothing young but a piece of chicken."

"As pretty as she is, maybe Pops is changing his ways." Spade continued to admire Fabiola.

"No, I don't see it," he assured Spade.

"But you can't be sure, since you didn't see him going out last night alone either."

Tonk took offense. "That's a low blow."

"No offense. I know you love Pops but I am about to get this motherfucker and beat the block. Let me know if you know hear anything."

"You know I will."

Fabiola ended her conversation with Toy after Spade walked off. Tonk was walking down the hall away from the crowd and Fabiola wanted to catch up with him, but another person got in her way.

This time it was the chick dressed like the pregnant nun that approached him.

"I know this is a bad time, but do you happen to know the combination to the safe that Casino keeps at my house? I need to pay some of the bills that Casino normally takes care of."

"Fuck naw, I don't know the combination to any safe anywhere. And if I did, I wouldn't tell you." Tonk was amazed at how these money-hungry bitches were scheming while Casino was lying in a hospital bed fighting for his life. "I do know this, though: I'll be by your place tonight to pick up that safe until I get word to do different—and it better be there when I show up."

"Excuse me, Miss," Jake said to the pregnant nun. "I need to talk to Tonk." She rolled her eyes and walked off with her tail between her legs.

"Where'd you come from?"

"I just got here," Jake said, giving Tonk dap. "How is shit going? And how the fuck did this shit happen?"

"Shit is still shaky. I'm not sho what went down. I heard five niggas just opened fire on him with techs while he was on his way inside Jackie's Halloween party. But right now," Tonk said, "I'm more concerned about my man's health and trying to keep some order around this here place."

"I feel you," Jake said, slowly shaking his head. There was an awkward silence between them. "Is Spade up here?"

"Naw, man, he just left him. Had you been here earlier you could have caught up with him."

Jake ignored where Tonk was trying to take the conversation and continued with his own. "I've been hitting that nigga all morning and he ain't answering." Jake took a step closer to Tonk. "Spade do got the work, don't he? 'Cause I need to cop. It's the first of the month."

"I'll let him know that you're looking for him when I talk to 'im."

Fabiola sat down and began to digest everything that she had seen and heard. Knowing that everybody wanted Casino's money and really didn't care about him made her really want to get in and see him even more.

Roxy came back and handed Tonk a coffee. "Here you go."

"Thanks, Roxy."

"Look, Tonk, I need you to get some of these people out of

here. And we need to make sure for Casino's sake that none of these damn beggars get back there to stress him out."

"You are so right. I want him to rest, that's all, so he can get himself out of here."

Fabiola decided that she couldn't expect Tonk or Roxy to help or understand why she needed to see Casino.

She thought for a minute and then finally it hit her: *Aunt Rose!* Her aunt Rose had been working in the hospital's dietary department since before Fabiola was born. She didn't hestitate to give everybody a piece of her mind and her ass to kiss when she felt they needed it. Her coworkers knew how she was, and everyone from the doctors to the janitors loved her. If anyone could figure out a way for Fabiola to see Casino, it would be her aunt Rose.

After a couple of minutes of scrolling through the numbers in her phone—not finding what she was looking for—Fabiola dialed her mother's number. After someone picked up on the other end, she asked, "Ma, what you doing?"

"Looking for you," Viola said. "I've only been calling you all day."

"I'd left my phone in one of my other pocketbooks earlier, and been tied up for the past six hours. What's going on?"

"For one, your salsa lessons have to be rescheduled because the instructor had an emergency."

"Is that all?" Fabiola mumbled under her breath.

"I heard that."

"I'm sure you did, Ma. You don't miss much."

"No, I don't. And if I were you I would want to remember how important it is for you to keep up with all your lessons, they'll keep you so much ahead of the game."

Fabiola joined her mother in unison, *"Because that's what it's all about, being on top of your game."*

"Stop mocking me, child."

Fabiola laughed. "Mom, just trying to add some humor to your day, that's it. You know I know you all too well. Why else were you calling me?"

"I need you to come by so we can get you prepared for the photo shoot. You know I've never stopped sending your music out, and one of the music execs that I met in New York finally responded. I sent him a package a week ago. He heard you sing, loves your voice, and wants to see photos of you," Viola said enthusiastically. "You know how they do; they want to see if your look is marketable, and you and I both know that it is."

"A'ight, Ma, that sounds good, but can you do me a favor?"

"What is it?"

"I need Aunt Rose's number."

"Did you hear me?" Viola asked. "I have some people lined up that want to take a serious look at you."

"Yes, I heard you."

"Aren't you excited?"

"Yes, Mommy, yes I am, but I need Aunt Rose's number." Fabiola wanted her mother to take off her manager's hat for a moment.

"Then why don't you sound like it?"

"Because I got some heavy stuff on my mind and I really need the number."

"What can be heavier than the great news I just laid on you?"

"Ma," Fabiola continued, "can you please just give me the number; it's very important."

"Not half as important as what I am saying. Do you understand this man has called three times asking about you?"

"Okay good. Mommy, we will get the pictures done. I promise. Now please give me Aunt Rose's number."

"What do you want with her?"

"I promise I will fill you in on everything later."

"All right then, but I need you to head over here so we can work out the details for the photo shoot."

"Okay," she agreed. "Now, can you give me the number, please?"

"Here's the damn number, girl. Sometimes I just don't understand you."

After writing it down, she said, "A'ight Mommy, thanks. Talk to ya later." She hung up the phone, but before she could dial the number she had written down, her phone rang. It was her boyfriend, G.P.

"Hey, G.P.," Fabiola answered. "Can I call you back in a minute? I need to make a call real quick."

"I just need to holla at you for a second, that's it. I've been calling you all day and the phone been going straight to voice mail."

"I didn't have my phone with me today."

"Well, I need to see you."

"Cool. Let me make this call real quick and then I am going to call you back."

"Promise?"

"Yes, I promise." Fabiola hung up the phone with G.P. and finally made the call to her aunt Rose, who was as crazy as a bedbug and loved Fabiola more than anything.

"Good morning," someone answered, "SPCA, can I help you?"

"Hello?" Fabiola said, confused.

"Have you had your dog spayed or cat neutered?"

"Huh?" Thinking she may have dialed the wrong number, she said, "Aunt Rose?"

"That's what's wrong with this world today; everybody's too

busy to look after the welfare of the little kittens and little doggies."

"I'm sorry," Fabiola apologized. "I must have the wrong number . . ."

"What number you trying to reach, Fabs? You don't want to talk to me because I'm an animal activist today?"

"Aunt Rose?" she questioned. "Why are you talking about four-legged animals?"

"Duh . . ." Aunt Rose mocked, "because the 'four-legged animals,' as you call them, can't speak for themselves."

Fabiola laughed. "I need your help, Auntie."

"Anything, sweety, as long as I don't have to lie, cheat, or steal to do it."

"No, you won't have to do any of those things." *She didn't say anything about smuggling,* Fabiola thought. "It's just a small favor, that's all."

"You always dragging on a damn conversation," Rose accused. "This isn't the last note of a song. It's a conversation, baby. You ain't get that from my li'l sister, that's fo sho. Yo mother never did beat around the bush, especially when it came to trying to get what she wanted."

"I need to get into the hospital to see someone," Fabiola finally blurted out.

"Oh chile, that's my domain."

Fabiola could hear the sound of dogs barking coming through the phone. "The SPCA or the hospital?" Fabiola teased.

"Both. But I was referring to the hospital."

"I need to get in to see someone, but I'm not on the family visiting list."

"A piece of paper never stood between me and what I wanted to get done. And besides, I think it's good for you to visit your friends sometimes. All of that time you spend singing, and this lesson and that lesson, running here and there, doing this and that, you need to have some fun of your own, you still young, girl. You can't keep living your mother's dream."

"It's my dream, too," Fabiola cut in, "but I do agree that I need a break now and then. That's why I really need you to help me get in to see my friend."

"You know I'll do anything I can to help you"—Rose raised her voice to be heard over the barking dogs—"after all, you are my favorite niece. Just don't tell Adora that I said that."

"I won't." Fabiola smiled.

"When do you want to see this friend?"

"Tomorrow, if it's okay with you?"

"You're gonna have to rise with the roosters."

"That won't be a problem."

"And you gonna have to come over and walk the dogs and cats for me one day."

"Again, that won't be a problem."

"And after you make it big you'll go back to school to be a vet-erinarian?"

"Ummmm, that might be a problem." Not wanting to lie to her aunt, she said, "We'll cross that bridge when we get to it."

Satisfied with her negotiations, Aunt Rose said, "Deal, baby. Meet me at six AM, where you dropped me off that time, and Aunt Rose gonna make it happen for you, you hear?"

The next morning, Aunt Rose was waiting at the prearranged spot when Fabiola walked up. Rose looked at her watch: 6:01. "You're late."

"I got caught in morning traffic."

"Just put this on"—Rose handed her a white smock—"and follow me."

They made it past the nurses station on Casino's floor without incident. "I'll check on you in about twenty minutes," Aunt Rose said. "If you need me before then—call."

"Okay. Thanks, Auntie."

The first thing Fabiola saw when she stepped into the room was Tonk asleep in a chair next to Casino's bed. Casino was awake.

Casino slowly looked up, connected to an IV. For a brief moment Fabiola felt sorry for him. He looked worn and haggard, like a piece of old leather that had been stretched to its limit. Fabiola wanted to let him rest, but she didn't come all this way to punk down. Fabiola's heart raced, and she felt unsure as she began to speak to him.

"Mr. Casino, please don't be alarmed," she said, tiptoeing closer to him. "I'm not coming to ask for any money, as I'm sure others have."

He looked like he wanted to respond, but Fabiola stopped him. "Save your energy, I can tell you're tired. I want to assure you that you can relax around me. I just want to say a few things to you." He tried to speak again but seemed to be having a hard time.

Fabiola's voice forced Tonk awake. He was upset at himself for falling asleep. "Do you want her out here, 'Sino?" he said, looking menacingly at Fabiola.

Fabiola looked into Casino's eyes. "I swear I mean no harm and I come with good intentions. You helped me and my family and I just want to repay the favor." She rubbed her sweaty palms together so she wouldn't fidget.

"No, let me hear what she has to say," Casino slowly said.

"Three years ago, we were getting evicted and you came in and saved the day. You allowed my mom and sister to live in your house and you haven't tripped on them for rent or anything. And I really appreciate you, more than you will ever know."

"You"—he took a deep breath and continued to speak slow—"are the singer?"

"Yes, you remember?" Fabiola got a little excited.

"He don't forget anything," Tonk added, then asked, "Did you get a deal yet?"

"Not yet, but I still haven't given up. I have a photo shoot tomorrow as a matter of fact." She then looked at Casino. "And that's why I can press forward, because of you. You didn't even know me and yet you believed in me."

"Ah, it ain't nothing." Normally Casino would have felt uncomfortable talking to a stranger, but he found it easy to talk to Fabiola. Maybe it was the pain medication or a combination of the meds, a pretty face, and her stroking his ego.

"Although it was something small to you, it was big to me. And we never got to repay you, so I'd like to repay you by simply being here for you in your time of need."

"Baby, I am okay." He pushed the words out. "I'm well taken care of."

Fabiola wasn't convinced. "I know, but please, please just let me do this. You've done so much for me and my family already, but if you could allow me to at least come by and check on you, I will feel better about my mom never being able to pay you back."

"You don't have to." He took another deep breath.

"I really want to. I can read to you, I can talk to you. I can sing you one of my future hits," she said with a tentative smile. "I can even watch out for the vultures, because you know they are circling the building, right?"

Casino smiled a little. "I know. They always are."

"I just want to know that you are okay. Because quite frankly, from what I've witnessed in the waiting room, some of the people don't love you for you but love what you got." Fabiola immediately felt that she had overstepped her boundaries and blurted out, "I apologize. I shouldn't have said that."

"You ain't lying," Tonk added.

"I could give Mr. Tonk here a break so he can go home and take a shower daily."

"Looks like she has sold herself—what you think, bro?" Casino asked.

"Shit, she sold me for sure," Tonk said.

"What's all this ruckus about?" the real nurse said as she walked in.

Casino nodded toward Fabiola and said to the nurse, "My daughter."

"She just came up here to check on good ole daddy dearest," Tonk added.

"She's so pretty, and you look too young to have a daughter that old," the nurse flirted as she passed him his pain pills.

"What can I say?" Casino blushed.

"He started out young," Tonk teased.

The nurse smiled. "Well, keep it down in here and"—she looked at Fabiola—"it is really outside of visiting hours and he needs his rest, so you're going to have to cut your visit short. We've made an exception for Mr. Tonk here, but we can't have another person in this room."

"I will," Fabiola agreed with a smile. "Tonk, what time do you want to go home?"

"You don't have to do that."

"I want to though."

"Well, anytime you come is cool but neither Spade nor I will leave his side."

"Well, what y'all gone do? Pee in a cup or something?"

Tonk smiled. "Not exactly, but whatever time you want to come is cool, just let me know."

"Okay, tomorrow I have a photo shoot at one. I may be caught up with that for a few hours, but I should be done and able to get up here around seven PM. Is that okay?"

"Sounds good to me."

"I will see you at seven tomorrow. Casino, do you want me to bring you anything when I come?"

"I think I'll be able to manage, but thanks."

Fabiola was overjoyed that Casino was going to let her visit with him. Mission accomplished.

★ ★ ★

"Click-click-click."

"Say 'superstar,' " the photographer stated before snapping the photo of Fabiola.

"Wait, wait," Viola called out. "Fix that one piece of hair," Viola demanded of Sheena, the hood hair stylist.

Sheena immediately went over to Fabiola and fixed the one strand of hair that was out of place. And she did so with Viola breathing down her neck to make sure it was done right.

"All right," the photographer said, placing his camera up to his eye, "let's try this again."

"Wait, wait!" Viola interrupted once again. "I think we need different earrings," she suggested.

Adora pulled three different pairs of earrings out of a big trunk that was filled with all kinds of accessories. She ran over and held them up against Fabiola's cheek to see which ones looked best. After choosing some jazzy, medium-sized gold-and-diamond hoops, Adora placed the other pairs back into the trunk and turned her attention to her sister, who looked absolutely stunning.

The shoot had been going on for more than four hours, but Fabiola never let her exhaustion show. Instead, she did what any superstar artist on the come-up would do: She sucked it up and did what she had to do. It didn't hurt that Maymount Park, where they were taking the pictures, was a beautiful spot.

"Now smile, say 'Money honey,' and look directly into the camera," the photographer said as the camera snapped a few more shots.

Fabiola switched poses like a pro, wondering the entire time how in the world the photographer could keep the camera lens steady over those pop-bottle glasses of his. She smiled even harder and chuckled at her own thoughts.

"That's right! Perfect smile right there," the photographer complimented. "Now I need you to be ecstatic, like you just won a Grammy."

That wasn't a hard roll for her to play at all; winning a Grammy was a lifetime dream of hers. "I'd like to thank the academy . . ." Fabiola got right into character with a smile bright enough to light up the entire park.

"That's it! Wonderful! A money shot indeed," the photographer said with a smile as he looked at the camera. "That's it. I think we got some really beautiful shots for you to work with."

"I think so, too," Viola agreed, as if unless she had, the photographer would have needed to have taken a few more frames.

"Give me until nine AM tomorrow and I will have the photos ready," the photographer stated while packing up his things.

"At your studio?" Viola asked.

He nodded.

"We will be there at ten." Viola extended her hand. "Thanks so much," she said, shaking hands with the photographer.

That works out for me, Fabiola thought. *I can get to the studio, see the photos, and be done with Mommy by noon so that I can get over to the hospital.*

The photo shoot that Viola arranged was a great success, and the pictures turned out amazing—considering all the events that surrounded the past twenty-four hours.

The long drive to perform at the infamous Chicken Shack, then to finally get home only to hear the news of Casino getting peppered with bullets, which resulted in rushing to the hospital and being there all day long; not to mention overhearing all the different people scheming on the man's money not knowing if he was dead or alive.

Fabiola couldn't believe how disgusting people could be. All of that drama just gave her the insight she needed to know what a *Boss* must go through, and if left up to her, she was going to be one soon.

Fabiola told Ricky that she was going to take a few nights off. Maybe he would learn to appreciate her after hearing the people booing his corny new songs and not having her there to bail his has-been butt out. Maybe when she returned, he would let her sing some of her own material.

The bottom line was that Fabiola needed a little time to relax anyway. She didn't know the last time she had gone to a movie or out to eat at a real restaurant. Well, that was what she was going to be doing late Friday night. She was going out on a date.

Trap Boy

Fabiola met Gregory Parham, who most people knew as G.P., a few months ago at a club in DC. At the time he was the perfect gentleman.

"Hello," he had said, approaching her after she had finished her set. "You have the voice of an angel." He extended his hand. "My name is G.P. and I need an angel in my life."

Fabiola smiled as she extended her hand to the complete stranger, who then took her hand and kissed it. His voice was straight old-school. He must have just watched one of those old Billy Dee Williams movies like *Lady Sings the Blues.*

But over the past few months, Fabiola learned that old-school he wasn't. He was lots of fun to be around—and nobody partied like G.P. Fabiola had promised him that she would spend some time with him, and now she was going to make good.

G.P. pulled up to Fabiola's mother's house—well, the house Casino had allowed her family to use—driving a purple Lexus LX 470, and blew the horn. When Fabiola heard him, she dialed his cell number and told him, "Look, don't anybody answer to any horns around here."

"I didn't mean nothing by it, Boo. You know I'm just anxious to finally get to spend some real quality time with you. Time with you has been hard to come by lately."

"A'ight then," she said, accepting his apology. "I'll be out in a minute."

Fabiola finished touching up her makeup and then pulled on her thigh-high boots on top of her Frankie B jeans. She took one look in the mirror and then slipped on the mink jacket that her mother had bought hot off a crackhead and stepped out ready for her date. When she got to G.P.'s truck, the wheels were so big she damn near needed a stepladder to get in the thing.

G.P. was a certified d-boy, dope dealer, trap star, or whatever the slang term for them was these days. He had tried to keep it from Fabiola at first but it was too entrenched in his blood. G.P. was the type of fella that needed to let people know that he was getting money and a lot of it. G.P. flaunted his cash. Normally, Fabiola wasn't interested in the trapper type of cats, especially the young and dumb ones, but she tolerated G.P. He did buy her nice things, made her laugh, and his sex game was indeed something a best-selling author could write home about.

"We going to that new club tonight," G.P. said when she climbed in the truck. "What's the name of it?" he asked. "The Diamond Mine—that's it," he answered his own question.

"I don't want to go to any club," Fabiola protested. "I thought we were going out to a movie and a restaurant." She felt like she was hanging out at work when she went to clubs.

"I'm trying to floss for my lady, the baddest bitch in the city. Fuck a tired-ass movie. Tonight we gon pop hella bottles of the most expensive bubbly they got . . . do it up in baller-status style. We gon make this grand opening legendary. Let me spoil you, let me show off those boots I bought you," G.P. begged.

That was one of the problems she had with G.P.: He could buy her clothes, make it rain all night on sweaty stripper chicks, and buy out the bar, but when Fabiola asked him to invest some money in her career he looked at her like she was speaking a foreign language. G.P. had no vision, therefore he failed to see her vision. The furthest his sight went was hustling narcotics; if it couldn't be bagged up in a plastic bag and sold . . . it didn't make sense.

Fabiola knew that a real relationship wasn't going to work out for them in the long run, but the last six months had been fun. She'd give him that. What girl didn't like to go on getaways to Atlantic City and New York City and receive expensive gifts? She worked hard and G.P. was just the distraction that she needed.

"I'll go if it means that much to you," she gave in.

"Thanks, Boo." He smiled, showing victory all over his face. "And I tell you what I'm going to do: After the club, I'll cook you a gourmet steak dinner at my house. One of dem steaks that Biggie rapped about."

"But"—Fabiola matched his smile—"I don't want no shit out you come two in the morning after we leave the club when it comes to my steak dinner. I don't want to hear you too pissy drunk to cook for me."

"Nah, I can handle my liquor, plus I can hook a steak up," he boasted.

"Okay, we'll see."

Every baller and wanna-be baller in the city made the grand opening of The Diamond Mine, which had three floors, with a different style of party happening on each one. Downstairs was hip-hop. Dance hall on the second level. And on the third, it was anything goes. That's where the pole was, and the strippers were putting that sucka to work—overtime! G.P. spent most of his time and money making it rain on the third level. He had women circling him like vultures all night long, and he was loving every minute of the attention. At that moment, it didn't matter to G.P. that the prettiest girl in the club was there with him.

Maybe it is time for me to upgrade, Fabiola thought as she looked at how engrossed he was in his surroundings. *He's never going to understand anything other than this.*

"Boo," she called out to him, but he didn't answer, since he was mesmerized by an African chick with a weave that stopped at the top of her apple-shaped butt, who was taking off her clothes to R. Kelly's song "Sex Me."

Fabiola directed her attention at her and realized that the girl was so seductive that Fabiola was intrigued a little herself, so Fabiola waited until the song was over and softly punched him on the shoulder. "G.P., let's go, I want to go home now."

"You gone give me my own private dance when we get home?" The girls lost his attention for a few seconds while he gave it to Fabiola.

"I sure will," she purred, sealing the deal with her bedroom eyes.

"Girls, my baby girl said enough." He kissed Fabiola on the cheek. "I hate to leave but I gotta go," G.P. informed the dancers and grabbed Fabiola's hand, but not before throwing the rest of his five-hundred ones in the air.

A couple of the strippers rolled their eyes at her while the ones about their money grabbed the ones. Fabiola could feel the daggers of hate stabbing her in the back as they walked into the musty smoke-filled crowd.

I don't know why they mad at me, shit I was a good sport as my man made it rain for them. Thanks to my man and my good sportsmanship they can all get off early tonight.

G.P. held on to Fabiola tightly and led her downstairs. Once they got to the bottom of the steps, someone tapped her on the shoulder, and she turned to look. It was one of her brother's women, Cheryl. "Hey, girl."

"Hi, how you doing? You heard from your brother?"

"I've been meaning to call him."

"Well, girl, you know I caught him with a chick."

"Really," Fabiola said, but it was nothing new to her. This was her brother's thing—women. Every man had a weakness. Some it was money, some it was cars, others it was drugs, booze, or gambling. But she didn't feel like lending a shoulder for the girl to cry on that night.

Just then someone else came over and interrupted the conversation. It was her girlfriend Shug. Shug and her had been best friends since ninth grade and they had been partners in crime ever since. They hugged.

"Girl, where you been?" Shug demanded to know, not even acknowledging Cheryl.

"I've been calling you," Fabiola said.

"Girl, I've been so busy and got so much to tell you."

"Sorry, Cheryl, I'm going to talk to you later," Fabiola said, dismissing the woman.

After Cheryl left, Fabiola told Shug, "Girl, you saved the day."

Just then G.P. gave Shug some dap and looked over Shug's shoulder. "Ahllll hell, my motherfucking nigga." Excitement filled his voice and whole aura as he embraced his friend. "Man, when the fuck you came home?"

"Yesterday."

"This calls for a motherfucking celebration," G.P. said and grabbed Fabiola's hand. "This my boo right here. This Fabiola and her friend Shug. This my boy Li'l John."

"Nice to meet you." She smiled at his friend.

A few of G.P.'s other homeboys walked over to say what's up, and that's when the party went to a whole new level. Under the circumstances Fabiola didn't even attempt to break it up. She just grabbed Shug's hand and pulled her along as G.P. took Fabiola's hand and pushed their way through the crowd to get over to the picture booth. If a person wasn't with G.P. and his crew, the only pictures that the other partygoers were going to get were the ones taken on their camera phones, because G.P. decided to rent out the picture booth for the rest of the night.

The song "All Eyes on Me" by Tupac came on just as they popped the first bottle and the bubbly exploded. G.P. knew that the deejay had played the song for him. There was no denying G.P. had not only the bar on smash but the entire club.

Dudes from all over the city were watching G.P., studying his every move. They were either admiring his style, hating on him, praying for his downfall, or scheming on his riches. It didn't seem to alarm him at all. Instead it fueled him and made him continue to ball out even harder. He liked that the fellas were watching him, but even more so, he liked the way their women watched him put on a show, wishing like hell that they were in Fabiola's shoes.

Fabiola held her own, off to the side, playing her position as if she was the queen of the place. Every so often G.P. would go over with the photographer in tow to snap some shots with her and him or her and Shug.

They partied, popped bottles, and danced the night away at the picture booth.

After the last call for alcohol, Shug left and Fabiola whispered in his ear as he held a bottle in hand, "Boo, I'm ready for my steak dinner."

G.P. put his arm around Fabiola and handed a guy their coat-check tickets. He began to give dap to all his homeboys and when their coats came, he helped Fabiola into hers and strutted out of the club with Fabiola on his shoulder as if she was his trophy.

The valet guy had the plum-colored Lexus truck dead in front of the club, so they didn't have to walk far to get in.

Once they had got to his house, Fabiola took her boots off while G.P. slipped on some sweats.

As Fabiola went to drop her overnight bag off in his room, G.P. realized that he hadn't taken the steaks out of the freezer earlier that day. While G.P. was waiting for the steaks to defrost, he tried his hand at seducing Fabiola, but she shut him down.

"A deal is a deal." She was as cold to that idea as the meat on the counter.

"Come on, baby."

"I'm still hungry. I'm starving," she said.

"A'ight, Boo, so let's make the compromise."

"Here we go." She sucked her teeth. "I'ma tell you right now, I am not going to eat no daggone peanut butter and jelly sand-wich."

"I wouldn't do that to my boo. Not my superstar. My song-bird." He leaned in and kissed her. "I got something better than that."

"What?"

"How about I'll run down the street and get some Chinese food and you freshen up so that I can have you fo dessert."

"Sounds like a plan," she said as she batted her long eyelashes at him.

He extended his pinky finger and she did the same, so that they could seal the deal. "Bet."

He put on his sneakers and got in his car to head to the Chinese restaurant. Before he reached the corner, he was ringing her cell phone.

"Hey, Boo," she answered when she saw it was G.P. calling. "I'm trying to clean the bathtub out. When the last time you took a bath in this thing?"

"I'm a man—I take showers. Baths is for broads."

"Oh, whatever!"

"So, how about a little phone sex? Give me a preview and convince me to hurry up and come back."

"You gone come back anyway, right?"

"You know that."

"Well, I could hit you off with a little sumthin', sumthin' now, I suppose," Fabiola purred as she got up to head back into the bedroom.

G.P. started to undo his pants, causing him to swerve and almost hit another car that was speeding in the opposite direction. "Shit, motherfuckers niggas," he spat.

"What's wrong, baby?" Fabiola asked.

"Nothing for you to worry your pretty little head about," he said. "The only thing you need to be worrying about right now is me. Now, wassup?"

"Wassup is I'm touching myself right now and I want you to do the same," Fabiola said as she put her hands under her shirt and began to cup her breasts, rubbing her fingers over her hardening nipples. "Stroke yourself for me, baby. Pretend like it's me touching you. Does that feel good?"

"Shit, girl, you're gonna make me have an accident." G.P. started to sweat as he moved his hand up and down his shaft.

"Naw, baby. Keep yourself in one piece, 'cause I'ma tear you up when you get home," she whispered seductively. Just then she heard something downstairs. The door squeaked like it did earlier when they came in. "Damn, that didn't make you come back home, did it?"

"What? What you mean? I told you that I was going to get the food, right?"

"Isn't that you downstairs? Because there's somebody down there."

"Hell naw, that ain't me," G.P. said, alarmed. "But I know what time it is though." The car that he had almost swerved into looked out of place when he first saw it, but he let his little head override his big head so he didn't pay it any attention. Now he knew what was going down.

He busted an illegal U-turn in the middle of the street. "Hide, or better yet get out the best way you can. Niggas want to come up in my shit, niggas gone die up in my shit. I'm on my way back."

"Huh? What?" G.P.'s words weren't registering in Fabiola's head quick enough, but her survival instincts kicked in and she was fast enough to lock the bedroom door and cut off the light.

"Man, I'ma hit you back. I need to call my niggas."

"G.P., I'm scared," she whispered as she looked around for a place to hide.

"You gotta fend for yo' self until I can get there baby. Hide or something. Hold that shit down 'til I get there. I'm on my way." He hung up.

Before she could get another word out, she heard the line go dead. Fabiola realized that she was on her own.

She heard the footsteps of what sounded like more than one person on the stairs, so she slid under the bed. Once she was under there, she felt like a sitting duck. Her life seemed to be flashing in front of her and she felt at any moment they would come in and duct-tape her, rape her, or maybe even kill her.

I am not going to die without a motherfucking fight, Fabiola thought as she made up her mind to take her life in her own hands and not put it in the hands of some thugged-out stick-up kid. There was no time for tears or waiting for a nigga to kick the door in and kill her. No—survival was the only option. Fabiola jumped up and opened the window. She threw her boots out the window before following and taking the two-story plunge.

She landed in some bushes that were below the window, then fell on the ground. She got up, picked up her boots, and began running for her life. She looked back and saw a guy coming from the front of the house toward her. She pretended to be Lynda Carter and ran like Wonder Woman. She knew her life depended on it. She ran off into the woods that were on the side of G.P.'s house and hid there until she heard G.P.'s tires skidding when he pulled up to the house. She continued to go deeper into the woods, scared to death and not even taking a moment to think or catch her breath or consider how wet her socks must be.

She heard gunshots and then a car speed away. A few seconds later, she pulled out her cell phone and called G.P.

"Yeah, Boo, where you at?" G.P. answered as if nothing had happened.

"Hiding in the woods," she whispered.

"Come out. I'm gonna to be waiting for you."

"Okay," she said to him with tears in her eyes as she made her way to the edge of the woods. G.P. was sitting in the truck waiting on her.

Once she got into the car and before she could shut the door, G.P. began rambling. "Shit is crazier than a motherfucker. Dem niggas was surprised as shit when they seen me." He spoke excitedly, as if he was enjoying the situation at hand.

She let out a long sigh and then noticed a pistol resting on the seat. As he pulled off and was driving away from the house, she pulled her wet socks off and put her boots back on.

"Yeah, I only wished I could have been there when those niggas came up in there. I wish you had gone to get the Chinese food instead of me. I would gave dem niggas the surprise of their fucking lives." G.P. was amped.

"Hello." She waved her hand in front of his face. "What happened to 'Hey, Boo, how are you? Are you okay? Are you hurt? How did you get out?' Just nothing, huh?"

"You alive, ain't you? Shit, niggas could have merked you."

"I know." Fabiola leaned back and closed her eyes and put her hand over her heart. "I was so close to losing my life."

"Yeah, but you didn't." He said, "I know it was probably one of them hating-ass niggas from the club. Mafuckers followed us to the house and shit."

"How they get keys to your house? Because they had a key. They did come through the front door."

He thought about it for a minute. "Shit, I don't know. Could have been dem motherfucking niggas in valet. I gave them my keys and they could have dubbed them." He picked up his cell phone and called somebody. "Dre, meet me on Third Avenue. We need to try to put our heads together and figure this shit out. Oh yeah, and call Jon."

Not Li'l John from the club. That dude ain't been home two days yet and he about to get caught up into some real live gunplay shit. This shit gets crazier by the minute.

Fabiola just listened, praying that he would hurry up and get her home.

He slowed up as they were approaching a stoplight. "Dre, see you in twenty, gotta handle my bizness." He hung up the cell phone as he ran a stoplight and then picked up speed.

"That light was red, Boo."

He ignored her. "Get down, Boo. Get the fuck down now," he demanded and reached for his gun. Before she knew it, G.P. was shooting out the passenger window at the car beside them. It all happened so quick, it was almost like she was in a movie.

Blahka! Blahka! Blahka . . . He let off six rounds from his Glock .40 caliber and caught the other car by surprise. The other car sped off and G.P. followed closely. Fabiola was balled up on the floor of the truck in a fetal position. She looked up and saw the fire that came from the gun as he shot out of the window and thought that she saw a bullet fly over her head.

The car in front of them swerved and G.P. tried to stay with it. He pressed on the accelerator and then slammed on the brakes, running dead into the back of the car. He pushed the car about a half block down the road while Fabiola screamed at the top of her lungs. Relentless, G.P. would not stop until the car in front of him winged a quick sharp right at the last second, making G.P. miss the turn. He didn't continue the pursuit, because he heard sirens coming from the direction the other car was headed. He decided to settle for a fast getaway.

"Nigga, drop me the fuuuuck off! Let me out of this gotdamn car! I'll fucking walk!" Fabiola yelled.

"Calm down, Boo."

"Calm down my ass. Let me out!" she screamed at him.

"I'm going to drop you at your mother's," he calmly told her.

For the rest of the ride G.P. was on the phone rounding up the troops to meet him around his hood. Before the car could come to a complete stop in front of her mother's house, Fabiola jumped out of the car and slammed the door.

G.P. rolled the window down and said so casually, "Look, I'ma call you after I get these niggas. A'ight?"

"Ain't no need, for real."

Fabiola stood on the sidewalk shaking her head in disbelief.

Why the hell am I going through this type of shit? Drive-bys, jumping out the window, running through the woods with no shoes on, dealing with this deranged trigger-happy nigga AND . . . I am still fucking hungry!!! I must be crazy my gotdamn self! What the hell am I thinking about? I could have jeopardized everything I've been working toward. Hell no! Something is majorly wrong with this picture!

Music Royalty

Fabiola was up all night and most of the morning applying ice to her ankle, which she had sprained jumping from G.P.'s window. The events of last night kept running through her mind like a scene from a DVD on repeat, only it was not created under the watchful eye of a seasoned movie producer. It was real, too real. If Fabiola hadn't escaped, no telling what could have happened to her. And to top it off, G.P. had the nerve to act like it was just another day at the office. He actually told her, "Shit happens."

Nigga please, Fabiola had thought to herself. *Not to me it doesn't.* And if she could help it, it would never happen again. Fabiola's mind was made up: She was done with G.P.

and all the rest of the young knuckleheads who were trying to pass themselves off as men these days.

While Fabiola struggled not to get her ankle bandages wet in the shower, she heard her phone ring. She knew there was no way she would have been able to get to it in time, so she let it go to voice mail. After her shower, she dried off, slipped on some lounge clothes, and climbed back into bed. She reached for her phone and checked her messages to find one from her mother, who was calling her from work. Although Fab wanted to rest, she had to meet her mother for their weekly lunch date, and canceling was not an option. Viola had left precise instructions. "Girl, I hope you ain't in bed; it's ten o'clock in the morning."

Fabiola shifted her foot, which was propped up with a quart-sized bag of ice lying on her ankle. "Well, whatever you're doing," the message went on to say, "I want you to meet me at the Applebee's on Laburnum at twelve-fifteen. Adora may not be there, so don't make me wait there alone. See you then."

Fabiola had held the phone out and looked while rolling her eyes. "No 'Not if you're busy' or 'If you don't have anything planned,' but *'See you then,'* "she said out loud before closing her phone. Regardless of her mother's delivery, she knew she had to get up and get moving. Viola had been on top of her business all of her daughters' lives. There was no denying that she loved her girls and wanted better for her daughters than what she had growing up. She loved her son, Ocean, too, but it was different with the girls.

After getting out of bed and dressed, Fabiola drove over to the restaurant and found a spot next to her mother's Honda. She eased her vintage Mercedes into the open space. As she flipped the mirror down on the visor to check her makeup, she realized that besides some slight bags under her eyes from not getting any sleep last night, she looked fabulous. She was wearing a brown velour sweatsuit and brown-on-brown Gucci sneakers. She put her fake Gucci sunglasses over her eyes and strolled into the restaurant.

"Are you eating alone, ma'am?" a skinny waitress standing at the seating station asked. She was wearing a pair of black pants that sagged at her butt, and a burgundy pullover polo shirt with the restaurant's name stitched on it.

"No," Fabiola responded. "I'm meeting my mother and sister. At least one of them should already be here." Fabiola gave the place a quick scan while she spoke.

"I do believe a member of your party has arrived. Follow me, please." The waitress led her halfway around the curved aisle, and Fabiola spotted her mother sitting at a table in the corner sipping on a glass of water with a lemon wedge on the rim.

Viola looked up and saw her daughter. Fabiola never could sneak up on her. None of her kids could. She always knew when one of them was around.

"Hello, Mother," Fabiola said, taking a seat. "Have you been here long?"

"No, only a few minutes."

"Sorry to keep you waiting. Where's Adora?" Fabiola asked.

"She's a bit under the weather."

"Ahlll, I gotta call her."

"You should." Viola changed the subject. "But Johnny Wiz said he loved your photos." Viola was too excited to answer her daughter's question. "I e-mailed the shots to his office yesterday, and his assistant got back to me this morning. How great is that?"

Johnny Wiz was the CEO of The Wizard Entertainment Group and was considered music royalty in the entertainment world. His father was one of the first black rock stars and his mother was an iconic Creole jazz singer. Together, his parents started the label. According to the media, from the time Johnny was old enough to be potty-trained, his second home was at The Wizard. He'd been doing odd jobs at the company ever since he was six. When he graduated from Harvard University, where he completed graduate programs in both business and law, he transformed what was a small independent family label into a major one.

With his father having long ago passed away and his mother's decision to *officially* retire ten years ago—at seventy—Johnny had been running the family's business. Despite a team of top-notch lawyers, advisers, and staff, though, his mother still wanted to have some say, so in the business the final word always came from the mouth of The Wizard. Having his mother in it drove him crazy, but what he could he do? Either roll with the punches or pick another career.

Fabiola had seen many TV specials on him and remembered that the walls of his office held more platinum plaques than he could keep count of. Fabiola always imagined that one day her name would be on one of them.

"Johnny the Wizard!" Fabiola squealed. "Momma, why didn't you tell me that you were in touch with The Wizard? The Wizard Entertainment Group is where I've always wanted to be."

"I did tell you that there were other people checking for you and that I wouldn't stop until we had a deal, right?"

"But The Wizard isn't just other people. He's . . . The Wizard." Fabiola was so excited she could hardly think straight. "Ever since I can remember it has been my dream to sign a contract with them."

"Are you ready to order yet, ma'am, or can I get you something to drink while you decide?" a waitress popped up out of nowhere to inquire.

"Hot tea, please—with two teaspoons of honey." Fabiola had read somewhere that hot tea and honey were good for overworked vocal chords and had been drinking the mixture ever since.

"Anything else?" the waitress asked.

"No, but thank you," Fabiola said

After the waitress was gone, her mother confided, "It was always a dream of mine growing up, too, to be a famous singer on The Wizard, living the life, with a ton of Grammys under my belt."

"I'm going to make it happen for both of us," Fabiola said. "Mark my words: Johnny Wiz is going to love me."

"What is there not to love, baby?" her mother boasted. "You have the voice of an angel, and you're gorgeous. You get your good looks from me." Viola struck one of her best glamour-girl poses.

"When I get the money from my first hit"—Fabiola was already thinking abut the future—"I'm going to buy us all a big house."

"That will be a blessing for sure," Viola said. Fabiola didn't respond. Viola could tell from the expression on her face that she was somewhere else. "A penny for your thoughts?"

"It's nothing."

"Tell that lie to somebody who didn't carry you for nine months."

"It's just that I feel this is the ultimate test."

"Why do you say that?" Viola wasn't sure where her daughter was coming from.

"Because Johnny Wiz is the best of the best. He *is* music."

"That's why he's going to love your stuff. The great always recognize the great!" Viola assured her daughter. "I know you are going to make me proud."

"I just want him to love me the way Hot Soundz loved me."

"Trust me: They would love to have you at The Wizard Entertainment Group, especially after the ordeal over at Hot Soundz. I heard that before Hot Soundz closed they had been engaged in a less-than-friendly rivalry with The Wizard since Johnny took over the reins from his mother." Viola had indeed done her homework.

"You're right, Mommy. I just really want this to happen in my life, like finally, for real."

"Ow," Fabiola exclaimed after accidentally bumping her ankle on the table leg.

"I didn't realize that you twisted it up that bad messing with that hooligan," Viola said.

"Well, that was just one more thing to keep me motivated. I can't take any more episodes like last night."

"I don't know what you saw in that boy."

"Me either," Fabiola said to her mother as she sipped her tea. "But I don't want to waste one more moment thinking about him."

"That's why you can't be dealing with those kind of guys—"

"Mommy, please," Fabiola cut her mother off before she could get into one of her drawn-out speeches about how important it was to have the right man. "I already know where you are going, and last night was the nail in the coffin."

Viola added, "You do understand something like this could have really destroyed your career before it even took off?"

"Yeah, Mommy, I totally get it."

"Good." Viola switched gears. "Did you ever speak to your Aunt Rose?"

"As a matter of fact I did catch up with her."

"You never did tell me why it was so important that you spoke to her."

"Mommy." Fab took another sip of tea, not really wanting to

tell her mother everything, so she stalled a little bit. "You remember Mr. Casino, right?"

"Yeah, of course," she said. "But what does he have to do with Rose?"

"Well, he was shot, and now he's in the hospital."

"That must have been the shooting they were talking about on the news," Viola said.

"He got shot Wednesday night on his way to a Halloween party," Fabiola said. "I went to the hospital the morning of the shooting and it was ridiculous how people were acting."

"I can only imagine. He's a pretty powerful man. But why were you down there?"

"I don't know, Mommy. He's just done so much for us. I felt compelled to see if there was anything I could do for him."

"What did you have in mind?" Viola asked, curious.

"I didn't even think that far ahead. Anything: fluff his pillow, get him water, read him a book, whatever . . ."

"I understand more than you may think, Fabiola. The man reached out and helped us during one of the lowest times in our lives and continues to help us every day by allowing us to stay in his property and not asking for a dime. I think it's really sweet of you to want to be supportive of him in his time of need. I'm proud of you." Viola patted her daughter's hand.

"I am really glad you understand, Mommy."

"I do understand totally, but I don't want you spending so much time there that you take your eye off the prize."

The comment her mother had just made wasn't what Fabiola wanted to hear, so she changed the subject. After a moment, Fabiola asked, "Mom, what exactly are we going to do about that daggone Ocean?"

"What has your brother done now?" Viola asked with a raised eyebrow.

"I ran into one of his girlfriends last night."

"What's so odd about that? If you live in Richmond you're bound to run into one of that boy's friends."

"That's my point," Fabiola said. "It's impossible to try and keep up with all of his women. It's starting to feel awkward when I meet one of his new conquests, because I always end up having to provide an alibi or corroborate a lie. It gets to be too much." Fabiola shook her head. "Why can't he just have two women like most guys his age?" They both laughed.

"They're crazy to put up with his foolishness," Momma said. "He don't look that damn good. I told him that I didn't want to meet any more women until he done bought one of 'em a ring and done proposed."

"And that hasn't stopped him yet, has it?"

The waitress reappeared. "Do you all need anything else?"

"Are you going to take Adora some food since she's not feeling well?"

"It's chicken soup at the house, she can warm that up."

"Just the check—that's it." Viola then redirected her attention back to the conversation at hand. "Well, at least I don't have to deal with as many women as I use to," Viola said. She looked at Fab's plate. "You barely touched your food. What's wrong, baby? You didn't like the chicken sandwich?"

"Just wasn't hungry."

"Wrap it up and carry it with you then."

Right on time, the waitress slid through the aisle balancing a tray of dirty dishes in one hand and their check in the other. She dropped the check off on the table facedown and kept it moving toward the kitchen.

"I just don't like when they try to be my friend, and then expect me to go against the grain when Ocean start acting up," Fabiola said. "I know Ocean got some bullshit with him when it

comes to women but he is my brother, and that's where my loyalty rests."

Viola dug into her pocketbook and came out with a few dollars to pay for the lunch. "Always remember that," she smiled as
she laid the money on the table. "Well, my sweets, I am off to
find out just how much Mr. Johnny Wiz loves your voice and
the ever-so-stunning photos." They both stood up.

"Thanks, Mommy."

"For what?"

"For everything: the lunch and just for continuing to make it
happen. I don't know what I would do without you."

A little moisture formed in the corner of Viola's eye, but she
didn't let it get any further than that. "You are so welcome,
baby," she said, leaning in to kiss Fabiola on the cheek. "You
seem about five inches shorter."

"I'm trying not to put that much strain on my ankle. I need it
as strong as possible for when I perform."

"You're right, baby, take it easy," she agreed. "By the way,
where are you going when you leave here?"

"To the hospital," Fabiola said, "to see Casino."

"I'd like to go," Viola said in more of a question form than a
statement.

"Right now it's immediate family only. Aunt Rose pulled a
few strings to get me in."

"Maybe when he's a little better then," Viola said, hoping his
fine self would be doing all right soon.

Code Blue

"CODE BLUE!" The nurse was running down the hall screaming at the top of her lungs. "CODE BLUE! CODE BLUE!" Doctors and nurses started rushing from everywhere in response to the emergency call.

Fabiola had just stepped off the hospital elevator when she heard the commotion. *Code blue?* In the movies someone was always about to die when they called that out. "Oh my God! Casino?" she whispered. She convinced herself that there was no need to panic, because although Casino seemed to be paralyzed, just yesterday he was alive and he seemed to be progressing. Then she saw three nurses make their way into Casino's room. Fabiola's heart dropped to the soles of her Gucci sneakers. When she tried to enter the room, she was stopped at the door.

"I'm sorry, ma'am, but no one is allowed inside right now," a nurse told her.

Casino's hospital room was a madhouse. The first nurse had sounded off the code blue less than sixty seconds earlier, and now the room was filled with medical attention. Three doctors and seven nurses; it was incredible how so many people could manage to be so efficient to save a person's life without getting in one another's way. The electronic line on the EKG machine barely showed a blip. "Why are his vitals so weak?" a young doctor asked while the primary doctor ripped off the patient's gown, preparing to give him the defibrillator.

"Three, two, one," he counted down before applying the steel disc to the patient's chest. "Clear." The force of the current caused the body to lift several inches off the bed. The doctor who administered the procedure looked at the EKG. No change. "Again." The doctor tried to jump-start the dying man's heart once again. "Nothing." The young doctor gave him a shot from a long syringe.

"We're losing him," one of the nurses said.

The head doctor in charge was annoyed by the nurse's observation. "Please don't waste what little time we have with the obvious, Nurse Parker."

"Y'all let the motherfucker die, huh?" Spade called out. He and Roxy had been in the room the whole time, unbeknownst to the medical staff.

"Excuse me," Nurse Parker said, "but the two of you are going to have to wait outside."

Fabiola was waiting by the door when Spade and Roxy stepped out. "Is he okay?" Fabiola asked.

"Muthafucka dead as a doorknob," Spade said. Fabiola felt a huge lump rise in her throat.

"How could you be so crude about Casino dying?"

"Who said anything about Casino? I was talking about the Indian dude . . . his roommate."

Relief flooded Fabiola's body. She had been taken on an emotional 180 in the course of a few minutes. "By the way, didn't I see you up here the other day?" Spade asked.

"You may have."

There was no *may have* about it; he wouldn't have forgotten someone as beautiful as the woman standing before him if he'd been beaten across the head with a bat and given amnesia.

"Well, my name is Spade." He smiled and offered his hand. "I'm Casino's son. What's ya name?"

"Fabiola."

"Fabiola? That's a beautiful name. Did your mother name you that or did you pick it yourself?"

"My mother gave it to me. She said that God told her to give me that name because I was going to be the fabulous one, and her name is Viola, so she combined her name with Fabulous."

"Indeed you are 'fabulous.' " Spade looked her over and licked his lips.

"So, how long you been fucking Casino, or do you just suck his dick?" Roxy never was one for a whole lot of small talk when she wanted to know something.

"Excuse me?" Fabiola turned to the lady that she remembered thinking was Casino's wife the first day she saw her at the hospital.

"I said," Roxy repeated, moving her neck a little bit, "how long you been fucking Casino?"

"I'm not sure what your relationship is to Casino, but I am sure that *my* sex life is none of your business." Fabiola didn't back down one inch. Spade was impressed by the way Fabiola handled herself. He knew firsthand that Roxy could be intimidating sometimes.

"Everything about you is my business when it comes to Casino, little Fab-be-ola." She let her name roll off her tongue.

"Then you are talking to the wrong person; it sounds to me like you need to be addressing your concerns to Casino—not me."

"Put your fangs away, Aunt Roxy, and be nice to our guest," Spade finally intervened. Turning his attention to Fabiola, he said, "Ms. Fabiola, please excuse my Aunt Roxy. We are all going through a real trying time right now, so tempers may tend to flare a little more than usual, although Roxy can be a bitch at any time."

"Watch who you call a bitch, young man," Roxy cut in. Fabiola took it all in, and although she was a bit intimidated, she smiled on the outside, as if Roxy hadn't offended her one bit.

"Now," Spade continued his conversation with Fabiola, "what did you say your relationship to Pops was?"

"You all can come back in now," the nurse said, wearing a haggard smile. The patient had pulled through and it was on to the next crisis. That was the way MCV operated. A lot of years during the late eighties and early nineties Richmond was labeled the "murder capital," and if it wasn't for MCV's top-notch trauma unit the murder rate would have probably been at least double what it was.

"I didn't," Fabiola answered Spade's last question as she headed into the room to see Casino.

"Well, if it ain't Whitney Houston." Casino smiled when Fabiola walked through the door.

"My voice ain't quite as good as Whitney's in her prime, but I'm not on crack either, so maybe one day it will be."

"Well, too bad for Whitney, and good for you. Crack is whack."

Spade wasn't sure about Fabiola and Casino's relationship, but after hearing the quick banter, and seeing the smile on Casino's face he knew she would be good for his spirits. And he had no intentions of letting Roxy sit there and run interference. "Come on, Aunt Roxy. Let's go down to the cafeteria." Spade read her eyes. Roxy didn't want to leave the young threat alone with Casino. "Come on"—Spade grabbed her hand—"she's out of Dad's age bracket anyway. She's more my taste." Spade winked at Fabiola as he and Roxy left the room holding hands.

Casino already looked better than he did the day before. He was wearing a pair of new plaid Polo pajamas and his hair had been freshly cut. His side of the room was filled with flowers, cards, and fruit baskets. He and Fabiola were alone for the first time, and Casino tried to break the awkwardness. "Are you going to sing for me?"

"I can. What would you like me to sing?" Fabiola took off her sweat-suit jacket, making herself comfortable.

"I didn't mean to put you on the spot. You can sing whatever you like, anytime you like."

"No problem. I'm taking requests, so you let me know what you want to hear."

"You know any Roberta Flack?"

"Yup," and she begin to sing "The Closer I Get to You." Her voiced carried outside Casino's room and a couple of people came into the room to hear her. After she was done with the song, people clapped, and so did Casino.

"Bravo! Bravo!" He smiled. "Your mother wasn't lying at all. I had no idea you were so talented."

"Thank you," Fabiola said, blushing. Although Fabiola got

compliments on her voice all the time, getting one from Casino surprised and delighted her.

"How did your photo shoot go yesterday?"

"It went wonderful. We picked up the photos today." Fabiola was surprised that he remembered.

"Did you bring any?"

"I didn't think you would want to see them, but I can bring them when I come tomorrow. My mother sent some of them to Johnny Wiz of The Wizard Entertainment Group. He heard me sing and now he wanted to see how well I come off on camera. You know . . . what type of look I give off, and if I'm marketable or not."

"Your look is one in a billion," Casino commented.

"Although you said it with the emotion of a cadaver, I'll take it as a compliment." She blushed.

"It really wasn't intended as one—just telling the truth."

Just then the StarQuest show came on on the television. "Can we turn the channel please?" Fabiola asked.

"Sure. We can watch whatever you want to watch, but the sick and shut-in usually gets the remote."

"If we were watching anything else I would never ask, but I refuse to help this show's ratings."

"Why? I like me some Melon Low." Casino smiled as he looked at the television. Melon Low was a big star in the eighties who had a big voice like Chaka Khan, the timeless beauty of Janet Jackson, and a banging body like J. Lo in her prime. Casino's response was no surprise to Fabiola, because every man—young and old—seemed to love Melon Low.

"About a year ago, I was on that show and Melon Low had no love for me, even though the crowd went B-A-N-A-N-A-S for me."

On-screen, Melon Low talked about the vision of the show and her passion to help up-and-coming singers.

"What she's talking is bullshit." Fabiola sung the word *bullshit* in the key of A minor.

"Why? What happened exactly?" Casino asked, unable to take his eyes off Melon Low.

"The crowd and both of the men judges loved me and the applause meter was off the charts, but she really ripped into me and said I didn't have what it takes to go to the next level, and that my look wasn't marketable."

Casino looked Fabiola over and said, "Well, we know that ain't true."

"Good thing I didn't have low self-esteem, because I would have never sung another note, not even in the shower."

"That's because she hasn't had a hit in—what? Ten or fifteen years?" Casino turned the channel to CNN.

"I know. I guess my first mistake was singing one of her old songs better than she ever sung it." Casino and Fabiola both laughed. "One of the judges came backstage and told me that Melon must have saw so much of herself in me and that it was scary for her to see a new and improved model right in front of her face. I reminded her of who she used to be. Thank goodness the other judge talked to me, because between him and my mother's encouragement I was able to get past the incident."

"Well, I'm boycotting the show and her jealous-hearted ass, too." Fabiola smiled at her new friend.

The two talked for a long time. Well, Fabiola did most of the talking and Casino listened intently. Fabiola had him laughing at her stories about the drama she experienced while doing gigs.

"I had no idea that your work was that hard," Casino confessed. He thought it was all fun. Singing and dancing.

"It goes beyond the stage, you know."

"How so?"

"The delivery is a large part of it, but having the drive to get there is the harder work, keeping not only my voice in tip-top shape but my body as well, staying fit, not eating chocolate or things that could break me out. These are things that I have to stay consistent with long after the curtain drops or the band stops playing."

"Well, I commend you for that."

They continued joking and enjoying each other's company, when Roxy and Spade returned as Fabiola and Casino shared a laugh. "Well, anything that can make two people laugh that hard in this gloomy muthafucka is worth listening to," Spade said.

They looked up after hearing Spade's voice. "Our secrets, son," Casino said.

"I thought we were a sharing family," Spade attempted.

"And you know I carry secrets to my grave."

Fabiola started to pack up. "I'm going to get out of here. I'll see you tomorrow." Fabiola touched Casino's hand, but due to his injury he couldn't really feel her touch. His eyes gave her the embrace back, however. "See you later, and be good, ya hear?"

"Don't worry, I will."

She grabbed her jacket and purse, then left.

On her way out the door, Fabiola heard Roxy ask, "What was that all about, Casino?"

Fabiola stopped in her tracks and waited outside the door for Casino's response. "Damn, Roxy, when did I start answering to you?" Casino said. "I might as well have a woman if I have to answer to one."

That's all Fabiola needed to hear—that Roxy wasn't his woman. Fabiola smiled as she walked away.

★ ★ ★

"How're you feeling, old man?" Tonk asked. He sat in the corner of the hospital room watching over his boss. Although there had been no other attempts on Casino's life, no one was taking any chances.

"The doctors say if things keep improving the way they are I may be out of here in a few weeks. Afterward, he says I'm going to need about six months of therapy and maybe I'll walk again without a limp." Casino's voice was a lot stronger than it had been.

"With all due respect, Casino, I don't give a flying fuck about what no quack that barely speaks English has to say. I'm asking you."

"I'll be out of this place in less than two weeks one way or another," Casino declared. "A month of therapy and I'll be walking. Two months and I may be dancing."

Tonk was happy to hear his boss sounding optimistic. "Those are pretty lofty goals for a nigga that never could dance before." Tonk stopped talking when he heard someone turning the doorknob. The doctor had already made his daily visit and the nurse wasn't due to make another round for at least an hour. Instinctively, Tonk's right hand slid under his jacket and gripped the handle of the .357 he kept holstered there.

"Whoa, big fella," Spade announced with his hands in the air, "it's just me."

"We weren't expecting anyone. You're an hour early." Tonk removed his hand from the weapon but the tension was still evident in his eyes.

"Yeah, I was in the area and thought you might be able to use the extra rest. Did I interrupt anything?" Spade removed the leather coat he was wearing, threw it on the end of the bed, and took a seat. "Besides, I need to talk to the both of you."

"You can start by getting your shit off the bed," Casino said, staring at Spade's multicolored, butter-soft leather jacket.

Spade moved the coat to the back of the chair. "My bad," he apologized, taking off the matching leather baseball cap.

"You look a little ragged, and I'm the one lying up in the hospital shot up. What's wrong?" Casino said to Spade.

"Every hour that I'm not up here I've been manning the streets trying to find out who shot you, and I've come up with nothing." Casino saw the frustration on his son's face.

"Don't let it get you all worked up, son." Spade liked when Casino called him that. Spade was actually the son of Casino's best friend, who had been killed. After his death, Casino raised Spade as his own. "We're going to figure this out together, the three of us."

"The three of us," Tonk echoed, then added, "Mouths are definitely closed on this one. Not even niggas in the after-hour spots are talking, and those niggas gossip like broads in a beauty salon when they want to."

"Maybe this shit was some type of omen," Casino said, causing both Tonk and Spade to look at him curiously. "I mean . . . I been doing this shit for too long. The drugs—shit—I do that shit more for sport than income. Maybe it's time for me to step back."

"Am I hearing this right?" Spade looked confused. "Are you saying you want out of the game?" Casino had been *that dude* since before Spade was born.

"Who said anything about getting out of the game? I'm a G until death. I just want to change the game up a little bit," Casino tried to explain. "When what you are investing in has more downside than upside it's time to reevaluate. And in this game the investment is your life. It's a young man's game, son . . . and a young man should be in charge of it."

"I feel ya, Dad," Spade said, understanding that Casino was practically gift wrapping the baton for him to take over the business and run with it if that's what he wanted—and it was. "But right now my main concern is trying to find out who crossed the line and give it to 'em like they tried to give it to you. Now, can you please go over with me again what you saw the night those clowns did the unthinkable?"

Casino thought for a few seconds about what had been on his mind nonstop since the shooting, then he spoke. "Like I said before, it was two tiny muthafuckaz, just a little taller than midget small, but not quite."

"Kids?" Tonk said with a wrinkled forehead.

"Maybe." Casino had been going over that possibility himself. "But they handled them tools like they'd used them before. Not with the skill of an old hand, but certainly not the awkwardness of a novice either." Casino sat back and thought about what he had just said. Two assailants, possible midgets, skilled at handling semi-automatic assault weapons? If he wasn't lying in a hospital bed unable to move his legs as a result of it, it would have been laughable. But Casino was in a hospital bed, and he was paralyzed from the waist down, and no one in the room was laughing. "I wonder how come I didn't remember that before," Casino almost whispered.

"Remember what?" the other two men in the room said at almost the same time. They were both looking at Casino.

"There is one other thing that I remember."

"Well?"

"If you shut up, I'll tell you." Spade put a lock on his tongue and Casino continued. "Before it went down, I'm almost sure they were sitting in a purple or dark-blue Impala."

"Are you sure about the car?" Tonk asked. This would be the first real clue they had in finding the jokers that were responsible.

"I would be willing to bet the farm on it."

One Monkey Don't
Stop No Show

Casino was looking and feeling better by the day. Tranquility, peace, and quiet were just what the doctor ordered, but it was also driving Casino a little stir-crazy. If it weren't for Fabiola's daily visits, Casino probably would have had Spade and Tonk sign him up out of there by now. Fabiola brought a welcome change whenever she visited.

Even Tonk noticed the change in his boss during Fabiola's visits. At first, Tonk was skeptical of Fabiola's motivation for wanting to visit Casino. Being as close as he was to a man like Casino who had power and extra money to toss around afforded Tonk the opportunity to witness the selfish and greed-driven characteristics of so-called friends or associates. Fabiola displayed none of the obvious or not-so-obvious behaviors. That's why whenever Fabiola came by, Tonk made it his business to leave the room. Sometimes he went out for a breath of fresh air or to the cafeteria to get a snack, but mostly he just sat in the hallway outside the door and allowed Casino and Fabiola some privacy. Today was no different.

Fabiola sat at the edge of the hospital bed as she'd done every day for the past week, laughing with Casino. She was wearing a blue-jean hooded Vera Wang–inspired jumpsuit that Adora had made for her after Fabiola saw it in a magazine and fell in love with it.

Adora made the outfit, but it wasn't *just like* the one in the photo. She took it a step further and added fur around the hood to give it a little more attitude.

"So, what do you think I should do about Ricky?" Fabiola got to the point. She had just finished telling him how Ricky had tried to fine her again for some foolishness. This time it was because she was talking on the phone in the van on the way from a gig.

"Can you be more specific?"

"He's just so extra. I don't know how to deal with all of his BS."

Casino considered the question for a few moments before he answered. "It seems to me you both need each other equally right now: You need his name to get booked in order to make money and circulate your name until your opportunity comes, and he needs your vocal prowess to be asked to come back after performing at these venues he's booking." Casino paused. "That's normally a recipe for a good relationship. But for it to be effective both parties must be aware of their need for the other."

"I never really thought about it like that," Fabiola said softly. When she began coming to see Casino she thought she would be helping a man in need; Fabiola had no idea that the visits would turn out to be so beneficial to her. "This may sound like a crazy question," Fabiola said to Casino.

"The only crazy questions are the ones not asked, young lady."

"Well, my question is," she said after being unable to remember where she'd heard that quote, "How did you become so insightful?"

"Experience," Casino said before biting into a giant red apple. "Experience is the best teacher of all things." Casino enjoyed talking to Fabiola about life's lessons. When he looked into her eyes he saw the future fighting to create its own destiny—not letting circumstances dictate it—and it made him want to protect her from the madness of the world.

"Surely you're not saying because a person is older they are smarter than someone that's younger?"

"Surely"—he paused for a second with his index finger in the air while he swallowed a mouthful of apple—"I'm not saying that at all. Experience and age are two completely different animals; one hasn't anything to do with the other. Every minute of your life you age, whether you like it or not. It takes virtually no effort. Experiences, on the other hand, whether yours or someone else's, are like a map of life. If a person lived their entire life making decisions based on experience—meaning he does what he does based on results he's already had or the results of other people doing what he's attempting to do—that person would live a virtually flawless life." Fabiola was thinking about the heavy jewel Casino had just laid on her when there was a knock on the door, followed by the doctor walking in.

" 'Ello, Mista Winn. How are you today?" the doctor asked in his Middle Eastern accent as he picked up Casino's chart from the end of the bed.

"That's the sixty-four-thousand-dollar question that I've been waiting on you to answer for me, doc."

The doctor finished reading the chart, put it back on the

hook, and began to examine Casino's legs one at a time by prob-
ing and lifting them in the air. First the right: "Um-huh"; then
the left: "Um-huh." Casino watched the doctor attentively. "I
have good news for you," the doctor said.

"That's the best kind, doc. Give it to me."

"Well, the swelling has gone down tremendously and it's my
expert opinion that you will be able to walk again, but you're
going to need quite a bit of therapy." The doctor smiled tri-
umphantly. "They have one bed available at The Sheltering Arms
Rehabilitation Center—they are one of the best in this region—
and I took the liberty of reserving that bed for you. I hope you
don't mind?"

"Not at all; you can take all the liberties you need when it
comes to getting me walking again, doc. Just be sure to check
with me first." The doctor looked confused. "It's a joke, doc."

"You are a funny man, Mista Winn. I like you. I wish I could
spend all my time talking to you, but I have other rounds to
complete. Have a nice day, Mista Winn."

After the doctor left, Casino looked at Fabiola. "This is going
to be our little secret, okay? I don't want anyone knowing how
close I am to getting back on my feet."

"Nobody will hear it from me," she said, making a zipper motion across her mouth.

"Good."

"I probably won't be able to get up here to see you tomorrow,
because I have an important lunch meeting with Johnny Wiz."

"That's good news. How come you're just mentioning it?"

"I wanted to save the best for last and leave you on a positive
note."

"I've heard of Johnny Wiz." How could he not have? The
man in some way touched half of everything being played on the
radio. "How did you arrange the meeting?"

"My mother met someone from his camp when I won the Hot Soundz contest in New York three years ago and they kept in touch. Finally the person passed on my stuff to Johnny Wiz," Fabiola said proudly. "I need to get a full glam workout: hair, nails, makeup, brows . . . the works." Thinking about the magnitude of the meeting started to make Fabiola a little nervous.

Sensing her anxiety, Casino said, "You're going to knock 'em dead. All you have to do is be yourself."

"I really hope so," Fabiola sighed. "My mother and sister are depending on me to make this happen. It's all of our dream. I have to do it."

Casino could see the dedication and determination on Fabiola's face. She was glowing with the hope for an opportunity to succeed. "I believe that anything can be achieved if we want it bad enough and are willing to put in the work."

"My mother and sister have sacrificed so much for me. I don't want to let them down."

"Your mother is a hardworking lady that wants the best for her children, especially one as talented as you."

"Speaking of which, she wanted to come up here to see you and thank you personally for what you did the day we were getting evicted, and for continuing to let us use your property."

"Tell her that her gratitude is appreciated, but that wasn't the reason I let you all stay in the home."

"Why did you do it then?" Fabiola had always wondered why Casino did what he did for her family.

"I did it for me."

"I'm not quite sure I understand what you mean by that," Fabiola said.

"I've done a lot of shit that people could say was selfish and fucked up. And they would probably be right," Casino admitted. "That's why on the rare occasion I get to help someone that really needs it, I relish the opportunity. It's my way of balancing out the other shit I do—the stuff that's not so good."

Now that Casino's health was improving, Fabiola was noticing, for the first time, how young he looked. If Casino hadn't told her his age—forty-five—she wouldn't have believed the man was older than thirty.

"Your mother can visit me when I get to the rehabilitation place. Looks like I'll have my own room and they won't trip off of all of my fans," he joked. "Now you go on and get yourself ready for tomorrow. I want you to knock that Johnny Wiz's socks off, and as soon as you're done, no matter how late it is, make sure you call me and let me know how it went. I don't want to have to wait until our next visit. The anticipation may cause me to regress in my rehabilitation."

"It's going to be late by the time we're finished."

"It's never too late for you to call me. You hear me, don't you? Never too late."

"You got it."

Casino smiled when she got up to leave.

Only Lunch

The call didn't come until after nine PM, and it forced Adora to be up all night long trying to get all of Fabiola's outfits together for her big day. She needed an outfit and accessories for the lunch meeting, one for The Wizard Showcase, and one to change into after the performance. The Wizard Entertainment Group was hosting a showcase to find new talent for the label. The A&R department moved around from city to city looking for new sounds and faces. The following day the showcase would be in Richmond. If Adora had anything to do with it, her sister was going to be the best-dressed performer any of those industry bastards had ever seen.

Viola was up with her girls for the moral support. She

was torn that she would not be able to go with Fabiola to the lunch date with Johnny Wiz. She had signed up last month to work some overtime at her job at the cookie plant, and it was too late to find someone to fill in for her. It was mandatory that Viola go to work or she would be fired.

"Besides, Ma, it's only lunch," Fabiola tried to assure her mother.

"Oh, it's lunch all right," Viola started. "Just probably the biggest lunch of your life. I don't care what you say, my gut tells me that I need to be there with you." Viola didn't downplay the significance of the moment one bit. "And don't order any shellfish; you know it sometimes makes you break out. Maybe they won't fire me if I take the write-up?"

"Mommy, you know good and well some of them folks at your job are already jealous of you and we ain't really made it yet," Fabiola warned. "Them ole hags can't wait to find a reason to get you ghost."

"Mommy, Fab will be fine," Adora interjected. "It's only lunch, and Lord knows she knows how to eat. You taught us proper table etiquette since before we even went to kindergarten. She's going to be on her best behavior, and thanks to me she'll look the part . . . fabulous Fab."

"Besides," Fabiola jumped back in, "you'll be at the showcase tonight, won't you?"

"I wouldn't miss that for all the overtime in the world," her mother assured her.

"For Christ's sake, Mommy, as soon as Johnny saw the pictures of Fab, he had the company jet fueled up and made arrangements to fly to Richmond personally to meet little sis. If that ain't making an impression on a nigga, I don't know what is," Adora said.

The girls put up such a great argument that Viola reluctantly went against her better judgment to not be with her daughter at what could possibly be a life-changing lunch.

The lavishly decorated Omni Hotel was happy to host The Wizard Entertainment Group's showcase. They went beyond the call of duty to make it feel like a home away from home for everyone involved. With the tour buses parked outside of the hotel, it didn't take long for the cat to get out of the bag that The Wizard Entertainment Group was staying at the Omni, and as a result the lobby was flooded with aspiring singers, dancers, rappers, and, yes, the groupies, too. And of course The Wizard was booked in the Omni's presidential suite. Due to his prestige and need for privacy, he asked that the hotel provide a five-star lunch for him and Fabiola in his suite.

Fabiola was at the reception desk of the hotel at twelve-thirty sharp. The lunch wasn't scheduled to begin for another hour but Fabiola wasn't leaving any room for error. *Only one chance for a first impression,* and Momma always used one of those famous sayings: *To be early is to be on time, to be on time is to be late, but to be late is to be forgotten. Never will I let something as little as time stand in between me and my career.*

"Welcome to the Omni Hotel, my name is Jenny. How may I help you?"

"Yes," Fabiola said, "I'm here to see Johnny Wiz for lunch. Can you tell me what suite he's staying in?"

"We don't give out our guests' room numbers." The desk clerk had been approached by young ladies trying to find out what room the music mogul was staying in all morning long.

"He's expecting me."

The desk clerk looked skeptical, but said, "Okay then. Give me your name and I'll check to see if you're on his registry for approved guests."

"Fabiola," she said, "Fabiola Mays."

The desk clerk's fingers danced on the keyboard of her computer for a fraction of a second and then stopped. After looking at something on the screen, the clerk tapped the keyboard a couple of more times. "Ms. Mays. Mr. Wiz is staying in our presidential suite. Here's the room number and a card to activate the elevator to go to that floor. Again, I'm sorry if I've caused you any inconvenience."

Fabiola wanted to rub it in but thought better of it. Instead she said, "No, not at all. You've been nothing but helpful to me." Once on the elevator, Fabiola looked around at the gold-tinted mirrored walls. The elevator carpet was thick and plush. The gold elevator buttons lit up like stars in the sky as jazz music serenaded Fabiola from what had to be the best sound system on any elevator in the world.

A girl could get used to this real quick, Fabiola said to herself as she puckered her lips in the mirrored doors. She then turned from left to right, checking out her profile. She was satisfied with what she saw. By the time the elevator reached the top level, Fabiola felt good. She knew that she was going to produce results and she didn't even have Mommy by her side to guide her. Fabiola took a huge breath as she stepped out of the lift. She was about to knock on the door of the presidential suite but she heard what seemed like a heated conversation going on inside and didn't want to interrupt. Plus, she didn't want to mess up her lunch date by barging into the middle of the heated debate. So she took a seat on the suede day bench outside of the suite.

"Mother, I thought you are suppose to be with friends in Switzerland, enjoying yourself. You are not suppose to be worried about business."

A voice over the speakerphone responded, "Son, you forgot I

am the business. Your father and I built this company before you were ever even thought of."

"Yes, I know, Mother, but I've been a part of this company since I was in your womb. So, literally, Mother, I was born into this. And I've watched and learned from every single business decision that has been made in the past thirty-five years."

"Yes, and I've been running this company for over fifty years, and I still feel that some of the artists you are signing are nothing that I would have taken a second look at."

"Yes, Mother, but this is a new day with new times and a lot has changed."

"Whatever happened to wholesome girls with voices like Roberta Flack, Aretha Franklin? You sure haven't picked any of those lately. That mess you been choosing sounds like cows screaming. It's a mess!"

"Mother, what time is it anyway in Switzerland?" Johnny knew that there was no use in trying to win an argument with his mother.

After the voices died down, Fabiola waited for a few minutes before knocking on the door.

A butler wearing a uniform opened the door. "Right this way, Ms. Mays. Mr. Wiz awaits you."

The butler took Fabiola's elbow, ushering her inside the suite. "May I take your coat?" Fabiola handed the butler her mink jacket.

She couldn't help but be impressed by Johnny and the way he went all out to make the lunch so special for her. "Mr. Wiz, I am Fabiola Mays. I admire your work, your company, and your overall vision. Been watching you on television for so long and it's such an honor to meet you." Fabiola extended her hand out to him.

Instead of shaking her hand, he grabbed it and kissed it. "The pleasure is all mine."

"This is really very extravagant," Fabiola said to Johnny Wiz. "Thank you so much for taking time out of your busy schedule to meet with me." Over in the corner, there was a man playing a soft song on a baby grand piano. Flowers were everywhere, perfuming the room, and lit white candles cast a luxurious glow. The whole setup was stunning.

"I am the president of the company, so my accommodations should be nothing less than presidential." He flashed his pearly whites, holding a glass of champagne in his hand. By the look of the emptied glass and the half-empty bottle sitting on the table, Fabiola figured he probably already had a few drinks.

Fabiola could not believe that she was standing before the great Johnny Wiz himself. He was even more overwhelming in person. She had studied his interviews on every music and business network that had ever had him on. His personality always overflowed with cockiness and confidence as he discussed his company and the entire collection of platinum recording artists that he had under his umbrella. Fabiola took it all in. Johnny Wiz had light-reddish skin with a dusting of freckles around his nose. His body was as fit as a pro athlete, despite the rumors that circulated about him having had liposuction and numerous other forms of cosmetic surgery. His hair was sandy brown and was cut short. But his most striking feature was his gray catlike eyes; staring into them made Fabiola feel like he could read her mind.

Johnny knew he was being studied, but he was accustomed to it; he used the time to look Fabiola over. He'd seen a lot of beautiful women, but the pictures of Fabiola did her no justice—she was simply gorgeous. "You are even more stunning in person than you are in your photographs," he said, putting his hand on her face.

"Thank you so much." Fabiola closed her eyes for a split second. "But I am more than a pretty face, Mr. Wiz, I am the total package actually."

He smiled and took another look at her. "You really are. You are beautiful and so very talented. Your voice is so old-school, but yet so fresh and new at the same time. I listened to your demo just about the entire way down here." He nodded. "You are definitely what this industry needs."

Yes! She thought. *I'm in!* That compliment meant everything coming from the head honcho of the music game. It was the stamp of approval Fabiola had been waiting for. *Finally someone gets this!*

"Thank you so much!" she said enthusiastically. "Would ya, would you," she said, getting all tongue tied, "like to hear me sing in person? I would like to show that I am not just a studio singer. I can really sing."

"You don't have to thank me, it's really the truth." He smiled at her. "You are very marketable. And I like how we'd be able to change your looks. You could be very versatile. I see you being a trendsetter in the best way."

"Thanks again. So let me sing for you . . .'"

Fabiola launched into an old-school song—"Someone Like You" by Patti LaBelle—to let him see that her voice is something that his mother would definitely approve of.

"Bravo, Ms. Fabiola! Bravo!" He stood up to clap. "You are right: You are so much more than a pretty face, your voice is absolutely beautiful. It really is, but at the end of the day, you are what you are, a pretty face who happens to have a voice that can be reckoned with."

"Thanks, Mr. Wiz. That means so much coming from you."

"Well, The Wizard loves your voice, your look, your energy, and he possibly is going to sign you."

"Oh my goodness. I want to scream."

"Please don't."

She laughed and he said, "So we must celebrate! Would you like a drink?"

"No, I don't drink," she lied to him. She wasn't about to drink at a business lunch.

"Not even champagne or a shot of Hennessy, perhaps?"

"No thanks," she said with a slight smile to let him know that she wasn't being rude. She was eager to get straight to the point. "There's a lot of things that I feel you all could do with me in regards to getting my career off the ground—of course *if* you decide to sign me."

"Sweets, we work with the best of the best. We have the cream of the crop on board in terms of producers, songwriters, publicists, studios, A&Rs, and artist development teams—these people make up the machine that drives my company. We not only work with platinum-selling artists, we create them. Everyone on our label is a huge star and we have pop, rock, and rap icons on our roster. The Wizard settles for nothing less than the best."

"Yes, I know this, and I didn't mean to offend you," she said. "I've been studying this industry practically all my life," she said.

Johnny put his hand on her face. "You know, you are so gorgeous that if you couldn't sing, I would probably make you my wife," he said, gazing into her eyes. "I didn't mean to digress from the topic. So, you say you've been studying the industry for a long time?"

"Yes, my sister jokes that I was only conceived to become a megastar."

"Well, I'm not sure if you *really* know how this music thing works or not. I mean the books and the television specials can't always depict the way things really work." He didn't give her a chance to respond. "I can take you to the top." He pointed up toward the ceiling. "I can make all your dreams come true. I can make you a rich woman with fame and fortune beyond your wildest imagination. But in return, what are you willing to give?"

"I am willing to give it all I got. I've already been doing a lot to get to this point. I've been taking voice lessons, every dance class you can think about. I work out seven days a week, eat the right foods. And I am willing to bring that same discipline to make the label happy."

"All you got, huh?" Johnny sat down on the burgundy-, green-, and gold-striped couch and looked at her.

"If you sign me I promise you I will be the hardest-working singer you've ever seen come through the doors of The Wizard Group. I will sing my heart out. I don't use any drugs, I'm not caught up with any men, nothing. All I focus on is my singing and songwriting."

"Good, because that's exactly what this industry is about: sacrifice. Sacrifice for all your dreams to become a reality." He took down another double shot of Hennessy, and by the look of his bloodshot eyes she could tell that he didn't need any more.

Fabiola began to pour out her heart. "I am willing to sacrifice, for my dreams, my career, and a better life for me and my family." Her voice betrayed a passion that seemed to come from her heart and soul, arousing Johnny Wiz even more than he had been when he saw her walk through the door.

"You are so beautiful." He slurred and then he stroked himself through his pants. Fabiola was mortified—she didn't know what to do or say. So she pretended like she didn't see anything.

"You do something to me that I can't put my finger on," he said in a seductive melody as he rolled his eyes in the back of his head and continued to stroke his bulge. All of his smoothness was going out of the window. He was losing cool points at a rocket-climbing rate, but still Fabiola kept her composure.

"You are in power now. At this very moment, you could make me do things that I'd be sorry for later. Write checks, sign you to a deal that my board members would question, make me promise ridiculous things that I would regret later." He released his dick from the restriction of his pants; it stuck straight up in the air. "What are you willing to do? Are you going to execute your power?"

Fabiola looked down in disgust. She was completely taken off guard by Johnny's boldness. She had heard of studio rats having to fuck their way into a recording contract, but she never imagined that one day she'd find herself in the very same predicament.

"Sir, the talent is in my voice."

"Yes, and a lot of girls have the talent and unfortunately talent doesn't always get you through the door. Hell, sometimes it doesn't even get you through the door." Him repeating himself let her know that he was a bit tipsy.

She didn't know what to do. All sorts of crazy thoughts raced through her mind. Should she get up and leave now? And then lose everything? Maybe she should call her mother, but then her mother would know that she really didn't have it under control like she said she did. She wanted to cry because it wasn't suppose to turn out like this, but she managed to keep her composure as Johnny continued.

"It's about sacrifice. You are twenty-one years old, old enough to make your own decisions. Take your destiny in your hand." He nodded toward his manhood.

Fabiola was dumbfounded. The chance of a lifetime was right in front of her. What she had been practically living every day of her life for, what her mother and sister had been sacrificing so much for so long in the hopes that this day would certainly come, was right there, and she didn't want to fuck it all up by making the wrong move in this delicate situation.

Johnny could tell she was fighting with conflicting feelings. "Touch it," he tried to urge her.

"Johnny, I don't want us to get into this . . . not now," she said in a soft but firm tone, not wanting to piss him off.

"Baby, you have to make up your mind. I'm very interested in you—all of you—but how interested are you in me?" He grabbed her hand and put it in his lap. He wanted her to stroke him but she didn't. "That's it," he moaned. Fabiola quickly removed her hand.

"Johnny, please don't let this get in between us," she begged.

"You got my time and my attention." He looked her in the eyes. "Now don't blow it," he said. "You are almost at the pinnacle of your dream, and you only have a few steps to take, but it's a long ways back down. You have to decide if you want it or not."

She looked at his average-sized freckled dick and knew that if she put it on him that he would want more, but that didn't necessarily mean that he would keep his word and sign her. Should she become a whore to the business? This was the day she had been waiting for all of her life, but she had no idea that it would come with this kind of price.

"Baby, it can be so, so e-zee for you. It's up to you." He was still stroking himself, licking his lips. "But you are running out of time." The pace of his stroke intensified. "It's either the bed or you can leave."

Fabiola knew that her entire life was at stake. *No one will know what I did but him and me.* She tried to assure herself as she kicked off her stilettos. Clips of her mother's overjoyed smile and her sister giving her a high five when she returned home with the deal flashed through her mind.

"That's right," he coached when her shoes came off and she began to undo one of the buttons on her blouse. "I know that pussy is so tight and wet for me." His tongue darted out of his mouth like it had a mind of its own. "Oh, Daddy-O is horny for your pussy." He licked his lips when she undid another button. He could now see the black lace bra she was wearing. "Oooh, I just can't wait for you to turn me out Virginia style. Show me that Virginia really is for lovers."

Tears pooled in the corners of her eyes as she watched him continue to stroke himself faster, talking to her like she was a whore. "You're making the right decision. You are going to be a huge star. America's sweetheart! I can see your name in lights."

Fabiola saw that Johnny was in ecstasy and knew that once again he'd get what he wanted, but just as quickly as the thought crossed her mind she snapped out of that thinking. "Johnny, I don't want to do this." Those words made him lose his erection.

"It's your choice. No one is forcing you to do anything. Either you do or you don't. If you don't—no deal; if you do—deal. Make your decision now."

Fabiola slipped her shoes back on and fastened up her blouse.

"The bed or bounce?" Johnny Wiz laughed.

"You're going to have to enjoy your bed alone, Johnny. I'm sorry that you feel as you do." Tears were in her eyes.

"I'm sorry, too. I'm sorry that you are such a selfish little bitch. Now get the fuck out."

"I'll make it to the top without you, Johnny."

"Over my dead body, bitch." Johnny lost his cool sitting on the sofa. "And I mean that. Get the fuck out. Do your talking while you're walking and don't let the door hit you."

"I would have liked for it to be with you, but . . ." She was trying to appeal to his logical side.

"Apparently not," he cut her off.

"Like I said, with or without you I'm going to see you at the top," she said, snatching her coat and pocketbook from the butler, who looked as if nothing unusual was going on.

"Bounce, bitch. Out of here," Johnny snarled.

"Enjoy your bed . . . ALONE!"

"Oh, it's never alone, you little bitch. There are thousands of bitches like you that will do what you won't. If you didn't know, you know now. You were lucky to get this high up. Bitches like you know what the business is from the get-go; they don't play Ms. I'm-a-Stuck-up-Bitch like you." As she was opening the door, Johnny continued, "That's right. Get the fuck out of my shit before I call security." Fabiola slammed the door, almost knocking the pictures off the wall. She was angry at how disrespectful he was to her and lost control.

From the other side of the door she yelled, "Only bitch-ass niggas call security, you freckle-face bitch." She thought of G.P., who never called the police. "They handle their own business."

Johnny got off the couch and walked over to the door. "Didn't I tell you to leave, bitch?"

For a split second she thought about all the poise, manners, and professionalism she was supposed to have, but Johnny Wiz had violated and they were indeed out the door.

"Bitch, you better get out of my motherfucking suite, you tramp-ass bitch," he said almost like he was talking out of the side of his neck.

She continued to speak up for herself. "All 'cause I wouldn't let you fuck me? 'Cause I wouldn't let you put your freckled dick up in me?"

"Actually I wanted to fuck you in your ass, bitch," he yelled through the door, not caring who heard him. "After I put it in your mouth. Now get the fuck from in front my door, bitch."

"Make me, punk muthafucka," she screamed back at him.

"Bitch, you are done in this world. You gon' be sucking dicks for a profession. The only place you gonna be able to get a job in this country is a whorehouse."

"We'll see. You can't stop me. And you know it. You will see me again."

"Yeah, when you're dragging behind your mother when she comes over to suck my dick and apologize for your dumb ass not giving me what I wanted when I wanted it."

By then, hotel security had arrived and escorted her off the premises—kicking and screaming. She sat in her car and cried like a baby. She couldn't believe what just happened to her. What was supposed to be only lunch turned into a fucking disaster.

A Smack in the Face

Fabiola went straight to Shug's house and cried on her friend's shoulders for several hours. They sat on Shug's couch with a small wastebasket in front of the sofa filled with tissues. "You can still make this happen, Fab. You just have to work even harder," Shug said as she hugged her best friend. It killed her to see Fab like this. "But whatever you do, you can't let your mother know what happened. If you know like I know, she'll snap. And knowing your mother, I am not sure on who."

"I know, but what if he flies back out without coming to see me perform tonight at the showcase? I really need that deal."

"He'll come to his senses once his dick goes down and

he hears you sing again. He's a businessman first and foremost, and you are as close to a sure things as there is."

"I really hope so. I said some real fucked-up shit to him."

"I know, and all you really did was defend yourself. Now, in the meantime you gotta put your game face on. For all you know this could have been a test."

"A test?" Fabiola echoed. Shug's suggestion offered her a bit of relief. "I hope."

★ ★ ★

Later at the showcase, Fabiola was backstage waiting her turn to perform. Butterflies fluttered in her stomach as she listened to the other people sing ahead of her. Fabiola had no idea what her destiny would be. She prayed for the best and tried to prepare herself for the worst, whatever that could happen.

Looking from behind the curtain into the crowd, Fabiola saw Shug, Viola, Adora, and her aunt Rose sitting together in the audience. As her eyes further scanned the auditorium, she saw Sheena, who had just been backstage applying the final touches to Fabiola's makeup, coming to take her seat beside the family. She could see the anxiety on their faces, all ready for her career to finally catapult to the next level. Then she looked at the music executives/judges table. Four members of The Wizard Entertainment Group were there. Johnny Wiz was sitting off to the side, along with a few other people that Fabiola knew were representatives from his camp. Johnny Wiz was as clean as the board of health, wearing a three-piece suit, sitting and watching intensely as the singer onstage in front of him performed.

Fabiola took a deep breath when the MC announced, "Coming to the stage is one of Richmond's own: Fabiooola Mays."

Fabiola took the stage in a beautiful hunter-green minidress that complemented her cocoa-brown skin. The dress fit her

body like a glove, hugging all her curves. Fabiola was last to perform, and the crowd was restless and ready to go home. She
launched right into her song, and her worst nightmare was coming true; for some odd reason the hometown crowd was cold.
But after the first verse, Fabiola pulled out the big guns, hitting
a note so strong it smacked every single person in attendance in
the face and demanded their undivided attention. Everybody
but Johnny Wiz, who got up, fixed his jacket, whispered something in one of the judges ears, and shook his head no. He then
motioned to the people who were sitting with him that he was
ready to go. In the process of gathering his entourage Johnny
Wiz made so much commotion that everyone's attention was on
him instead of the stage. At that moment Fabiola wanted to
break down, run off the stage, and cry, but she didn't and continued her song to its final note.

Viola had no idea why Johnny Wiz was leaving in the middle
of her daughter's stellar performance. Getting up from her seat,
Viola quickly walked toward him. She was moving so fast her
shawl kept falling from her shoulders.

"Mr. Wiz," she called out to him. "Mr. Wiz."

He stopped in his tracks, turning to give Viola his undivided
attention. "Yes, what is it, Mrs. Mays?" He took one look at her
and knew she was Fabiola's mother. Fabiola was the spitting
image of her mother.

"Please, sir, call me Viola." She smiled. "Why are you leaving
in the middle of your new big star's performance?"

"Because I'm not interested in her anymore," he answered
bluntly. "Not quite what I thought she would be," he said in a
way that he knew would cut Viola like a knife.

"What do you mean? She has the look . . . the look you said you
were looking for. You said yourself that she was gorgeous, and we
all know she can sing with the best of them. There is no denying

her gift." She was trying to plead her daughter's case. "I don't know what happened in there tonight, but it was no fault of hers."

"It isn't about what happened in there tonight," Johnny Wiz said to her in his trademark calm melodic voice, "but rather what didn't happen today at lunch."

A surprised Viola asked, "What happened at lunch? I was under the impression that everything went perfectly."

"You see, Viola, your daughter doesn't quite understand how this industry works."

"But she does, totally, and what she doesn't grasp, I will enlighten her about."

"Well, it's a little too late for that." He shook his head a little and gave her a half smile. "You see, we have over two hundred girls a week coming by the office wanting to get in my company however they can. They will do anything just to see me. I mean ANYTHING! Your daughter didn't feel she had to play by the same set of rules. A man in my position isn't used to being denied what he wants."

Viola understood perfectly. "I'll talk to her. I'll convince her to do whatever you need her to do. She won't have a choice. Just give her another chance," she begged.

"There are no second chances with The Wizard. Seconds come at the diners where she'll be waiting tables."

"Please, Mr. Wiz, please, I am begging you." As he walked away, Viola ran behind him like Scarlett O'Hara at the end of *Gone with the Wind,* just begging and pleading for another chance. But she wasn't humbling herself for her own benefit. No, this wasn't for her at all; it was for her daughter. On second thought, it was for her; this was her dream, too.

"Step away from Mr. Wizard," his giant security guard ordered.

Johnny Wiz turned around and said, "Your daughter blew it at lunch. Her name is shit in this industry."

"Please, Mr. Wiz, I will do whatever you need me to do to make this entire situation right."

"Good. I already told her what you need to do to me to make this right. Just ask your daughter. She knows in depth how you can get back in my good graces." He fixed his coat and walked off.

"Mr. Wiz"—Viola ran over after him—"please . . . please."

Another security guard stepped in front of Viola, blocking her path to Johnny Wiz. "I'm going to have to ask you to step away now," he said in a no-nonsense voice. "Please, ma'am, don't make me use force. I really don't like beating up women, but I will if I have to."

Viola stood there with tears in her eyes, devastated, not knowing what to do. But one thing was certain: She was going to get to the bottom of this, and Fabiola had some answering to do.

She rushed to join the rest of the family backstage. Viola grabbed Fabiola by the hand. "I need you to come with me. Adora"—she looked at her other daughter while maintaining a firm grip on Fabiola—"finish packing your sister's things and we'll meet you outside." Viola led Fabiola to a restroom and locked the door. Shug followed closely behind while Sheena helped Adora. Shug knew that everybody thought that shit had hit the fan, but the hurricane was about to come through once Viola got to the bottom of the events from earlier today, and Shug knew that her best friend would need her.

"What happened earlier today?" Viola paced back and forth while Fabiola leaned on the sink.

"Mommy, he tried to make me have sex with him."

"And?" she said, looking at her youngest daughter.

"What do you mean *and*?" a shocked Fabiola repeated, not believing what she had just heard. "*And* I decided that I wasn't going to ho myself to him."

Viola hauled off and slapped Fabiola across the face. Fabiola grabbed her cheek as tears rolled down her face. "You have fucked up every fucking thing that I have worked so hard for. All the shit that I've done for you is in fucking vain." But Viola wasn't finished. "You have just about signed your death warrant to the key people at the top of the food chain. I worked my ass off your entire life to get you here and this is what you do to me. You selfish little bitch, you!" Viola screamed. "What was so horrible about giving the man a little pussy if that's what it took? You fuck G.P. and all those other sorry motherfuckers who ain't giving you shit but a wet ass, and the nigga that's going to make you rich and give you an opportunity to be a star you turn your nose up at him like he's some type of monster!"

The tears were rolling down Fabiola's face uncontrollably now. Even though G.P. was the second person she'd ever had sex with, the harsh words from her mother still hurt her.

"How dare you do this to me? To your sister? How dare you do that to Johnny? Do you know how much it cost to gas a jet and fly across the country to see you? How fucking dare you?"

"How dare I? How about *how dare him* for trying to make a prostitute out of me?" Fabiola looked up at her mother, mascara running down her face. "You know what, Viola, because there's no need to call you Mommy, a mother would never want her child to prostitute herself for a music deal with an asshole like Johnny Wiz." Fabiola shook her head. "For a moment when I was inside that room with him I considered it. I thought, What would I lose if I just let him have sex with me one time? Well, right before I let him put his nasty perverted hands on me the answer came: my self-respect. My self-respect would be the cost. If I don't have my self-respect and my word, I don't have shit, Viola." Fabiola wiped the tears from her eyes. "I'm sorry I fucked up *your* dream! And all I can say is that at forty years old with a little luck you'll be able to have another child to make your dreams come true. Thank you for everything, Viola."

Fabiola stormed out of the restroom into the waiting arms of Shug and Adora. "Boo, I am sooo sorry this happened to you. I am," Shug said.

"Hey, Fabiola, I just wanted to say hi and to tell you how unfortunate it is that things didn't go the way you intended them to go tonight," Toy taunted, interrupting their group hug. "Oh, and if you need a real job, the hospital is always hiring."

"Toy, this isn't the time or the place for yo shit," Shug added.

"She has a real job"—Adora stood up for her little sister—"she's a singer. Thank you very much."

"Oh, you're such the protective big sister, huh?" Toy sneered.

"You ain't seen nothing yet."

"Don't be mad 'cause your sister can't keep her man, and I know why." She raised one eyebrow.

"And if you don't want me to be the grand finale getting your ass tore out the frame, then you better get the fuck outta here, bitch." Adora looked Toy up and down and Toy knew that she meant business.

After Toy stormed off, she said, "One day we'll see. It'll all come to light."

"But you get the picture, bitch." Adora screamed back at Toy.

"Was Toy's ugly-ass about to get beat down?" Sheena tried to bring some humor to the tense atmosphere. She caught the tail end of the spat as she was coming back in from putting her bags in her car.

★ ★ ★

Fabiola lay in bed crying most of the night, and when she wasn't crying she wondered how things would have been different had she made the decision to sleep with Johnny Wiz.

Pulling a Rabbit
Out of a Hat

Getting off the phone with Rose, who had cussed her out for two hours straight, only confirmed what Viola knew in her heart: She had crossed the line. Fabiola was right; no real mother would have asked her daughter to sell her body, especially not for a record deal. What did that say about her confidence in her daughter's talents?

Although she felt bad, she couldn't help but reflect on just how close they had come to true stardom. Viola held the cell phone in her hand. Should she try one more time? she wondered. No, it was no use. Every time she had tried to call her daughter, she either got the voice mail or the call just got disconnected. But Viola wasn't a quitter, and she refused to let Fabiola become a quitter either, even with their backs against the wall.

"You have another visitor, I see," the nurse said, nodding toward the guest sitting in Casino's room. They had just returned from a physical-therapy session. "Do you want me to help you with your shower now, or shall we attempt it later?"

Casino looked into the eyes of the visitor who had the exact same eyes and features as the young lady that had been coming to see him every day for the past few weeks. Even if he had never met her before, Casino would have known that this was indeed Fabiola's mother.

"Later," he told the nurse, while looking in Viola's eyes.

"Then hit the call button when you're ready," the male attendant said with a smile as he exited the room.

"Pardon my intrusion, Mr. Casino," Viola said after the nurse left the room, "but I didn't know where else to turn."

Casino observed the desperation on Viola's face. "Please, call me Casino, and lose the 'Mister.' And you're not intruding at all. It's a pleasure to see you. Your daughter tells me that you were concerned about my well-being after the small misfortune I suffered."

"I hardly call being shot as many times as you were a small misfortune," Viola pointed out. "From my understanding, a man half your age may not have survived the injuries that you suffered."

"Then I'm glad I wasn't half my age."

Viola couldn't help but laugh. Sensing something heavy on her mind, Casino said, "You said you had nowhere else to turn. How can I help you?" he asked.

"It's Fabiola." Viola cut to the chase.

"Is she okay?" Casino asked. Viola didn't miss the concerned look that crossed his face. Seeing that this man cared about her daughter helped her not to feel as uneasy as she had been when she came in.

"First, I need you to promise me that you won't tell her I came here."

Casino replied, "I can do that. Now, what's going on?"

"She's not in any danger; not physical danger, anyway," Viola said. "She's more of a danger to herself than anyone else."

"That can be the worst kind of danger," Casino said, "but if I'm going to be of any help, you're going to have to be just a little more specific."

Viola thought about the last conversation she shared with Fabiola. "You selfish bitch," she had said to her daughter. Shaking her head, she brought her attention back to Casino and continued, "You know how when some children are young, you can ask them what they want to be when they grow up and they give you an answer so fast it hardly looks like they thought about it? Then a week or so later you ask them the same question and they give you a different answer?"

"Indeed, my son wanted to be a lawyer when he was a kid . . . then a fireman . . . then football . . ."

"Well, since Fabiola was old enough to talk the only thing she ever said she wanted to be was a singer and songwriter, and she's damn good, too. Most of them studio tricks whose music is being played on the radio can't hold a note to Fabiola, but all of that means nothing in this industry if you don't get the right break or maybe get under the table and please the right man."

"I'm not sure what it is you think I may be able to do?" Casino questioned.

"Fabiola has known that she could count on me from the time the doctor showed me images of her on the ultrasound," Viola said proudly. "I breached that faith yesterday. Her losing faith in me may have caused her to lose faith in herself, and if she doesn't believe in herself she might as well be dead."

Those words hung in the air for a while before she continued.

"She has lost respect for me because I said some harsh words to her out of anger. She highly respects your opinion. I need for you to reinforce her faith in her ability to pursue and obtain her dream."

"Although that's a pretty good start, I think it takes a little more than faith to accomplish a dream," Casino said. Then, feeling a sharp pain in the thigh of his left leg, Casino kneaded it with the palm of his hand.

"Are you okay?" Viola asked with a look of concern.

"Best feeling in the world right now," Casino said, still rubbing his leg. "It was only a short while ago that I couldn't feel anything in my legs. I'll take a cramp any day." He switched back to the original topic. "Besides faith, what will it take to carry Fabiola to the next level?"

"A radio hit."

"Then what's the problem? I've heard her sing. She's amazing. Is it money?"

"Money will always help, but her biggest hindrance is being stuck in this little city unable to network with the people that do for a living what she needs to happen," Viola said. "Relationships are very important in this industry."

"More important than the finished product? Nothing in business is more important than the bottom line."

"Try telling that to one of the most influential men in the entire music industry. A man who yesterday suddenly developed a personal vendetta against Fab because she wouldn't let him have his way with her."

Casino paused as he took in this information. Viola held her breath, wondering what he was thinking and if he could help her. She looked at him sitting in a wheelchair. Any other man might look helpless without the ability to get up and walk around the room, but Casino seemed to exude power from every cell of his body.

"There's always more than one route of travel to reach a desired destination," he finally said.

"Is that so?" Viola asked attentively. "I'm all ears."

After Casino told Viola what kind of tricks he could possibly pull out of the hat, Viola only had one question. "Would you like to go into the record business with me?"

"We could explore that later, for now let's just focus on getting Fabiola on the right path."

Casino's words were like music to her ears.

★ ★ ★

The incident with Johnny Wiz placed Fabiola into a vulnerable state of mind, but it was nothing in comparison to the way she felt after being slapped across the face and called a selfish bitch by her mother. And the pain of it all was no less severe a day later.

The only people Fabiola had spoken to since the showcase were Shug and her sister. Ocean called once; probably because his mother asked him to check on his little sister. The only reason Fabiola answered the phone was because she didn't want to give him any reason to come over to the apartment. Shug was enough company as it was. Fabiola wished that she would have never let her in, but she didn't want to be alone either—she didn't trust herself alone.

"Gurl, you got to get yo ass out that bed and do something." Shug stood over Fabiola's bed. Fabiola pulled the covers over her head, dressed in a pair of old gray sweatpants and a white athletic T-shirt.

"Do what? All I know how to do is write and perform, and a nigga took that away from me." Fabiola's voice sounded sullen coming from under the comforter.

"I don't know, gurl, but you ain't gonna find the answer in

bed under the covers!" Shug said and stood there glaring at Fabiola with her hands on her hips.

Fabiola didn't want to listen. She just wanted to go to sleep, but she was afraid she might never sleep again. Why did everything have to be awful? She had lost everything. Everything. From out of nowhere the phrase *All I got is my word and self-respect* popped into her thoughts. Suddenly, she kicked the comforter off—startling Shug—got out of bed, dragged herself to the bathroom, and began to get herself together. If the mirror was any indication, it was going to take a minute.

Shug asked, "Where you going?"

"I got a promise to keep."

★ ★ ★

Two hours later Fabiola stepped into Casino's room looking and smelling like a new woman.

"So, how's everything going, hummingbird?" Casino asked and then shot a glance at Tonk.

Tonk got up from his seat. "I'll be close by. Y'all need anything?"

"No, thank you, Tonk," Fabiola said graciously. He nodded and left the room. "You look a little tired—how come?" Fabiola asked Casino, not answering his earlier question.

Her attempt at being evasive didn't stand a chance of going unnoticed, but Casino played along. "Maybe because I don't sleep well my first night in new places—never did. Plus, I was up half the night waiting for your call."

"I like this place better than MCV." Fabiola played the selective-hearing card. "How're the nurses treating you? They better be rolling out the red carpet. And you better be cooperating with your therapy." Fabiola sealed her lips with a pointed index finger and a smile.

"The nurses seem to all be great. I'm being treated like a king—as I should be—and therapy is kicking me in the ass, but at the end of the day I'll win that battle as well," he answered. "Now, are you going to tell me what happened?"

She risked a peek at his face with those big beautiful brown eyes of hers.

"With what?" she continued to play like all was good in the hood.

Viola had confided in Casino everything that went down, but asked Casino not to say anything to Fabiola about it.

"Judging by the look on your face, the meeting with the magnificent Johnny Wiz, the big lunch meeting," he said.

Fabiola dropped her gaze. "I don't really want to talk about it."

"A problem can't get solved if you keep it bottled up inside. Yesterday, Johnny Wiz was the topic of the day. You were supposed to call me last night to share it all with me. I never got the call, and now you say you don't want to talk about the man. This tells me that you *need* to talk about it, and then maybe we can figure out where to go from here."

"Goodness gracious—I don't know where to start," she confessed. "Do you want the *Reader's Digest* or the blow-by-blow version?"

"I've always been more of a boxing fan." He pressed a button, causing his bed to move to the full upright position.

"Johnny Wiz is a jerk," she blurted out.

"Most of us can be jerks every now and again. Some a little more than others is all."

"He was a bigger jerk than most," she capped.

"I see. But if we let that be grounds to kill all deals, nothing would get done in this world. You have to be able to move past that. Him being a jerk isn't going to slow you down, is it?"

"I can try to move past it, but I don't think he can." Fabiola rubbed her hand through her hair. "A lot of mean-spirited words were thrown around."

"So you bruised the ego of one limp-dick muthafucka—the show doesn't stop there."

"But he's one of the most influential limp-dicks in the industry," she countered.

"There are no *buts*. Do you have what it takes to be a star?"

"No doubt about it," Fabiola answered with more confidence and authority in her tone than she actually felt. "I've known I had what it took since I was a baby."

"Then fuck Johnny Wiz. One monkey don't stop no show."

Fabiola was eye to eye with Casino, and she was staring at confidence—confidence in her. "What do you suggest that I do?"

"I know this guy that dabbles in the music business. He has Grammy-nominated work in his portfolio for producing and writing, and he owes me a few large favors. I've called in one of those favors by getting him to help you make a record."

"He lives here?" Fabiola asked in disbelief.

"No. He's in New York and he's expecting you to arrive on Sunday evening. His studio and expertise are going to be yours Monday and Tuesday and you come home on Wednesday."

"Oh my God, Casino," Fabiola cried out. "This is too good to be true." She was already calculating the little bit of money she had saved up and how much the trip was going to cost her to be in New York for two days.

"No. You're too good to be true, and don't ever let anyone tell you different. And I have one more thing for you." He ran his hand down the front of his pajama top, smoothing out the wrinkles. "Look in the bottom drawer of that dresser." Fabiola did as she was told. "The little wallet," he said, "belongs to you. You didn't think I would send you out of town without any spending money, did you?" The wallet was filled with five large. Fabiola cried tears of joy as she hugged Casino.

"Thank you. I promise I won't disappoint you or let you down."

He smiled. "I know you won't."

The Big City

Heavy rain and high winds up and down the East Coast were the cause of more than the airline's usual amount of flight delays. So many unsatisfied customers were lying around, asleep inside of LaGuardia Airport, that it was starting to look like a giant slumber party that no one wanted to attend.

Fabiola's flight finally made it to its destination, more than two hours after its scheduled arrival, but the important thing was that she was there—New York City. This was only the second time she'd ever been to the big city; the first was when she won the talent show. Hopefully, this time the final outcome would turn out better. After making her way to baggage claim, Fabiola found more than just her luggage.

"Are you Fabiola Mays?" the man holding the sign with her name on it asked. He was wearing the traditional black chauffeur's uniform.

Just like in the movies, she thought. "Yes, that's me," she spoke up. "I'm Fabiola, but how did you recognize me?"

"Your eyes lit up when you read the sign."

Fabiola gave the chauffeur a quizzical look.

"I've been doing this for a long time," he said with an Eastern European accent. "My name is Traupee. Now, how about we go find your luggage?"

Casino never mentioned a car service. What other surprises might he come up with? She smiled. After Fabiola pointed out her suitcases as they traveled around the carousel, Traupee put everything on a cart and led her outside.

Following Traupee out of the building, she sucked in a lungful of polluted New York air without complaint. It was an upgrade from the canned air that the airports and planes were manufacturing. But she hadn't come to New York for clean air; she was there to feed her hunger pangs for success and her starvation for stardom by taking a bite out of the Big Apple.

"This is your car, Ms. Mays." The driver interrupted her thoughts.

"Thank you," she said, sliding onto the backseat of the black-and-gray Chrysler 300. The driver shut the door for her, placed her bags in the trunk, and soon they were pulling into the mad airport traffic.

"The hotel is about thirty minutes away," the driver informed her from the front seat.

Fabiola felt her way through her pocketbook digging for her phone. After finding what she was looking for, she dialed

Casino's number. "I finally made it," she said after hearing his voice on the other end. "Safe and sound."

"Good. When you told me about the delays I was concerned about you."

"Aaaww." Fabiola was warmed by his comment; she could hear the sincerity in his voice. "Well, I'm on my way to the studio now."

"Excellent! Now, can you do me one other favor?" Casino asked.

"Is Beyoncé one of the luckiest, hardworking chicks in the game?"

"Don't forget to call me as soon as you leave the studio, or before, if you run into any problems—big or small—while you're there."

He sounded like he was getting his strength back, and although she didn't really know him before the shooting, it was easy to imagine what he would be doing after he was back on his feet and out of the hospital. She envisioned him moving around, calling shots, and making things happen for all those around him. It brought a smile to her face. "Of course I will, Casino, but only if you can do one other thing for me?"

"Name it."

"Tell me how I will ever be able to pay you back for your generosity."

He said five words before ending the conversation: "Accept nothing less than success." And the call was over.

While she was thinking about what he had just said and all he had done, the phone rang. Maybe that was him calling back. "Casino?"

"Nope, it's me," Shug said. "Where you at, gurrrl?" Shug and Adora had dropped Fabiola off at the Richmond International Airport about five hours ago.

"Gurrrl, I'm in the car service en route to the hotel."

"Car service?" Shug screeched. "Umph, you doing big things, ain't you?" She didn't even wait for Fabiola to answer her question. "Well, by the time you take your shower, we'll be parking our car and hauling our shit up to your room."

"What?" Now it was Fabiola's turn to be surprised. "And who is *we*?"

"Me and yo sister—who else?" she said. "Every star needs an entourage. We may not have been able to afford those last-minute high-ass ticket prices that Mr. Casino blessed you wit, but that wasn't going to be enough to stop us from being there wit our girl. We just wanted to make it a surprise. We on the Jersey Turnpike now. Surprise! Bitches are on the way!"

"Damn, that's crazy. Y'all dropped me off at the airport and damn near beat my butt to New York."

"All that bullshit they take you through at the airport these days. Gurrllll, when you were taking off yo damn shoes and sitting on the tarmac listening to your iPod, we were on I-95 making our way."

"For a whole lot less money, too," Fabiola heard her sister scream in the background.

"Well, call me when y'all get here. I'm not gon' talk to y'all butts all the way up 95."

About sixteen minutes later the driver pulled up in front of an enormous hotel located across from Central Park. "This can't be where I'm staying," Fabiola told the driver. "This place is beautiful . . . and it looks expensive."

The driver checked his paperwork. "This is the place," he confirmed.

Fabiola looked at the paper she had in her pocketbook and agreed, "That's what it must be then."

Casino didn't half-step when it came to good taste. The hotel was beautiful. The high ceilings, gold décor, and plush carpet looked like something from an episode of *Lifestyles of the Rich and Famous*. By the time she checked in, took a shower, and got comfortable, as promised her entourage was pounding on the door with a cart full of luggage. They all hugged.

"This shit is off the hook, girl," Adora said.

"It is real nice," Shug added.

"It's kinda like the one we stayed at when we came up here for the Hot Soundz competition, except it's better in every way," Adora said.

"That dude likes you for real," Shug informed her best friend.

"I think he just likes helping people out. Some people are just like that."

"Maybe he wanted you to get familiar with it because one day he plans to marry you here," Shug teased.

Adora opened up the hotel room window and screamed, "GRIP YOURSELF NEW YORK CITY!"

Although they stayed up all night, first thing in the morning the three girls caught a cab to the Brooklyn studio where Fabiola was scheduled to meet with the producer. After ringing the bell a tall brown-skinned guy wearing a Sean John outfit let them in, offered them a seat, and walked off. Fabiola expected the place to be a little plusher. The studio was basically two rooms with a closet for a sound booth. The first room doubled as waiting room/entertainment room. There was a late-model big-screen television wired to a Sony PlayStation on the far left wall, surrounded by five beanbags. As far as furnishings, the rest of the waiting area consisted of an old brown-and-tan sofa and table set that probably came off the assembly line some time during the late seventies. A handwritten sign that read QUIET! GENIUS AT

WORK was taped to the wall, alongside posters of artists from the seventies and eighties. Fabiola, Adora, and Shug looked at one another and then took a seat on the antique sofa.

From the sofa, Fabiola could see a dude sitting behind a table with a lot of electronic equipment, wearing headphones. *He must be Taz, the producer,* she thought. He was a funny-looking man with light skin, big ears, and a crooked nose that stood out even more with the Cartier glasses he wore sitting on top of it. The lenses of his prescription glasses were so thick they made his eyes look distorted. He was screaming in a loud deep voice at the girl that was in the booth trying to sing. When the producer wasn't screaming, making demands, and cussing, he was bopping his head back and forth with his hand cupped over the earpiece of the headphones. The girls watched intensely.

"Fab, you can outsing that bitch on your worst day," Shug said.

"She's good," Fabiola admitted. "I think that's Royce." Although she didn't show it, Fabiola was a bit starstruck for a second, not believing that she was about to record in the same studio as the R & B sensation Royce, a female artist who was signed with The Wizard Entertainment Group. She had three hit singles off her first album, which went gold, and was working on her second.

"That is her, chile; I could spot that bad weave anywhere," Shug said, getting a laugh. "We need to introduce that poor girl to Sheena."

"You ain't lying," Fabiola cosigned.

"Hell, nah," Adora cut in, looking at them like they were crazy. "We ain't about to turn the competition on to our best-kept secret."

"I know that's right," Shug said.

"Stop! Cut the music," Royce announced. Her voice boomed

out the studio speakers. "I'm not singing this line, Taz." She was shaking her head as if to say, "no way, no how."

"Stop crying," Taz screamed back, "and just sing the fucking song."

"I don't feel like I should be singing these types of lyrics." Royce exited the recording room.

"You sing what's on the paper. That's it, that's all."

"It's too explicit." Royce held her ground.

"Why do I always have to get stuck with the hard-to-work-with musicians?"

" 'Cause you in this bullshit-ass studio," one of Royce's side-kicks said.

Taz stood up. "You do what I tell you to do. Now get back in the damn booth and sing the damn song."

"*Pick a spot on my body and fill it with your love* . . . I'm not no fuckin' ho. This is supposed to be a love song not a fuckin' freak show."

Fabiola wondered if Johnny Wiz had slept with her. She had learned after her meeting fiasco that it was rumored that he had slept with every woman that came through the company's doors.

"I'm not changing my song," Taz said. "That's it! Fuck that! Period!"

"I'm not going to sit here and let you talk to my artist like that," Royce's manager, Petey, stepped in with a little bass in his voice.

"I will talk to whoever I fucking feel like talking to, however the fuck I feel like it," Taz held his own.

"Why are you being so stubborn, Taz? It's only one line of one song," Petey tried to reason.

Royce was pacing the floor running her mouth. "I ain't gonna sing shit."

"She can sing the song the way I wrote it or get the fuck out of my studio."

"Hold on, Taz, I'm paying for this studio time," Petey said.

"You ain't paying for shit, the record company is," Taz reminded Petey. "And they ain't sent the check yet, so as far as I am concerned it's charity work I'm doing now."

"Fuck this, Petey," Royce demanded. "Call Johnny. We'll see what Johnny has to say about this." She smirked at Taz as if she had just trumped him. "He is not going to like you talking to his favorite girl singer like this."

Fabiola's question was answered. Johnny definitely had put that freckled dick of his up in her. Royce was under Johnny Wiz's spell.

"Call him," Taz taunted Petey. "Johnny Wiz don't run shit over here in this motherfucker."

Petey wanted to be able to handle the situation without involving Johnny, but Taz had forced his hand. He pulled out his cell phone and stepped toward the waiting room to make the call. Royce stormed off to the restroom.

"You running in that bathroom to snort a little of that shit, huh? Maybe some of that love boat will make you get yo mind right enough to sing this song."

"That phone call with Johnny gonna make you change the song so that I can sing it."

"This shit is too crazy," Adora said to her sister. "Damn sis, we thought you were going to be entertaining us but shit, this is just as good. You know I likes drama!"

After hearing a knock, Shug yelled to Taz, "There's someone at the door!"

"Well, get it then," he screamed back, looking at her as if it shouldn't have been that difficult for her to figure out. Then he screamed at Royce through the restroom door. "You can call anybody you want to call. I ain't changing shit."

Adora opened up the door and three girls came in, sashaying

past them straight into the studio with Taz. One of them bent down and licked the inside of his ear.

Petey walked back in the room with Taz. "Here." He handed Taz the phone.

"Hold on a minute," Taz told the groupie. He then took the phone out of Petey's hand and spoke into the receiver. "What up?"

Fabiola tried to keep up with the one-way conversation while tuning out all the small talk of the other girls that had just come in.

"I ain't changing the song," Taz spat. "It's my song. I wrote it." He paused to listen. "I know it's one line, that's why I ain't changing it. I'm tired of compromising my work. . . . Then if I change it, I gotta give that bitch fucking credit on a song I wrote." He listened for a minute, then spoke again. "Johnny, no disrespect, but I'm not going to change one word for the bitch, so if she want to blow the opportunity to be on a hit, then that's up to her. I really don't care either way. She can sing the song or bounce—her decision." Taz handed the phone back to Petey and followed the groupie into the other bathroom.

"It's your choice," Petey said, looking at Royce. "You don't have to sing the song if you don't want to."

"Let's go." Royce grabbed her bag and followed Petey out. She tossed her hair over her shoulder, holding her head high as she walked out the door.

It didn't take long for everyone in the studio to figure out what was going on in the bathroom. Homegirl must have had one helluva head game, because for the next four and a half minutes, the only music in the studio was Taz's moans.

Fabiola, Adora, and Shug just looked at one another; each one was waiting on the other to give the word to get the fuck out of there. But none of them said anything.

Taz came out of the bathroom fumbling with his pants and

sporting a satisfied smile on his face, when he noticed that Royce and Petey had left. To be sure, he walked to the waiting room. No Royce or Petey, but Fabiola and the other girls were there. "Which one of y'all can sing?" he asked.

Fabiola raised her hand.

"What the hell you waiting for then? Get up off your ass and get in the damn booth. We got a fucking hit song to finish. Shit!"

"I know that's right," Shug commented, "what one won't do, another will." She turned and gave Adora a high five.

"Where's the song you want me to sing?" Fabiola was cool and willing to roll with the punches.

"This is the song." Taz handed her the paper with the lyrics on it. "First, I'm going to play you the melody, then you can sing it however you feel. We'll go back and smooth it over afterward."

"No problem." Fabiola looked at the handwritten song, then glanced at her friend and sister with raised eyebrows and walked into the booth, closing the door behind her.

Taz tapped the mic. "Can you hear me?"

"Yes."

"Okay, good." He dropped the music and she listened for a minute, then he spoke into the mic. "I'm going to cue the music now; just sing what you see on the paper." The moment Fabiola began to sing, Taz became entranced. He didn't scream at her. He didn't stop the session. He just kept smiling.

"That's my sister right there," Adora bragged. "Do your thing, gurrl."

"Sang that shit," Shug cheered.

A star was being born right in the middle of his studio. Taz was still bopping his head with a giant smile on his face when she came out of the booth. "What's your name?" he asked. Things had moved so quickly he didn't even know the name of his new star performer.

"Fabiola." She smiled. "Casino sent me."

"It don't matter who sent you, what matters is that we now have a hit on our hands." Fabiola could hear the potential in the song as well, but she held her cool. While Shug and Adora went berserk, Fabiola only smiled. She had to keep her game face on. The last thing she wanted Taz to think was that she needed him so bad that he felt he could invite her into the bathroom next.

"Are you up to finishing the song and maybe one other?" Taz offered.

"I'm definitely up to it." Fabiola smiled again.

"Then let's get back to work. You need water, weed, or anything?" He was patting his pockets as if he could pull whatever she asked for right out of his pants.

"I don't do drugs, but water would be fine."

"You sure that's all you need?" Taz was far more relaxed and accommodating with Fabiola than he was with Royce. Maybe it was because he was as excited about the song as Fabiola, or it could have been a result of the mind-blowing head he had received in the bathroom.

"If you had some hot tea that would be great."

"Somebody make my star some tea. We need to treat this voice like precious cargo."

Fabiola smiled while looking up to thank God. But she was careful not to get too overjoyed. She'd seen a sure thing slip from her fingers time and time again.

Seven hours later the song was done. Everyone danced around the studio hyped up. Fabiola called Casino and played the song for him over the phone.

"I like it," Casino said, happy to hear the excitement in her voice.

"You do?"

"Yeah, it's hot and sounds like it's a hit," Casino assured her.

When Taz came to the studio the next morning, he found Fabiola waiting for him on the stoop writing in her notebook.

"Where your li'l posse at?" he asked.

"I left them asleep in the hotel," Fabiola said with a smile. "But I couldn't wait to get back here and get back to work."

"Good," he said. "I like a hard worker."

"I've been working on some songs. Would you mind listening to them?"

"A'ight."

After a few hours of working on some songs that Fabiola had written, Taz sent her out to the corner store for a snack and some fresh air. While she was out, he made a phone call.

"Yo, Johnny," he said into the phone, "this Taz."

"I know who it is; it's the nigga that kicked my artist out of his studio yesterday," Johnny responded.

"That's old news, baby. I got something that'll make up for that ten times over."

"I'm listening." He hid his curiosity behind a sigh.

"I found a thoroughbred. The song 'Touch Me' that I wrote— the one that you really liked?" Of course Johnny knew what song he was talking about; it was the same song his girl Royce was supposed to have done. "Well, this chick I found did her muthafuckin' thing with it."

"Really?" Johnny asked. He was always on the lookout for new hot talent. Today an artist was the next big thing; tomorrow she was old news. "This thoroughbred, is she marketable?"

"Do a chicken have feathers? Hell yeah, she's marketable. She has the face, the body, swagger, and the voice. And there's something new about her voice; she's not trying to do what everyone else is doing. I'm telling you, Johnny: She's the real deal, sho nuff, Holyfield. None of that put-together studio shit that's being played on the radios all day. This girl is"—Taz tried to come up with a proper comparison—"a cross between Aretha Franklin and Gladys Knight with some new-age shit thrown in." Johnny had never heard Taz this excited about anything. "You should stop by and hear the song. . . ."

"What's her name?"

"Fabiola, and she's from Virg—"

"I know her," Johnny cut him off, "and she doesn't have what it takes—too many problems."

"What type of problems?"

"Drama, drugs, ghetto, ahh, man, just too many issues, too many to iron out," Johnny lied.

This couldn't be the same girl I spent the last day and a half with, Taz thought. "I was with her all day yesterday and didn't see a sign of any kind of drug use. From what I could tell, she seems like a hard worker."

"Well, I don't want anything to do with her ghetto ass or her momager. And if I were you I wouldn't fuck with her either."

"I think you got her mixed up with someone else. The girl I'm talking about is the sweetest, most humble girl you ever want to meet—a real Southern belle."

"It's her all right. She almost tricked me, too. I almost made the mistake of signing her awhile back."

"What happened?"

"I saw through her charade just in time, that's what happened," Johnny said in an annoyed tone.

"Aren't you the same person that told me that as long as an artist can record and perform, the rest of the bullshit could be worked out?" Taz didn't feel like Johnny was being totally honest with him.

"Not this one. She's a lowlife."

"I hope this has nothing to do with what transpired between me and Royce?"

"You crossed the line with Royce, but that's not it," Johnny told him. "Been there, done that. Tell you what: Give me a call next month when I may be able to stomach some more of your bullshit, and I will send you studio work, but in regards to that Fabifolla or whatever her name is? She's definitely out of the question, next month, next year, or the next life." The phone went dead.

When Fabiola returned from the store, she noticed a sour look on Taz's face. "What's wrong?" she asked.

Taz shook his head, then removed the Cartier glasses from his face and wiped the thick lenses. "Let's get back to work," he said.

While he and Fabiola were working hard at trying to create a mini promotional album, Taz couldn't stop thinking about the conversation he had had with his brother the night before. Travis was doing his time in West Virginia now. Other than to let his brother know that he was doing fine, Travis expressed one other thing to Taz: to make sure he played fair by Casino.

Casino had met Taz's younger brother, Travis, while they both were serving federal time in Atlanta. Travis never forgot how much Casino looked out for him, and made it known that if ever he could do anything to return the favor, all Casino had to do was ask.

Time flew and by the wee hours of the morning, Taz and Fabiola had gotten a lot done in a short time. They had recorded four songs, but only "Touch Me" was completely mixed. "So, you go back to Richmond tomorrow, huh?"

"Yeah," she nodded, wishing that she could stay in the city longer and work in the studio. She was truly in her element. She had been waiting for the opportunity to be able to do what her heart yearned to do.

"Give this to Casino." Taz handed her the CD they had made together. "I told him he could have the single. All he has to do is press it up and get it played; that'll get you some buzz and create a fan base for you."

Fabiola took the CD. "Sounds good," she said, "but do you really think it'll be that easy?"

"You got a manager?"

"I had one." Fabiola really missed her mother, but she wasn't able to forgive her for what she said.

"Well, you need to get one—and fast. You should concentrate on your music and let your manager iron out the details with the business. Some artists wear themselves thin trying to be artist and manager. It's not a good look."

"I hear you. I really want to thank you for everything that you've done." She looked at the CD clutched in her hand. "You've truly been a blessing to me, and trust me when I get on, you don't have to worry, I got you big-time!"

"It's my pleasure. I normally charge a minimum of thirty thousand for a beat and a song, but I believe in you and I want you to make it; that's why I gave it to you. Well, that and a couple of other reasons." He took a deep breath. In a low voice, he added, "The man that sent you to me, Casino, my brother owes his life to him, and this is partial repayment for that also. But how do you compensate a person for something like that? Between me and you, I don't know what you did to Johnny Wiz to piss him off, but he's trying very hard to block your road to stardom."

"I know. It got very ugly between us." Fabiola dropped her head. "He tried to make me sleep with him, which I didn't. But I play that episode in my head every day over and over again." She looked up at him, and confessed, "Sometimes I wished I would have, but then I ask myself what that would have really meant."

"This whole entertainment thing is a dirty game, and especially fucked-up for women. Most of the times it ain't who you know but who you fucking, but being an industry whore has its downsides—trust me. That shit is like rolling the dice. Sometimes you get put on but there are some who just get used." Taz consoled her. "As I said, you are very gifted. Let your talent and wit get you to the top. Don't be discouraged! I see a lot of people come and go in my studio, but you have what it takes to make it. Believe me. And I am here if you need me."

"That means a lot to me."

"I mean it. Now you better get out of here. Don't you leave in a couple of hours?"

"Yes. Thanks so much for everything." She hugged Taz and he kissed her on the cheek. He knew she had a real long road ahead of her with Johnny Wiz as her foe.

Everything Happens
for a Reason

Two weeks had passed since Fabiola had gotten back from New York. She had been pounding the pavement trying to figure out how to get her song played on the radio. The task was proving to be harder than she thought. She tried taking radio djs out to dinner, sending them gift baskets accompanied by her CD, and even giving it to a couple of family members of djs to pass along. Nothing had worked. She was supposed to return to New York in a few days to continue recording her album. It was just too much work. She needed a manager in the worst way. But one thing Fabiola could say was that being on the grind so hard made her appreciate her mother's hustle. She had way more respect for Viola, and on top of it all, she missed her mom.

★ ★ ★

Fabiola got to the facility where they were taking care of Casino a little earlier than normal. She had a few other appointments she had to meet later, but didn't want to miss her time with him. To be totally honest, Fabiola was getting way more out of the visits than he was now, but that wasn't the reason she kept coming. When she got to the door, she could hear a woman's voice.

"Speaking of things that are unaccounted for, we haven't calculated any of the charity work that you seem to be doing," the voice said.

When Fabiola walked in, she found Casino sitting on the edge of the bed and Roxy stationed on a chair across from him. Fabiola hadn't seen her since Casino had left the other hospital. Roxy wore a gray-and-white pinstriped business suit with matching heels. The briefcase she carried was half empty, because the rest of the contents were lying on the bedside table, where she was carefully going through them. The paperwork contained most of Casino's legal holdings—at least the ones that she had been in charge of anyway. Roxy gave Fabiola a hard stare, and Fabiola returned it pound for pound before walking over and planting a kiss on Casino's cheek.

"How are you feeling today?" She smiled.

"I'm feeling like I'm in the company of a star." He was sitting with his back straight as a board, hair and goatee groomed, wearing his ever-present fresh pair of pajamas.

Roxy started putting the papers back in the briefcase. "We can finish this at another time?"

Funny how a man that's lying up could be so powerful that he could make so many things happen for so many people from a hospital bed, Fabiola thought as Roxy put the papers away.

"Yeah, we'll do that later, Roxy," Casino said, dismissing her.

"Ciao, for now." She smiled at Casino before cutting her eyes at Fabiola. "Later for you."

Roxy strolled out the door.

An hour and a half had gone by when Fabiola peeked at her watch. She hadn't realized that much time had passed.

"Where are you going when you leave here?" Casino asked her.

"It's Adora's birthday, and my mother always cooks and has cake and ice cream like she did when we were kids. She has always made a big stink out of all of our birthdays."

"The more I hear about your mother, the more I like her."

Fabiola didn't respond to his comment. "So, I may go over there."

"Why do I hear uncertainty in your voice? Do you have something else to do?"

"No, not really," she sighed. "It's just that me and my mother are on the outs right now, and I don't want to go over there and mess it up for Adora."

"Why are you all on the outs?"

"Long story." Fabiola shook her head, and although the hurt was apparent on her face she tried to camouflage it with a smile.

"Okay, well, I'm waiting."

"She sometimes acts as if it's her career and not mine, and that how I feel doesn't even count."

"Well, with all due respect, she has sacrificed a lot to make sure that your career moves in the right direction."

"And, Casino, I really do appreciate that, more than you or she could ever know. I mean, knowing everything that her and my sister and even my brother have sacrificed for me pushes me at times when I don't feel like going to this session or that dance class or even to band rehearsal. So I am grateful for every single thing that they have given up for me. However, sometimes my mother doesn't know where to draw the line."

"I understand where you are coming from."

"I don't think you do. I really don't think you do." Fabiola knew that Casino couldn't possibly have a clue.

"I do, more than you could imagine. I may not know every detail, but I am a man of great understanding."

"I believe you, but my mother is mad at me and said some rather ugly things to me because I wouldn't sleep with Johnny Wiz to get a deal."

Casino wasn't the least bit surprised at all.

"It's like just because this man has the power to make our dreams come true she wants me to compromise my morals and self-respect and forget everything that she taught me."

"You know, my dear, parents are not perfect. They make mistakes, too."

"Yes, I know," she said slowly.

"Now, you are not perfect either and you have to forgive her and move on. There is no need in carrying around ill feelings, especially not toward people who really do love you and want the best for you."

Fabiola thought about what Casino said the entire ride over to her mother's house. Fabiola used her key to open her mother's door. It was the first time she'd set foot in the house since their argument. "Happy birthday to you . . ." Fabiola sang out loud as she stepped in the house.

"I know that's not my—"

Fabiola cut her mother off. "It's only me, Mom—the selfish little bitch."

They stared at each other for a moment. Fabiola could see the regret and sadness in Viola's eyes.

Finally, Viola spoke. "Baby, please forgive me. I didn't mean those things I said to you. Even the best mothers make mistakes." Viola dropped her head in shame. She only hoped her daughter could hear the sincerity in her voice.

Fabiola was still angry, but she loved her mother and knew that no matter what, Viola only wanted her to succeed. After all the years of support she offered her daughter, the hustle and the grind, she could somewhat understand how Viola might have gotten beside herself there for a minute. Taking all of that into consideration, Fabiola felt her heart start to soften.

"Yeah, Fab, at least she didn't try to make you prostitute yourself when you were ten years old or no shit like that," Ocean joked.

"You always mess up a good moment, don't you?" Fabiola play-punched her brother. Then she turned back to Viola.

"Ma, I forgive you. And I'm going to give you a chance to make it up to me."

"Anything, baby," Viola said.

"First, please don't ever make me feel that I can't talk to you when something goes wrong. I should have been able to call you and tell you the blow by blow, but I was afraid."

"You are so right, baby."

"Next, I do appreciate all that you have done for me. I do. But understand that I am not a machine. I am a person."

"I know, baby. I love you so much. I do. And I sometimes forget that this isn't about me, it's about you," Viola said and pulled her daughter into her arms.

Adora walked into the room while her sister and mother were hugging. "Aw, what a perfect birthday gift, my two favorite ladies are speaking again."

Then Adora flipped the moment. "Now, where the heck is my present?" she said to Fabiola.

"You just said . . ."

"You know I was joking. I want a real present."

"I left it in the front room. I'll get it for you."

"No need, I can get it myself." Adora went in the other room and spied a large package. Wondering what was inside, she started opening the gift by first removing the multicolored bow, then the gift wrap. It was the new sewing machine that she'd needed. "Thank you, sis," Adora screamed back to the kitchen. "I love it."

"You're welcome." Fabiola was in the doorway of the room where her sister was.

Viola was still trying to figure out what she had to do to get back in the good graces of her daughter. "Okay, baby, what do I have to do to make it up to you: clean your toilet and scrub your floor?"

"Of course not, Mother."

"Then tell me what you need."

"We'll chat about it later. I don't want to talk about it until after Adora's celebration. This is her time, not mine."

"There are no I's in this house, only us," Adora let it be known. "So whatever you have to say, let it out. Plus, by now I am used to it."

"Oh, cut it out, now that's why I am going to wait."

"No, the hell you ain't. It's my day and now you better tell us."

"Well"—she looked at her mother—"I want you to be my manager again. I need help getting my new single spun on the radio."

"Oh my God!" Viola shouted, jumping in the air. If she had leaped any higher, she would've hit her head on the ceiling. "Adora told me that the song was hot. It drove me crazy not being able to hear it."

"I am looking for a manager this time, Mom, not a mom-ager."

"I can do that," Viola said, her voice charged with excitement.

"I do need my mother in my life, too, you just have to know how to separate the two," Fabiola warned.

"You got yourself a deal." Viola kissed Fabiola on the cheek, and Fabiola truly felt happy again for the first time in weeks. The time away from her mother had made her appreciate the hard work that her mother did for her.

"Who do I need to talk to about my stylist ideas?" Adora smiled at her sister. "You or Mom—I mean your manager?"

"My manager," Fabiola said seriously.

"Do you think Casino would be interested in investing in a record company with me?"

"That might be a good idea, because Casino said that he was going to pay for us to do a video for the single." Fabiola was excited when it came to talking about Casino.

"And not to mention, I think Casino likes you," Viola said.

"No, I just think we understand each other and he really believes in me," Fabiola said, trying to convince her mother, but inside she wished she was right. "Besides, he's got Roxy."

"I heard that chick has been chasing that man around for years, and if he ain't married her yet, then the odds are he won't."

"Baby sis, you know you got yoself a sugar daddy," Ocean teased.

"Shut up!"

Fabiola struggled with her emotions. As much as she tried to deny it, her feelings for Casino had grown at a tremendous rate. He was the complete opposite of all the knuckleheads she had dated in the past.

It's Party Time

The girls were on their way to the grand opening of the new club called The Den. Shug was driving, Adora was riding shotgun and pulling on a blunt, while Fabiola was chilling in the backseat thinking about what it would be like when she finally became famous. The radio dj was broadcasting live from The Den and playing mostly "get crump" music. Shug slowed the car to a stop for the red light and looked over to Adora. "Girl, you gon' smoke all the dang weed?"

"I'm not Fabiola, I do blow trees," Adora shot back.

"If you know what I know, sis, you would hit it til you finish, cuz Shug's ass be blowing more than some dang trees," Fabiola commented from the backseat.

"You got that right," Shug said with no shame in her game.

"That's why I smoked my half first." Adora took one last toke of the exotic weed and then passed the rest to Shug.

"Fuck you, Adora." Shug took a hard pull on the stogie while trying to hold the smoke in and said, "Like you got virgin lips up on your face."

Fabiola's phone vibrated, and she fished through her tote bag in search of her incessantly vibrating cell phone. *Where in the hell is 609 from?* Fabiola thought. She'd gotten several phone calls in the past two days from that number, but hadn't answered because she didn't know the number or because she was just too busy.

Pushing the call key, Fabiola answered, "Good evening." There was a momentary silence. "Hello?"

The caller said, "So, you think you got what it takes to make it, huh? Congratulations."

The voice sounded sort of familiar, but Fabiola couldn't make it out. "Thank you," she said, "but who may I ask is calling?"

"I'm that easily forgotten? Funny how fame or shall I say chasing the dream corrodes the memory."

Fabiola didn't have a lot of time or patience to waste on random prank phone calls. She had adopted Casino's no-tolerance policy on bullshitting. Just when she was about to hang up, the caller spoke again.

"It's me, Johnny Wiz. You do remember me, don't you?"

"Of course I remember you," she said, but thought, *How could I forget you? You tried to take advantage of me in more than one way.*

"Well, I just wanted to tell you congratulations and to encourage you to enjoy everything that comes with fame."

Fabiola was taken by surprise by Johnny Wiz's call and his acknowledgment that she had fame coming, not to mention his gracious behavior. Before she could thank him, though, he continued.

"Because it won't last for long, you stuck-up bitch."

Fabiola wanted to scream something back through the phone, something that would make her feel better about the situation, but it was no use; he'd already disconnected the call.

"Girl, who was that on the phone giving you fever?" Shug could tell that Fabiola was a bit distracted.

Dumbfounded, she couldn't even respond because she was trying to make sense of the entire conversation herself.

Then she heard what she knew was the beginning of her song playing. "Turn the radio up," Fabiola demanded.

The radio jock's voice boomed from the speakers. "I'm going to give y'all partygoers a little treat. This new joint was produced by The Tasmanian Devil, and it's so hot I need to wear gloves just to spin this joint!" The song started playing in the background while the radio personality continued, "Here it is . . . Richmond's own, but about to be internationally known, Fabiola Mays's new joint, 'Touch Me.' "

The girls erupted in cheers when Fabiola's song came on.

"They playing my song!" Fabiola shouted. "They playing my song!" Fabiola felt higher than any legal or illegal drug could take her.

Shug turned the volume up as loud as it would go, put the car in park, jumped out the car, and started dancing. Adora and Fabiola followed her lead. Before they knew it, they were singing, dancing, and screaming at the top of their lungs. *"Pick a spot on my body and fill it with your love . . ."* The girls got louder when they got to that particular line in the song, rubbing all over their bodies in the middle of the street. Cars were going by blowing their horns; some flashed their lights and some even made sexual propositions, but they ignored it all. The only thing they were focused on was the tune blaring from the radio. The moment was worth a billion dollars. No one could steal it, destroy it, or take it away.

Fabiola was so caught up in the moment that she had forgotten all about calling anybody else to let them know about her song being played on the radio. "Dora, Dora!" she screamed to her sister. "Call Mommy and tell her to turn to the radio station. I'm going to call Casino."

The blue lights from the police cruiser must have had the effect of a strobe light, because no one stopped dancing when the officer pulled up and got out of his squad car. Officer Brown initially thought that they were having car troubles, but judging by the girls' behavior it was clear to him that they were on drugs.

Officer Brown walked up to the women with his hand near his gun, just in case. "What's going on, ladies?"

Adora addressed the cop. "My sister's song just got played on the radio." The officer followed her eyes to Fabiola.

"Why didn't you just pull the car over?" the officer asked. "You know I could give you a ticket for this?"

"How about we give you an autograph instead and just call it a warning?" Shug offered with a small chuckle, not really giving a damn what the officer did.

Officer Brown was only twenty-seven, and truth be told he was kind of excited for Fabiola himself.

"Where're you all on your way to?" he asked.

"To The Den, the new club in Shockoe Bottom."

"I'll let you go without a ticket on one condition," Officer Brown said. "You have to follow me to the club so that you won't start any more impromptu parties at traffic lights. Deal?"

"Deal," they all agreed. The car was filled with giggles all the way to the club.

When Fabiola and her crew arrived at the club, word got out

that they were in line. A bouncer walked up to Adora and asked, "Are you Fabiola Mays?"

"No, I'm her sister, that's Fabiola." She smiled and pointed to her sister.

"Well, the owner of the club wants you and your guests to come in compliments of him and enjoy the VIP treatment of The Den."

"Are you serious?" was all Fabiola could say.

When they walked past the black velvet ropes and into the club, the dj played Fabiola's song, giving her a shout-out. "Ladies and gentlemen, Fabiola Mays is in the building. I repeat, there's a superstar in the house."

Everyone started looking around for the new local star. Once they spotted her, Fabiola didn't disappoint. She was working the black-and-white zebra-striped backless catsuit that Adora had created for her. They had taken their seats in a private booth in the VIP section when G.P. bopped up. He was wearing a colorful Dodgers jean outfit and a pair of alligator Air Force Ones.

"I'm glad you saved me a seat." G.P. didn't wait for a response before scooting in the booth beside the new star. "Waitress"— G.P. waved his hand to flag down the passing hostess—"we need three bottles of your best champagne."

"Are you aware that our best champagne is three twenty-five a pop?" the waitress said with a roll in her neck.

"No, I wasn't aware and frankly, Scarlett, I don't give a damn," G.P. admitted. "Matter of fact, bring us six bottles."

"Oh, and don't forget the twenty percent gratuity to go with that," she cooed, warming up to the big spender.

"I got you, momma." He winked at the waitress, letting her know that she could count on a good tip from him.

"Thank you, sir. And how would you like them: all together or one at a time?"

"All at the same time. Y'all got ice buckets big enough for them all?"

"I'm sorry, no, we don't."

Fabiola sat back and watched the exchange. G.P. always was a showoff.

"Then bring them all together in individual buckets." He handed her a hundred-dollar bill. "We having a party." The waitress took off to fill the order and G.P. told everyone that would listen that Fabiola was his wifey. They danced and drank the night away, and as always G.P. was the life of the party.

A few bottles of champagne later, the club was wide-open. "If you ain't up in The Den tonight for its grand opening, you done messed up," the dj said over the airwaves. "Are we having a crazy time up in this piece or what?"

The crowd went berserk. "Hell yeah's" and "damn right's" could be heard from everywhere. The radio personality played Fabiola's song one last time, but this time he delivered a microphone to the VIP booth where she was sitting and asked her to sing along. Fabiola was caught off guard; she had no intention of performing when she left the house. She was just out to have a good time. Who would have thought that her night would take a turn for the better?

"Fuck that shit up, gurrl. Do the damn thang," Shug screamed, cheering Fabiola on.

That was all the encouragement Fabiola needed to set the club on fire with her electrifying vocals. The record didn't even do her live voice justice. When she finished her miniperformance the entire club gave her a standing ovation—most yelling for an encore.

By the time Fabiola split from the spot, the alcohol had taken a toll on her, making her drunk and horny. The liquor had her so torn up that she barely realized she wasn't riding in the same car she came in. G.P. was driving this one, and soon they pulled up to the Sheraton Hotel, where G.P. got them a room. All the champagne they had consumed made Fabiola's mouth taste dry and pasty.

"G.P., can you go get me something to drink—a water or soda?"

"Baby, I'm fucked up. I'm not carrying my ass back out this room 'til da morrow," he said. Handing her a few one-dollar bills, he said, "Here, you need to go get us both something to drink from the soda machine. It's on the third floor."

G.P. plopped down on the bed, and Fabiola sucked her teeth. *Are there no more gentlemen left in the world?* she thought to herself. *If he was any indication of today's chivalry, the women of the world were in trouble.*

Fabiola left the room, heading to the vending machine. The walk seemed to revive her some. She decided on water for herself and a soda for G.P. and headed back upstairs, regretting that she had consumed so much liquor. *Damn girl, you know this shit ain't really good for your body,* she thought to herself. When she stepped off the elevator she saw police all over the hallway rolling about twenty deep. Soon she heard a familiar voice.

"Why you mafuckers all up in my shit? I ain't got shit on me," G.P. screamed at the police, who wore black nylon jackets with DEA stenciled on the back. "A nigga can't even make love to his girl without you mafuckers harassing them."

"Once we find what we came for," one of the DEA agents said, "you gon have plenty of time to make love. They gon love yo pretty ass up at Lewisburg."

Fabiola didn't have to hear any more. Fabiola busted a U-turn and made her way to the lobby to call Shug to come and pick her up.

"Girl, what the hell is my life turning into?"

"You are living the life of a superstar. You know dem stars always got some type of bullshit going on."

"But this is not how I want my life to be."

"The difference between you and them is that you have a down-ass friend that will come and pick you up from wherever and whenever."

"I know." Fabiola was quiet looking out the window the entire ride home, thanking God for allowing her the opportunity to get out of the room before it got raided. Deep down inside, she felt like a complete fool. She had such an explosive night, her single got played on the radio, her live performance was unbelievable, and then she damn near got herself arrested.

As Shug pulled up in front of Fabiola's house, she said, "You cool, or you want me to come in?"

"Naw, girl, I am good. I just really want my life to have some structure. I sometimes feel so empty. I have no real boyfriend and it seems like when the music stops playing, I want someone to hold me. You know?"

"Yeah, I know."

"Shit, who knows, maybe G.P. ain't the one."

"Well, we know he ain't the one for you. You know we both know who you need to be with," Shug said with a devilish smile.

"Who?"

"Casino, that's who," Shug said, and Fabiola could not hide the schoolgirl smile that spread across her face.

A New Beginning

Fabiola was trying to shake her hangover and the loud ringing of the phone wasn't helping her at all, so she grabbed the phone as quick as possible.

"Hello," she said as she held her head to try to stop the pounding sound.

"Good morning, Superstar." The warmth in Casino's voice quickly soothed her head.

"Hey," she said in a tired voice, but perked up a little when she heard her song playing in the background.

"What's wrong? You still sleeping? Did I catch you at a bad time?"

"You should know by now that it's never a bad time when it comes to you, Casino."

"Then why don't you sound like a young superstar that just got her first single played on the radio?"

"Honestly?" she asked.

Casino shot back, "Why not?"

"Well." She took a deep breath, ashamed to admit the truth. "I have a slight hangover." She stretched the truth a bit, knowing that it was more than just a slight hangover. "You wouldn't believe my night if I told you."

"You can tell me about it when you come over. Maybe I can nurse you the way you did me."

Surprised to hear the good news, she asked, "Since when did you get home?"

"This morning, they let me come home providing that I go back for therapy a few days a week and take it easy."

"Casino, I am so happy that you are in the comfort of your own home and that you are doing better. You have sure come a long way."

"So, you making the drive over here or what? It would be nice to see you."

She smiled to herself thinking of Casino calling for her to come visit. "I know it would be nice to see you as well. Give me about an hour to get it together and I'll be there." Fabiola had never been to his house before and the thought of going to see him excited her. "I'm going to need the address. Do you want me to bring anything?"

"I'm good. I've got everything I need. I just would like to see you outside of a damn therapy ward or hospital."

"Now, are you sure that you don't me need me to bring you something to eat?"

"No, star, I am going to cook for you."

Fabiola couldn't wait. Her hangover was now officially gone. She got up and showered—careful not to mess up her freshly done hairdo—and put on a pair of her favorite jeans with a pair of Gucci heels and matching bag. She took a look in the mirror: fabulous.

★ ★ ★

"Here's that glass of water."

"Thanks, Tonk." Casino was feeling a lot better now that he was back in his own house. Noticing the odd look on his friend's face, he said, "What's on your mind?"

"What are your intentions with her?" Tonk asked.

"With who?"

"Who else? Fabiola."

"What are you now," Casino joked, "my father?"

"No. But I've been your friend for more years than I care to remember, and I see how the room gets brighter when she walks in."

"I tell you what," Casino said, "I tell you what my *intentions* are if you tell me why you ask."

"Because I care about you and I don't think you need anything that'll be a distraction in your life right now," Tonk shared. "We're in uncertain times. It's not a good time to bring new faces into one's circle."

"*Uncertain times,*" Casino echoed. "That's one of the reasons why I not only want her around, but need her around."

"What do you mean?"

"I believe in her, and I trust her," Casino confessed. "She's a very talented lady and just needs the right person investing and guiding her through her career. I'm that person." Casino imagined that's what Puffy thought when he first discovered Mary J. Blige—and look how she turned out. He wanted that same stardom for Fabiola, only he wanted her to both start and end on top—no drama in between.

"So you are getting in the record business now?" Tonk asked.

"From getting to know Fabiola over the past few months, I know that she wants two things: to be a star and have someone to love her. I have big plans for Fabiola, but she's been looking for love in all the wrong places. I care about her and want to take her under my wing, so I'm going to make her my woman and make sure that all decisions made are in her best interest. She showed loyalty for me in my time of need, and now I'm going to be there for her."

Tonk raised his eyebrows. "Well, boss, I've never heard you talk about a lady like that. And if you want to be in the music business, then I'll do whatever I can to make sure that happens."

★ ★ ★

Casino's mansion was built on four acres of Hanover, a county located on the outskirts of Richmond. Fabiola pulled up in the circular driveway. When she looked at the brick Colonial-style house, she fantasized that she lived there and was returning home from a long tour. *One day,* she said to herself, and then snapped back into reality as she rang the bell. The chimes were music to her ears. . . . Then someone clicked a few latches, and there was Casino clad in a shadow-striped pair of black silk pajamas and robe. He was taller than she remembered. Now that he was standing like a tall, confident stallion, his presence was even more commanding than before.

"You got here faster than I anticipated. I planned to have on real clothes when you saw me this time," he said with a laugh.

"You look good in pj's; they fit you well," she complimented.

"Thank you," he said and opened the door wider. "Welcome to my humble home," he said with a sweep of his hand.

"Who decorated this place?" She looked around, admiring his

home. The furniture was the finest she'd ever seen in person and rivaled anything she had seen on television or in magazines.

"I had some help," he admitted. "You don't like it?"

"No—no," she said, "that's not it at all. It's beautiful!"

As he led her into the sitting room, she noticed a shiny ebony grand piano. "Oh, this is so beautiful. Who plays?" she asked.

"Nobody plays. It's just for decoration. As a matter of fact I can make it play by itself, but I have to read the book to figure out how to do it."

"Wow!" She was amazed. "May I?"

"If you like." He gestured with his hand.

Fabiola sat at the piano and Casino joined her. Casino was mesmerized. Fabiola played beautifully as she sang "Tell Me Something Good" by Chaka Khan. After she finished they were both silent for a moment.

Casino clapped for her. "Very impressive, Fabiola. You are truly talented: You sing, you play the piano, you never cease to amaze me. That was the first time that I ever even heard that damn thing play, and I must say that you playing really made me appreciate the fact that I am home."

"Then, as an entertainer, I think I've done my job." She smiled at him as she stood up.

"You can play it anytime that you want to."

"Thank you so much, Casino." She hugged him. "You know no words could ever say just how much I appreciate you and all that you've done for me. Not just for helping my family when we didn't have a place to go or all that you've done to sow into my career. But also for all the wisdom and knowledge that you've passed on to me."

"You are worthy. I have never met anyone like you, Fabiola. And I've been running these streets a long time. I never met a young girl as sweet and genuine as you. And I never got to thank you for coming to check on the old man."

"That was the least I could do, Casino. But aren't you supposed to be in the bed resting?"

"I've had it with beds for a minute. Turns out the doctor kept me in the therapeutic center a week longer than I actually had to be there. For some reason he thought that if he let me go home that I wouldn't get the rest that I needed."

She smiled. "Looks like the doctor outsmarted you, and he was probably right."

They moved over into his den, which was filled with green-and-black, odd-shaped, oversized soft furniture.

"So, I didn't interrupt your company this morning when I called you, did I?" Casino fished around.

"No, not hardly," Fabiola said nonchalantly with the wave of her hand.

A trace of a smile flashed over his face.

"So, Mademoiselle Fabiola, what exactly are you into?"

Fabiola admired the aquarium that doubled as a wall separating the family room from what looked like a study. Fabiola tilted her head, not understanding the question. "What do you mean? I'm into a lot of things: As you know I like to sing, I like to read, I like to laugh and have fun, I like horoscopes, I belly dance. I like a lot of things."

"I mean your sexual preference. Do you like women or do you like men?" he bluntly asked.

"Women? Why would you ask me something like that?"

"No offense, it's just that I've noticed that a lot of young girls these days like girls. It seems like a growing fad, and I've never seen you with any men nor have I heard you really talk about any that you are romantically involved with."

"See, that's what I really don't understand about men. Let me get this right: A woman is a whore if she fucks around, but if she doesn't then she's gay."

"I don't make the rules—well, not all the rules anyway."

"I love men," she declared. "No doubt about it!" She paused for effect. "However, now I'm all about waiting for the right man . . . the right situation."

Casino smiled as she continued.

"I mean, let's face it. I've known I was going to be a star my entire life. Now the entire world is about to know my name. I can't just be with any Joe Blow—a nigga that's going to have me jumping out of windows half naked to avoid God only knows what, or riding through the middle of drive-bys with him, or the police kicking our hotel room door in looking for drugs."

"You sound like you're speaking from experience."

"I am."

"Then you're right, you can't be in those kinds of predicaments. You have too much to lose."

"Sometimes it has to smack you in the face for you to get it. You know?"

They were interrupted by the doorbell. Casino went over to the intercom. "Who?"

"It's me, Casino," Roxy said.

"What do you want?"

"What the fuck do you mean what do I want—to come in. To know why in the fuck you didn't tell me that they were discharging you. Open up the door, Casino."

"Fab, excuse me for a minute. I have an unwanted guest."

Fabiola nodded but she didn't know what to think. She hoped it would come down to her having to put her foot in Roxy's butt.

Casino went to the door. "Roxy, you are not welcome here."

"And why the hell not?" she screamed. "Oh, because your little young bitch is over here? What, you got that bitch swinging from a chandelier?"

Casino spoke in a deadly calm voice. "Stop being disrespectful—you're embarrassing yourself. Now, pull yourself together and get off my property with some damn dignity."

"Casino, what is it?" Roxy was hurt. "I've always played fair with you. I never stole from you and always patiently waited for you to sow your oats. I never complained when you dated this woman and that one. I handled all your business for you and never ever took one dime."

"Yeah, but you betrayed me; a violation that is normally punishable in a much more severe way—much more—but due to our history I'm doing you this one last favor. I'll let you continue to enjoy life, and all I ask in return is for you to get the fuck off my property and out my life."

Roxy stood in Casino's doorway sobbing. "Casino," she hiccupped his name between cries.

"Don't, Roxy," he said firmly to her and then shut the door in her face.

Fabiola could not believe her ears and she wanted to jump for joy. Instead she looked up to heaven and smiled—God is indeed good! Now maybe she could have Casino to herself.

Casino joined Fabiola back in the den. "I apologize for the distraction."

"What happened? What did she do?"

"I can't discuss it; it will make my blood pressure go up."

"And Lord knows we don't want that." She said it in a joking way, but the truth is always in a joke.

Casino changed the subject. "Tell me about last night."

"Now last night will make my blood pressure go up for sure," she said, but she told him anyway.

She filled Casino in on the details from the night before. He was quiet for the most part while she spoke.

"Spade told me that he heard that you went to the club last night performing," he probed. "That type of stuff got to stop. You've got to keep your nose clean. I know I'm not telling you nothing that you don't already know."

She agreed. "You are so right."

"You should use your spare time to enjoy nice dinners, movies, plays, and things of that nature."

"Yes, I would like that!" She let out a deep sigh, saying, "And those are all things that I would do if I had a man to do them with."

Casino nodded in agreement. "Well, what kind of men do you like? I might know somebody."

"Please, not your son. I've heard about Spade." She smiled and shook her head. "He's a little too wild for me."

"I was thinking more of a very dear friend of mine. He's maybe twenty years your senior, a nice-looking fella, has a salt-and-pepper goatee." Casino stroked his face.

"Really? I think I could be with an older man, but I've never had a man that much older than me."

"He's never been with a younger lady before, not even when he was a young buck."

"Do you think that we would be able to get past the great age difference?"

"I think so. The way I see it, as long as two people have the same philosophies about life and are willing to team up to get the things they want and have understanding and respect for each other, age shouldn't make a difference."

"So, do you think that he and I could make it work? Enjoy ourselves and share lots of good times?" Fabiola was hoping that her wish was finally coming true.

"Well, we've been doing that for a few months now, so actually we've had a relationship, we just haven't crossed the bridge to the intimate part of town. The important thing is that I want you to know that I have your back."

"And I have yours."

He kissed her on the cheek.

"Damn, that's all I get? A daggone peck on the cheek? And you just told me that I am going to be your woman?"

"I've never been a big kisser, so you are going to have to work with me."

"Okay, but two questions?"

"Shoot."

"How come you never dated a younger lady? And does it work?"

"I never found a younger woman with enough to bring to the table. Most seem like they just want to run wild."

"Some do, but some old ones are that same way. You shouldn't stereotype."

"You are right. And then most young girls think that sex is the answer to everything."

She laughed. "How ironic you should say that. Most men are sure that sex is the answer to everything."

"Sex too fast can destroy a relationship."

"But I don't want you to have to turn to someone else, since I do realize that it has been a long time for you." She was thinking of some of the other women she had seen at the hospital on that first day.

"I don't want you to get it from somewhere else," he assured her. "I turn down more pussy than I accept on a regular basis. It's not about who I can fuck, it's about who I want to fuck."

"One more question. What's the deal with you and all your fans?" Fabiola said with a slight chuckle.

Casino answered, "I have a couple of intelligent ladies that I've known for years, some I was with. Some I wasn't. I'm not really interested in any of them and I never gave them reason to think there was anything more to the relationship, if you want to call it that. Only you." He grabbed her hand. "That's it, that's all."

Fabiola was thinking about what that meant when she heard another voice, or maybe two, in the house. Although Casino never said so, up until that point she thought they were alone.

"Pops, where are you? I need to talk to you." It was Spade's booming voice.

"Why are you yelling?" Tonk was sitting in the kitchen drinking a cup of coffee while he cleaned the .357 he had been carrying for the last ten years.

"Hello to you, too, you antique-gun-carrying mu'fucka," Spade joked. "Pops!"

"In here," Casino shot back.

Spade followed Casino's voice. "Pop, I need to talk . . ." He switched gears when he saw there was company in the house, and they were holding hands. "I knew it; I knew y'all two had something going on."

"You didn't know a damn thing."

"The hell I didn't. It was in your eyes, the way you looked at each other."

Casino and Fabiola looked at each other and smiled.

"Not true," Casino said to the young man he had raised as a son.

"Tell that to somebody that don't know better, Pops. Every time she visited you, you lit up the room with your smile. That's the only reason I never put my G down on her, because I knew. It was the only time you actually gave a fuck if a woman came to visit or not, so I knew something was up."

"Is there something you want?" Casino asked, changing the subject.

"To speak to you in the other room. It's important."

Casino asked Fabiola, "Do you mind?" Fabiola assured him she didn't, and Casino and Spade walked off to have some privacy.

"What's on your mind, son?" Casino said once they were alone.

"You getting shot," Spade blurted out. There was no use in him beating around the bush. "That can't go unpunished."

"And it won't." Casino put both his hands on Spade's shoulders and looked him square in the face. "But for now, all we can do is be patient and wait. Sooner or later the bitches that shot me are going to slip up and say something, and when that time comes . . . we take care of our unfinished business in a way that'll make their friends' friends wish they didn't know them."

The Body's Calling

Later that night, Fabiola and Casino were together in his upstairs master suite. She adored his bedroom; it was her favorite room in the house yet. It was huge, and the focal point was the tall four-poster mahogany super-sized king bed, truly fit for a king. In the far left corner from the end of the bed was a life-sized Roman-looking statue of a half-naked woman. Fabiola made herself right at home in the warmth of the gold- and earth-toned colors of the suite.

Casino was sprawled out on his stomach across the bed while Fabiola sat up next to him, feet curled under her butt, giving him a massage. Casino turned over onto his back and suggested, "You know what? You've been pampering me so much over the past few months I think it's about time I give you a massage."

"Sounds good to me." Fabiola shrugged, totally game to be on the receiving end.

Casino rubbed his hands together. "Get undressed so that you can be more comfortable." Fabiola looked into his eyes as she undressed. Casino was pleased by what he saw—her body was flawless. The long erect nipples of her firm C-cup mountains looked as if they were coming out of circles of deep chocolate. Her tiny waist made her hips and silky smooth dairy bottom appear to be more pronounced than they really were. Casino was mesmerized but he didn't let it show.

Fully naked, Fabiola gladly took Casino's place sprawled out across the bed on her stomach. Casino positioned himself on her lower back, careful not to press all of his weight onto her. Gently, he began kneading her shoulders.

This man definitely knows what he's doing, Fabiola thought.

Moans spilled from her lips as she enjoyed the treatment. "I didn't know how much I really needed one of these," she purred. It felt so good.

Casino worked his strong hands down, maneuvering them in a circular motion; her moaning and limp body was indication to him that he was making all the right moves. Fabiola was in nirvana, but she had no idea how much Casino was enjoying his work until she felt a third arm poking in the small of her back. She smiled a little. Moments after that, he leaned over and planted soft wet kisses on the back of her neck. "*Oooooh,*" she crooned, unable to hide the fact that his hot tongue touching her skin and his manhood grinding against her ass was turning her on in a big way. She wanted him inside her; every second that he wasn't felt like an hour. The anticipation was driving her crazy, and then something happened that rarely happened to her: She felt unsure of herself.

She knew that a man like Casino was very experienced, and the fact that she might not be able to deliver to his expectations made her nervous. She was afraid of not giving it to him the way that he was accustomed, but that didn't keep her from desiring him. Luckily for Fabiola, her body took over where her mind was ambivalent. Fabiola pushed back toward him, hoping that he would get the hint, and it didn't take long before he did.

He pushed his finger in between her second pair of lips. She was soaking wet. He put his finger in his mouth. Sweet. Casino wasn't small by any standards, and by the way her pussy gripped his finger while warming her engine Casino knew he had to be careful with her. He started with just the head. She tensed a little, sucking in a breath. After dipping the head in and out a few times, he explored a little farther. With each gentle thrust he added an inch; working it in little by little. Once she had taken all nine inches he lost control and began pumping faster.

"This pussy is so tight," Casino panted. Before she could panic from the anxiety of not pleasing him, he added, "And so damn good."

Fabiola was matching him thrust for thrust now.

"Are we supposed to be doing this?"

"Two consenting adults."

"Yeah, but the"—she moaned—"the hospital and all."

He didn't answer her question but his moans let her know that his heart could take it. "You like that?" he asked, not really expecting an answer, but pleased with what he heard.

"I—I love it," Fabiola declared.

"Tell me how much?" Casino pleaded. Hearing Fabiola compliment him while he made love to her was an aphrodisiac for Casino's ego and his libido.

"This much," Fabiola panted, popping her juice box like a Luke dancer.

After about eleven or twelve more strokes, Casino's toes curled, and he froze midthrust in the pussy. If she hadn't turned it up a notch after that, maybe he could have recovered, but she did, and he didn't. Casino's floodgate was released.

"I need to get back in shape," Casino breathed heavily, somewhat embarrassed. "Build up my endurance."

"Maybe it was just that good," she boasted. "Having a younger woman may be what you've needed." A smile crept across Fabiola's face because she knew she had pleased Casino.

Heavy Rotation

The buzz started to build for Fabiola and radio stations from New York to Miami were getting lots of requests for Fabiola's new work, putting her song in heavy rotation for a week straight. Then suddenly, in the blink of an eye, all that seemed to change. All the stations stopped spinning the record without notice. When Viola called several of the local stations in an attempt to try to find out why they removed the song from rotation, no one would speak to her or return any of her phone calls. If anyone knew what was going on they weren't talking. Even the local mix djs had unknown issues with playing her song, and usually they could play whatever they wanted within reason.

"Mommy, someone has to know something." Fabiola was talking to her mother on the phone while she lay in Casino's arms.

"No one will return my calls, baby. I spoke to this one guy off the record and he said they can't play it anymore. That's all he would say. But don't worry; I am still trying to get to the bottom of it." Viola wanted to make her daughter believe that everything would be all right, but deep down inside she wasn't sure if she even believed it. What they needed was a miracle, but Viola wasn't going to tell her daughter that.

Heartbroken, Fabiola hung up the phone. "No one will give a reason why my record is no longer getting any airplay. Everyone my mom talks to gives her the runaround." Casino could see the frustration in her face.

"I don't know why this is happening—why the heck can't I catch a break in this industry? Maybe it ain't meant to be." Tears were forming in Fabiola's eyes but she didn't cry.

"It's a law of nature that it must rain before the flowers can bloom." Casino tried to lift her spirits. He believed somewhat in what he told her, but he also didn't believe in coincidence. "Now listen to me carefully. Do you or your mother know who's in charge of making the decision about what songs get played on the radio?"

"I think it's the program director."

"I need you to be sure. Call your mother to ask her who's the motherfucker that's calling shots. We need to know who the real boss is."

Fabiola called her mother and found out that the operations manager was over the program director, so he was ultimately the one in charge.

Once she told Casino what her mother said, he kissed her on

the cheek. "Don't worry," he said. "Everything will be all right. I promise."

Fabiola knew that she was placing a lot of faith in Casino, but he was her superman and had made everything happen thus far. She looked into his eyes and felt a little better.

★ ★ ★

Airproof Airways controlled more than forty percent of the FM radio stations in the country, and at forty-seven years old, Mike Moss was the vice president of programming for the entire East Coast region. As the head honcho, he was the one that told the local operations managers to instruct the program directors what to play on the radio, when to play it, and how many times.

Mike was looking around the parking lot trying to remember where he parked his Cadillac DTS—the Christmas present to himself. There it was, right where he left it way in the back of the lot, far from every other car and with less risk of getting dinged by any other car. Everybody knew that Mike exercised religiously four times a week at the Philadelphia Fitness Center. All he wanted to do now was get home, get a bite to eat, relax, and watch the Lakers play the Mavericks on cable. After getting in the automobile and pressing the button that brought the engine to life, he felt a cold piece of steel tap the crown of his head.

"I don't have any money," Mike said. "You can have the car and my credit cards though."

Tonk, the man holding the nine-inch-barrel .357, said, "You can keep your car and credit cards, but you may lose your life and those close to you if you don't cooperate with me."

"Who are you?"

"That's not important, but what *is* important is that the man that sent me here wants you to do him a favor and he doesn't take no for an answer, so listen carefully. All he wants is a song played on the radio."

"You could have done that over the request line, you didn't have to commit a felony," Mike said.

He ignored Mike's attempt to humor him. "We want the song in heavy rotation: every other hour, Monday through Friday. That's sixty spins a week during the weekdays and every hour on the weekends."

"What song?"

Tonk said the title slow and deliberate so that there would be no misunderstanding, "The name of the song is 'Touch Me' and the singer is Fabiola Mays."

"It's not as easy as it seems. As a matter of fact I like the damn song myself, but it's bigger than me or you."

"You gotta do better than that."

Mike looked around without moving his head, praying that someone would come to his rescue, before just telling the truth. He took a deep breath. "If this ever gets out, I could lose my job. If you repeat it to anyone I will deny it to the bitter end."

"If you don't stop procrastinating you're going to lose more than your job."

Mike Moss didn't need any more encouraging. "This girl you're talking about has somehow managed to piss off Johnny Wiz."

"And?" Tonk gazed into Mike's eyes, still clutching the gun.

"And Johnny Wiz is a very powerful man. He called me personally to say that if I continued to play that song, he would pull his sponsorship money, the under-the-table payola, and forbid his artists to do promotion on our stations. He said he wouldn't allow them to perform at our summer concerts and he would no longer make sure we get his artists' music before anyone else. Damn near half the stuff we're playing on the radio are artists that are under Johnny Wiz's umbrella. It would destroy us if we didn't have access to them." Tonk didn't say anything, so Mike kept talking.

"I wish I could help you, because I don't even like the arrogant little fuck, but in this industry, Johnny Wiz is not a person to get out of favor with. My bosses would kick me in the street so fast it wouldn't even be funny. The man has at least thirty top-selling artists at any given time, and no disrespect to you or your boss, you only have one and she's still an unknown."

"I get it."

Tonk returned back to Richmond and reported to Casino everything that he'd learned from Mike Moss. When he got to Casino's new office at the Ghetto Superstar record label that he'd created, Tonk found his boss surrounded by boxes of pressed-up singles of Fabiola's song. Viola had told him earlier that they were having problems with distribution—even the mom-and-pop stores weren't taking the record.

Casino was sitting at his desk thinking about his next move, when he caught a glimpse of the man that was causing them all the trouble. Johnny Wiz was doing an interview on one of the video channels talking about an upcoming tour of his artists sponsored by Hypnotic. It hit Casino right then and there. "I know what's got to happen," he said out loud.

First, he called Taz and began telling him what he had in mind. After briefing him, Casino added, "I need you to be able to get me an in-da-streets dj, not one of those industry chumps."

"Then you want K-Slay or DJ Envy," Taz said.

Casino didn't know too much about either one of the men, so he would have to take Taz's word. "You got a number and a relationship with one of them?"

"Sure do, I fuck with both of them. Good thorough cats that ain't on none of that shady bullshit."

With one phone call, K-Slay was spinning the song as if it was no big deal. It was a hot song and that's what K-Slay did—play hot songs.

Casino wasn't finished. Now he had to put the fire under Johnny Wiz so that he could understand fully that the heat was on.

The Heat

On Monday night, a rose-colored 500 SL Mercedes Benz pulled up in front of The Bridge Night Club amidst a sell-out crowd waiting to get in. The spot was located on the Upper East Side of Manhattan and was the latest must-be spot in the city on Thursday nights; they had a different hot performer each week.

Royce and Petey exited the Benzo, giving the keys to the valet. "I still think we should have gone in from the back," Petey warned.

"I want to be with my fans," Royce said. "They love me and I love them."

People started screaming, pushing, and shoving when

they saw Royce exit the Mercedes. "That's Royce over there!" someone yelled.

"That's my girl," screeched another.

"Damn, that bitch is fine," a dude said to his friend.

"Who's that clown she's wit?" the friend responded.

Royce wore a rose, tailor-made print dress that fit her petite frame to a tee. The dress matched the color of the foreign car she was driving and complimented her chocolate complexion too well. Petey took her hand and smiled. "That dress is strangling yo ass. Let's get you inside before I have to get the National Guard to keep these fools off of you."

"You stepped on my shoe, nigga! Watch where you muthafuckin' goin', fool!" a two-hundred-pound plus-size black guy, who was standing near Royce and Petey, said to a light-skinned dude.

"First of all I'm Puerto Rican—not a nigga—and fuck you and your sh—"

Before the light-skinned dude could finish his statement, he was corrected by a straight right to his left eye.

"Oh, shit," someone said. "Did you see that?"

"Hell yeah," another person responded. "He knocked that muthafucka out!"

The light-skinned dude wasn't at the club alone, and when his friend saw him stretched out on the ground, he fired a punch at the man that had hit his friend. But the guy ate the punch and sent him to meet his light-skinned friend on the ground with a left hook. At that point all hell broke loose. It was like the Royal Rumble on one of those wrestling networks. Fists and feet were flying all over the place and no one was exempt—not even a superstar.

A chick dressed in Goth clothing snatched a handful of Royce's hair, pulling it clean off her head. Until that moment no one had known that Royce's trademark flowing black hair was a wig.

Underneath the wig Royce had on an old black stocking cap with a big hole on the side of it. "Y'all bitches then done it now." Royce let loose with a punch of her own, grazing the cheek of the Goth chick who snatched her wig. "And get that fuckin' camera out of my gotdamn face," she said.

When it was all said and done, eleven people ended up in the hospital, three in serious condition. Petey had to be flown away by chopper to the emergency room to tend to a knife wound in his side, but he would be okay.

★ ★ ★

The next evening, Johnny Wizard's controversial rap group Zinc was having an album release party in the civic center in Cleveland. It was a great turnout, and many old-school and new-school artists were in attendance. Everything was going fine until someone called in a bomb threat, causing the building to be evacuated.

"I'm sorry, but no one is going to be allowed to go back into the building tonight," the fire chief announced.

"You can't do that," the event promoter protested. "The Wizard spent over seven hundred thousand dollars to put this event together. It's being covered nationally. If you shut it down it will be a disaster!"

"I just did," the chief said bluntly.

The next night, The Wizard's "Move the Crowd" tour in Chicago was taking place, which was a media-covered extravaganza. Everybody was interested in the hot, young multiplatinum gangster rapper from Compton—Death Wish. His songs "Fear Nothing," "Got Dat Gat," and "Felon" garnered him national attention. Were his songs art imitating reality, or reality imitating art? That was the question among most music intellectuals. Most real street toughs labeled him as a fraud, but Death Wish dismissed them as envy-filled haters who wanted to be him.

The stadium event was booked to capacity and everyone was on their feet when Death Wish was introduced to the stage. Then it happened. Gunshots roared through the air. "Get down!" someone on the stage yelled. The dj dove off the platform. People in the crowd were being stampeded or worse; some ran toward and others ran away from the stage. Meanwhile, random shots continued to ring out. It didn't matter who fired the first shot or what that person was shooting at—the stadium was now the scene of a miniwar. Chicago was a city of real gangsters and gang members who didn't need a whole lot of encouragement to buck their gats.

Death Wish dove behind a set of large speakers for cover and pulled out his phone.

"9-1-1," the lady on the other end of the phone answered. "What is your emergency?"

"Send the police," Death Wish choked out the words. "Somebody is trying to kill me."

"Slow down, sir," the dispatcher said. "Can you tell me your name?"

"Death Wish."

"Is that your real name?"

"My name is Jr., Bartholomew Kitten, Jr."

"Bartholomew," the dispatcher repeated, "how old are you?"

"I'm thirty-seven."

"And where are you right now, Bartholomew?"

"Why you asking me all these damn questions, bitch? I'm hiding behind a fuckin' speaker. I knew these niggas in Chi-town were crazy. They trying to kill me. I'm not like them, I grew up in the church choir—I'm no gangster."

The dispatcher could hear the fear and desperation in his voice. "Don't worry, Mr. Kitten, the police are on the way."

"It's about time. I am a tax-paying citizen," he cried.

Later that night another Wizard artist suffered a setback: Jupiter Jazz's tour bus was vandalized. All of the tires were flattened and someone spray painted JOHNNY WIZ IS A WOMANIZING PERVERTED BISEXUAL BITCH on the side of the bus in neon-green script.

"And the disasters for The Wizard didn't end there," the female correspondent featured on "Music Lifestyles" reported as she went through a laundry list of misfortunes that had befallen Johnny Wiz's artists that week. "Meanwhile, at the hotel of another one of The Wizard's artists, Slakey Jake and his entourage were robbed at gunpoint of all their jewelry. The estimated value of the stolen goods was over a million dollars."

Johnny turned off the television in disgust, and was deep in thought when he was interrupted by his secretary's voice over the intercom. "Mr. Wiz?"

"What?" he yelled a little too loudly, startling her somewhat.

"I have Zink's manager on the phone. Also, Petey and Royce are here to see you."

Johnny was in no mood to talk to anyone. "Take a message."

"It's about the security, sir."

"I told them that I have the best security money can buy," he spat, "and shit just happens sometimes. This week was an aberration." Now all he had to do was to convince himself of that.

Casino was almost in tears. He hadn't laughed so hard in a long time. "Job well done," Casino said proudly to Tonk.

"Thank you." Tonk smiled, glad he could be of assistance to his boss and longtime friend. "What do you think that nigga Johnny Wiz is doing right now?"

"He's fucked up, I'm sure."

"You betta bet that Johnny Wiz is somewhere hiding, not taking one single phone call," Tonk said. "He should know that you don't play with fire, because you will get burned."

Security Issues

Nathan Walshenberg was a legend. With more than forty years in the music biz, Nathan's work was not only still relevant, but prevalent. He was responsible for launching some of the most iconic pop, jazz, and R & B stars of all time. The mention of his name garnered the respect and admiration from old-school, new-school, and up-and-coming artists alike. Most performers only dreamed of one day being in the same room with a man of his stature and greatness. Once a year in his hometown of Philadelphia they got a shot to rub elbows with Nathan.

It was Nathan's thirtieth annual red-carpet charity dinner for underprivileged children. At $50,000 dollars a table, all the heavy-hitting players were in the building to show respect for Nathan and support the cause on this beautiful star-filled night. Held in an elegant, elaborate tent that was decorated like a sultan's castle, Madonna, Diana Ross, Diddy, 50 Cent, Sting, Elton John, Eminem, and Dr. Dre were just a few of the stars that were out and about that night.

Nathan and Casino went a long way back, but this was the first year that Casino was in attendance despite twenty years of personal invites from Nathan himself. Casino never had a real reason to rub elbows with any of the people in attendance. But Fabiola had entered his life at just the right time, and ever since the shooting he knew he wanted to take his life in a new direction. The $50K was a small investment for Casino, because it not only put him in a room filled with influential key players, it would also put him in the company of Johnny Wiz.

Johnny Wiz almost hadn't come; he was still trying to maintain damage control over all the disastrous events that had taken place last week. He may have appeared as arrogant and as confident as ever, but on the inside it was a different story. He was worn out mentally and in total despair. He was even worried about something crazy happening at this event; something that would cause him more problems—problems with Walshenberg. He was listening to the imaginary news report that was playing in his head of how something else related to him went wrong. In the middle of his thoughts, someone approached him.

"Johnny Wiz," Casino called out, greeting the man in front of him eye to eye. Casino smiled and grabbed two glasses of champagne from the tray of a tuxedo-clad waiter. "How are you? You look like you could use one of these."

Johnny Wiz eyed Casino as he tried to remember where he knew the man from, but he couldn't place the face. Since only "key players" were invited to this function, Johnny didn't want to offend anyone that could be beneficial to him in the future, especially now.

"Yeah, I do," he said with an outstretched hand.

"I heard about all the security issues you've had recently. A damn shame. It must have caused an uproar with your artists and sponsors." Casino's sympathetic manner put Johnny at ease.

"Yeah, things got pretty awkward for a moment," Johnny said, the champagne—his third glass—loosening his tongue and helping him to let his guard down a bit.

"I can imagine." Casino sipped his drink.

"When you get to be as successful as I am, you have many enemies. It could be anyone," Johnny confided in Casino, who had a way of getting complete strangers to confide in him.

"You pissed off a lot of people, huh?" Casino smiled. "That's what happens when you are at the top of your industry; you have to make tough decisions, and everybody is not always happy."

"I'll drink to that." And he did, tilting the glass back to finish the last drop. "You seem like a man that knows his business. What do you do?" He waved the waiter over for another glass of champagne.

Just then Nathan approached them.

"Casino, my man." Nathan extended his hand. "So glad to see you."

Johnny watched as Nathan embraced Casino, and he could see the brotherly love between the two men.

"When do you fly back out?" Nathan asked.

"I'm here for a couple of days."

"Good, you must stop by for dinner before you leave. I am sure that the Mrs. would love to see you."

"Does she still cook a hell of a pot roast?"

"Still the best."

Johnny wanted to know the connection between the two. As he sipped on his bubbly he wondered why he didn't already know Casino. He watched Nathan and concluded that Casino must be a real stand-up guy or somebody important to know, if he had actually sat down to eat at Nathan's house. He knew how protective Nathan was of his wife and family.

"You two met, I see." Nathan finally acknowledged Johnny. "So there's no need for any introductions."

"Yeah, we did." Casino nodded, but Johnny was too embarrassed to admit that he didn't know who Casino was.

"Well, Johnny, you may be able to seek out some of Casino's expertise. I know it saved me years ago." Nathan lowered his voice a little bit. "His consulting is the best money could buy." Just then someone from Nathan's staff came to whisk him away. "Casino, call me," he said before leaving.

Casino looked at Johnny and knew he had the fish on the hook. "You asked me before Nathan joined us about what I do. Well, I have a top-notch security team that can make all your recent issues go away." Johnny looked into Casino's eyes and there was something about his manner that told Johnny that this man had the power to do what he promised—that plus the fact that Nathan seemed to have so much confidence in him. Johnny Wiz was willing to do whatever he had to do to make his problems go away, and especially to get his nagging mother off of his back. If that took some money to fix it, then so be it.

"Where do I send the check?" Johnny said with a smile and a chuckle. Casino didn't respond, but instead put his glass up to his lips, never losing eye contact with Johnny. "Seriously, who do I make the check out to? I'm willing to bet that you are a man of your word."

"You can bet your last on that. Even when all the chips are down, all we have is our word."

"So, Mr.—you know we've been talking and I didn't even get your name or your company?"

This was going easier than Casino had expected. "Mr. Winn. Casino Winn."

"Well, Mr. Winn, do you really think you could help a new friend out with his pest problem?"

"But of course," Casino said. "I'll be glad to help out a new friend, not to mention that any friend of Nathan's is a friend of mine."

"Then it's settled. All you have to do is tell me what it's going to cost me."

"That's what's so great about friends; I wouldn't take a friend's money. It's about brotherhood. It's about us being the lowest on the totem pole." Johnny Wiz was a bit offended, because he didn't consider himself at the bottom of anybody's anything. Normally he would have said so, but at that moment he just listened as his new friend continued. "We, as black men, have to help one another, and if I can help a brother out of a bad situation, I will. If the shoe was on the other foot, I would want to think that I could count on you to help me out."

"Definitely, brother." Johnny nodded and extended his hand. "Anything you need, Casino, anything." Johnny leaned in a little closer. "If I can help out in any way, shape, or form, let me know."

"Do you mean that?"

"Of course!"

"Well, maybe there is something you could do for me. I have a very talented artist that I am working with. She's as talented as they come, yet I'm catching hell trying to get her career off the ground. You know this industry—it's unbelievably hard to get radio spins, exposure, concert appearances, distribution. And the thing of it is, I promised this little lady that I would make it happen for her."

"Don't worry about it. Consider it done." Johnny shooed off Casino's concerns with his hands. "Those are all such small things, my brother. I have radio by the balls, and distribution by the jockstrap. In fact, have you heard of my rapper Teflon Don?"

"My girl loves him."

"Well, he has a hit song that we need someone to sing the hook on. It was written for Royce, but with the wig incident I'm not ready to put her on a project like this. I can have the track sent to you. Once she hears the track, later in the week I can fly her up, put her up, let your girl drop the vocals, and it'll be as simple as that. This will give her lots of exposure." Johnny Wiz passed Casino a cigar. "What do you think about that, friend?"

"That would be wonderful." Casino lit the cigar. "My girl really can sing, too."

"What the fuck?" Johnny threw up his hand. "If she can't, then once we get done with her in the studio she will sound like she can," he assured Casino with his signature Johnny Wiz cockiness.

Both men were sitting, enjoying their cigars together, celebrating the beginning of a blossoming relationship. Casino thought about Fabiola and smiled. He didn't feel that now was the time to burst Johnny's bubble and reveal Fabiola's identity, but that time would come soon enough.

Collaboration

By the next morning, Fabiola and Casino had an appointment at one of Johnny Wiz's studios for her to collaborate on a song with Teflon-the-Don. Before arriving, Casino had already told Fabiola that Johnny Wiz had somehow had a change of heart.

They rode the elevator to the eighteenth floor of The Wizard's offices, and when the doors opened Fabiola felt like she was stepping into pure extravagance. The marble floors glistened, the ornate oak furniture looked stately, and expensive, beautiful artwork adorned the walls. An assistant greeted Fabiola and Casino and offered to escort them to one of the recording rooms. All of Johnny Wiz's staff had already been told to give Casino and his artist the

VIP treatment. Before they made it to the studio, Fabiola went to the restroom and Casino was intercepted by Johnny Wiz. He greeted Casino with a handshake.

"So, everything is all set up for you. I've given strict instructions to my entire staff to treat your artist with the same treatment as they would our own artists. Speaking of which, I never even got your artist's name."

Casino saw Fabiola walking up behind Johnny, returning from the restroom. "Here she comes now." Johnny turned to lay his eyes on Casino's pride and joy.

It couldn't be, Johnny thought.

"Fabiola, meet Johnny Wiz. Johnny, this is our next megastar." Johnny Wiz just about shit a brick.

"Yes, the very talented Fabiola Mays," he said, taking her hand into his and kissing it. "We've met before," he mentioned to Casino as he tried not to sweat.

"Really?" Casino played dumb, enjoying every minute of watching Johnny eat crow.

"Yes, we have," Fabiola said. Johnny looked at Fabiola and didn't see one uncomfortable bone in her body. She appeared as confident as ever and looked at Johnny warily.

"We met before a while back and had a little misunderstanding." He smiled. "And it was nothing but that—a little misunderstanding."

"Johnny, you know it was more like a big misunderstanding!" she informed him.

"Yes," Johnny said with as much humility as he could manage, "you are right, Ms. Mays. It wasn't small. Indeed it wasn't. But let's say, for the sake of argument, that I was having a bad day which resulted in our misunderstanding becoming an ego moment, which sometimes *us* men have." He smiled at Casino, looking for him to agree.

"Well, those times are dead concerning Fabiola, right?" Casino said, not matching Johnny's smile.

"Yes, of course. As far as Ms. Mays is concerned, I think we should focus on why we are here: getting her album off the ground. I've done so much more with less, and for you the sky is the limit! You can't deny, Ms. Mays, I've told you before you are very talented. So, let's let bygones be bygones. My good friend Mr. Winn and I have big plans for you."

"Why thank you so much, Mr. Wiz."

"Call me Johnny," he instructed, sounding corny.

One of the employees cut in. "Mr. Wiz, Teflon is waiting in the studio."

"Ms. Mays, let's not keep him waiting. Once you put your vocals down we've got a surefire hit and we all are going to make lots of money."

Fabiola loved the idea of doing a song with Teflon Don; he was one of the hottest rappers out right now.

"Come this way and let me show you to the studio and introduce you to the producer you will be working with," Johnny said.

The equipment was state-of-the-art and was unlike anything she'd ever seen. Hands down it was the Bentley of recording studios and made Taz's studio look like skid row in comparison.

Teflon-the-Don was in the studio although his part of the song was already completed, and he seemed genuinely pleased to be working with her. When she walked in she was a little nervous, but Teflon greeted her, "Fabiola, it's nice to meet you." He kissed her on her cheek.

"It's such a pleasure to be working with you." She put her pocketbook down.

"Naw, li'l momma, the pleasure's all mine. Yo, I fucks with that 'Touch Me' shit. You wrecked that shit. And I know with me and you together, our shit's gonna do numbers."

"I pray," she said modestly.

Teflon made sure that Fabiola was comfortable in the studio and catered to her as if she were his little sister making it easy for her to drop any nervousness she might have had.

Once Casino saw that Fabiola was all situated and in her zone, he asked Johnny, "Can we go somewhere else to talk business in depth, man?"

"Sure." Johnny led Casino to his plush office.

Sitting behind his oversized oak desk, Johnny said, "My artists have concerts and events lined up this week. Can you assure me that everything will be taken care of?"

"You can let everyone know that you have the best security in the country and all is well. Just supply me with an itinerary of their appearances and make sure that Fabiola stays happy, and I will personally stay on top of your issues."

"I spoke with Nathan again this morning, and he assured me that if the situation can get under control, then you are the man for it. Having Nathan speak so highly of you and cosign for you is enough. I really appreciate this, man. You're saving me a lot of Tylenols and Motrin."

After meeting Fabiola, Johnny Wiz suspected he had been played and that meeting Casino after the week's fiascos wasn't as much of a coincidence as it appeared. But he wasn't mad, because game recognizes game. Although he hadn't been played in a long time, the tables had been turned on him and all he could think was: May the best man . . . or woman come out on top.

Casino stayed at the studio a little while longer after the conversation with Johnny, and once Fabiola took a small break he told her he was leaving.

"Call me if you need me, baby. I have to make a few runs, okay?"

Although there was a peace treaty in effect and Teflon had

gone out of his way to make her feel comfortable, Fabiola knew that she was still on Johnny's turf and didn't want to be left alone there, because in her eyes Johnny still could not be trusted. She decided not to ask Casino to stay because she didn't want to appear to be too clingy. "I'll be just fine," she said. "But don't forget that you promised to take me to that Italian restaurant tonight."

"How could I? You've only been reminding me since last night." He gave her a peck on the lips and left.

Everything went according to plan. Teflon and Fabiola completed the song, talked about other projects that the two of them could come together on, and most of all Johnny was on his best behavior.

"You can always stay in town for a few more days and work on another song that one of my producers think would be great for you."

Teflon watched as Johnny kissed ass.

"I'm going to have you all moved over to our host hotel, which takes care of all our superstars and their guests."

"No, that won't be necessary."

"I insist. Fabiola, I don't know if you get it or not but you are about to be America's Sweetheart. I don't think you understand."

Fabiola was in shock, because she couldn't believe Johnny's transformation. He was the complete opposite of the man she had met in the hotel in Richmond.

Johnny provided a limo to take Fabiola back to the hotel to meet Casino. She called Shug from the back of the limo.

"Hey, guurrrl!" Fabiola yelled into the phone.

"Hey, gurl, my butt! I've been waiting to hear from you all day. Why haven't you returned any of my calls?" Shug sounded off.

"I'm going to tell you all about it, but right now I just have to let it marinate myself." This was all like a dream come true to Fabiola. Success was so close that she could practically taste it. "Right now I'm just riding in my limousine," she said teasingly, twirling her finger through her hair, "on my way to my presidential suite in the Waldorf Astoria Hotel. Nothing much, actually, dahling," she said, looking out of the window in the New York City traffic and wearing a smile that could light up the entire city. "What you doing?"

"A lot less than you, best darling," Shug laughed. "I'm about to head out to the mall. Where's Casino?"

"Doing whatever it is he does," Fabiola said in a playful tone.

"Then while Casino's not around I need to give you the heads-up that G.P. is out of jail and you know he been checking for you."

"How about long story short, right now, I could give a fuck about G.P.'s ass. I just want to be happy and live out my dream and be with the man of my dreams."

"I know, but I gotta keep you on your toes."

"You right, thanks, girly." Switching the subject Fabiola said, "Girl, I really hope this works out so that I can buy my mother a house finally."

"You will. I know you will. You are right there."

"Oh yeah, did I mention that I just got finished recording a song with Teflon-the-Don?" Fabiola finally lost her cool and started to scream, "Did you hear me? Teflon-the-motherfucking-Don!"

"You lying!" Shug trumped her scream. "Oh my God!"

The radio in the limo was set on Strong 99, where hip-hop and R & B played all day.

"Girl, Charming Ching-a-Ling is on the air. I'll hit you right back. Let me hear the gossip." Charming was the hot jock that everyone loved to hate. She got every piece of gossip before it hit the wire or anything mainstream, the streets, the underground, or the grapevine, and if she didn't get it correct, she made it up—anything to make her show controversial. Dishing dirt was her forte and no other jock could fuck with her when it came to throwing mud. She barred no blame, and was always on the top of her game.

"This is the new joint by Fabiola Mays." "Touch Me" played in the background. "For the fellas, this PYT looks just as good as she sings, and she can sing her damn aspirin off," she said in her strong upstate New York accent. "But girls and boys don't think I've gone soft and won't produce the goods on our PYT. It turns out that Ms. Fabiola 'Fabulous' Mays is dating a man at least thirty years her senior. That there is just plain ole weird." Charming offered her unsolicited opinion—as always—across the airwaves of her syndicated show. "I'm working on getting more details on our newest Pretty Young Thing as I speak. So stay tuned in, ya heard?" "Touch Me" continued to play full blast.

Fabiola was upset that her relationship with Casino was put out there for the world to know—she had nothing to hide—but she was vexed that they were making it sound like something perverted and not the genuine love that it had grown to be. She was on the verge of changing the station and never listening to it again when something happened. As she checked her makeup in her compact mirror, Fabiola noticed that the girl looking back at her wasn't vexed at all. How could she be so immature that she almost let her emotions and ego cause her to miss the big picture?

Girl please, when Charming Ching-a-Ling gossiped—good or bad—to her millions of listeners on the radio it translated to one thing: Fabiola "Fabulous" Mays had motherfucking arrived.

She called Adora screaming at the top of her lungs to share the good news.

"Girl, things are so good here. I just made a song with Teflon-the-Don and how about they're playing my song on the radio again and Ching-a-Ling was talking about me on her show."

"For real! Congrats li'l sis!" Adora was equally excited by all she heard. "Well, you know we've all been waiting to hear from you. DJ Lonnie B been playing your shit on blast here."

"Oh my God. I am so excited."

When Fabiola got back to the hotel, Casino was waiting with champagne and a rose-petal-laced bed. After taking her to dinner they spent the rest of the night in each other's arms, until he broke the news to her.

"Spade called me and I have to fly back home immediately."

"What's going on?"

"I'm not even sure. All I know is that it is important." He gazed into her eyes and gave her a firm look, took her hand, and said, "Please, baby. Respect that I don't discuss my business with you. That's the only way to keep you out of prison with a conspiracy charge."

Fabiola wanted to know, but at the same time she had to do as her man asked, so she just nodded.

"Do you think that you will be all right in the city alone?"

"I'll be fine. The question is, will you be fine? That's what I am worried about." She took a deep breath and poured out her heart to Casino. "It's hard for me to see you just ride into the fog knowing that I've seen you almost dead before. I couldn't stomach that."

He cut her off. "It won't be that hardly. More like Spade may know who left me for dead. Now, I would feel better if you let me buy a ticket for one of your friends to fly in and stay with you until you leave in a few days."

"I'm a big girl, don't worry about it. I'll be fine. I want to work on some more songs with Taz, and besides Taz will make sure that I am a'ight. Plus, I'll be keeping myself pretty busy. I've got an interview with Charming Ching-a-Ling the day after tomorrow," she assured Casino.

"This is a big city to be in alone."

"I know, but I'm only going to be here a few more days, and if Shug or Adora came down they'd probably get bored and end up doing their own thing anyway. And not to mention I think my mom may be coming to town because I think she's going to be meeting with that publicist."

"That's right." He remembered. "Well, promise to call me frequently to let me know that you're all right. Can you do that for me?"

"I'll do anything for you, Mr. Winn."

The next day after finishing up with Taz at the studio, Fabiola got a call from Teflon, who asked her if she'd like to grab something to eat with him. She met him and about ten members of his entourage at Shelly's restaurant. They sat in a private back room, and several bodyguards were there to make sure nobody came in who wasn't invited.

Fabiola arrived in a Jolly Rancher–green halter Capri-style jumpsuit. From the time she entered the restaurant, all eyes were on her. Was it the jumpsuit or her walk that demanded everyone's attention as she made her way to the back of the restaurant?

Teflon tapped the dude sitting next to him on the leg. "Get up so the lady can have a seat." Teflon stood to greet Fabiola. "It's nice of you to come." Taking her hand in his, he said, "Have a seat." He handed Fabiola a menu. "Are you the most beautiful person in the room everywhere you go?" he flirted.

"Compliments will get you everywhere," she half joked. She was impressed and surprised by his diction and manners. He was nothing like the persona he portrayed in his videos and interviews, but Fabiola knew she was here for business and not pleasure.

"I'm not going to bore you with the obvious then: You're lovely to look at, a great singer, and you have a mean two-step game," he said. "That's a lethal combination. You're gonna go crazy far in this business."

"Do you really believe that?" She couldn't help blushing from the compliment.

"I do. Every syllable of it. The press is gonna have a field day with you. They love a pretty face and a talented entertainer. Just be careful of the pitfalls and pit bulls."

After placing her order with the waitress, Fabiola said, "Teflon"—it sounded like she sung his name—"I have complete respect for you, almost as much as I have for my man." She hoped that she hadn't bruised his ego, because a man with money and power can be difficult to deal with, but she wanted to let him know about Casino up front to avoid any "misunderstandings."

"Dude's a lucky man. I wish to one day be as fortunate with mines."

"You will."

There was an awkwardness between the two of them that Teflon broke. "You know, be aware of Johnny Wiz. He seems to like you a lot and have an appreciation for your talent."

She shook her head. "I don't think so."

"I saw how he was doting on you and practically kissing your ass. All I am saying is though the man writes me a lot of big checks and shit, I don't trust him as far as I see him, and even then." He shook his head. "That dirty motherfucker will smile in your face and stab you in your eye." He picked up his glass. "So take heed, baby girl."

The Ching-a-Ling Show

"I'm live in the studio with Fabiola," said Charming Ching-a-Ling. "So, Ms. Fabiola, first I'd like to give you a big-city welcome."

The studio at the radio station was warmer than Fabiola anticipated, and Charming Ching-a-Ling wasn't as glamorous as Fabiola imagined from listening to her over the airwaves. Charming was a chicken wing away from being a size 14 and stood about five foot six. Though she was a little thick she maintained it well—it was all solid. She wore a Strong 99 FM baseball cap over her long straight hair, and the cleavage from her implants peeked out of her black Strong 99 FM wife beater. Her dark-blue stretch jeans were strained to their limit by her butt implants.

"Thanks so much! I love New York."

"You're actually from a town in Virginia, right?" Charming asked as if she really weren't sure of the answer. But make no mistake about it: Charming Ching-a-Ling had done her research.

"That's right," Fabiola confirmed.

"You have that real down-home Southern belle air about you. Your mannerisms and all. I love how naturally pretty you are, not a lot of makeup. You know, my God, some of the people who come through here, ump, ump, ump"—she shook her head—"they really can give Tammy Faye Baker a run for her money." She smiled warmly at Fabiola.

Fabiola laughed at the dig, while trying to guess some of the people Charming was referring to. Charming kept the show moving right along. "New York City, you know I give props where props are due, and no one has a problem with that. It only gets complicated when props are not due and I talk about it." Charming's thick New York accent kicked in. "But that's neither here nor there today. Seriously, Fabiola is really pretty—just as pretty as her pictures."

Fabiola knew to bring her A game to the Ching-a-Ling show, because that's what Charming did: she gossiped and talked about everything from baby daddies to fashion. Lord knows, Fabiola didn't want Charming calling the fashion police on her, like she did some of the other celebrities, on or off the show. So she just smiled on the outside and was happy on the inside that she had met the "Charming Approval."

"I can tell that you are extremely fashion conscious, Fabiola. Most of the time you're dressed like you stepped off of Fifth Avenue. You really be getting your grown and sexy on."

"Actually, that's more of my sister's department—Adora." Fabiola was glad to give her sister credit. "She's always been into fashion and design for as long as I can remember. She puts together all of my outfits."

"When you say for a long time, how long are we talking?" Charming was famous for throwing mud, but not today. Viola had given her daughter charisma, and Fabiola's charm could mesmerize a snake.

"Since I was like three or four years old."

"Wow, she should look into her own clothing line. Big shouts out to Adora!" Charming yelled.

"Thanks, sis!" Fabiola gave her sister a shout-out, then redirected her attention to the conversation at hand. "She will, all in due time. She's been spending so much time trying to make sure that I have what I need that she hasn't been able to focus on anything else. But now hopefully she will have time."

"That's sweet of your big sister." Charming shifted the subject. "So, I've heard that you have been spending a lot of time here. Is it because you are dating Teflon-the-Don?"

Fabiola was shocked the rumor mill had created that lie, and she hoped that Casino didn't hear it and take it to heart. *Well, he knew better anyway. Casino knows my heart belongs to him and him only,* she thought to herself, but she showed no emotion and calmly told Charming, "No, we're not dating at all. We did a song together called 'A Boss Chick.' If I must say so myself, the song is hot. As a matter of fact, I have it with me today to début it on your show. We wanted you to be the first place to spin it."

"That's really big, and thanks for letting us be the first to hear it." Fabiola smiled, but Charming wasn't finished with her. "A song isn't all you two have in common, because my sources tell me that the two of you were engaged in an intimate dinner, and he was spotted in Giuseppe Zanotti on Madison Avenue buying you shoes." Charming batted her eyes and put on a cardboard smile as if she had Fabiola cornered.

"We *were* at dinner a couple of weeks ago and shout-outs to the people over at Shelly's—their food is really delicious—but the intimate dinner you spoke of was more of an innocent get-together with ten or so other people in celebration of the new song we had just finished recording a day earlier."

"And the shoes are also innocent?" Charming's eyebrows rose. "Because I know for a fact that Teflon doesn't even shop for himself, sooooo for him to go into the store and shop for you . . . it must be special."

"That was just a thank-you present for singing on his song. That's all."

"Well, insiders told us that he got you a Rolex watch as well. Surely that isn't just a thank-you present."

"I don't know anything about a Rolex watch from Teflon."

"I see that you are wearing one now?" Charming's red lips shot the questions out. "And a really nice one at that. Y'all let me say this: Ms. Fabiola has a Rolex on that looks like it's from Antarctica, with all that ice on it making wintertime in New York look like Miami in May. Okay?"

"Thank you so much, but this is from my man. He got this for me as a congrats gift when 'Touch Me' became a hit."

"Very nice, and he happens to have very good taste. Is he your sugar daddy?"

"He's older than me and he treats me like a lady should be treated, but he's hardly a sugar daddy." Fabiola took the stabs but didn't bust a sweat.

Not being able to rattle her, Charming Ching-a-Ling changed gears. "Now, how was it working in the studio with Teflon-the-Don?"

"It was wonderful. He was so easy to work with and calm spirited. He welcomed me into the studio and our chemistry was phenomenal, which I think impacted the song, making it ever so hot to death. We got the song down in no time."

Charming looked Fabiola in the eyes to see if she could find any indication that there was something going on between the two, but she saw nothing. "Well, Ms. Fabulous, let's play the song. Would you do the honors of taking us to your song?"

"But of course." Fabiola introduced the song. "New York City, it's my pleasure to bring to you first, my second début song, 'Boss Chick.'"

At the end of the song, Teflon-the-Don called in.

"Charming, why are you giving this nice girl such a hard time? Haven't we spoken about that before?"

"Sure have." Charming laughed it off. "Fabiola knows that it's just my job. Shoot, I have to eat and baby needs pampers, milk, and shoes, and besides Fabulous Fabiola is over here holding her own just fine. Now, how about you tell my listeners how it was to work with her?"

"It was gangsta in its own way."

"Give us the behind-the-scenes scoop on the Fabulous Fabiola."

"I mean, her name says it all . . . Fabulous. She has a wonderful spirit and to sum it all up she's one of the hardest-working women in show business. She's dedicated to her craft—a perfectionist indeed." Teflon gave Fabiola high praises.

"Now, Teflon, you've been known to be a real ladies' man. Is she one of your chicks?"

"Charming, you need to stop it. But to keep you eating, I'll let you know that we are colleagues who happen to have a hit song in common and a great friendship."

"You haven't answered the question. It seems like you are beating around the bush."

"No, we are not dating nor have we had a one-night stand nor do we have a love interest. Fab is happy and has a man, and I respect that. And I look forward to working with her again sometime in the future."

"So, who are you seeing these days? If it ain't Fabiola in your life, who is the lucky girl in your life, then?"

"Nas couldn't said it no better: Money is my bitch."

Teflon-the-Don stayed professional and kept the interview positive.

After the call with Teflon, Charming and Fabiola bumped a little girl talk in between a few more hot tracks. Off the air, they really vibed well; Charming even promised to show Fabiola some exotic out-of-the-way boutiques in the city. Back on the air, Charming put a caller through.

"We have another caller on the air," Charming said to her listeners.

"Hello," Fabiola said. "Can I have your name?"

"You might as well take my name since you done stole both my songs, and you trying to be me."

"What?" Fabiola was caught off guard.

"You heard me, you fake wanna-be-me-ass bitch. You stole my song, and now you trying to steal my place and my sound. You are trying so hard to be me, but you don't want to FUCK wit me."

"Honey, I don't know who you are but it sounds like you have some issues of your own, because I don't do karaoke." Fabiola chuckled a bit. She figured out who it was and she had no intentions of letting any one punk her, especially a disgruntled industry hoe. Besides, controversy sold.

"You little thieving bitch, you."

"Excuse me, I've never been one to steal and I sure wasn't the one that stole that cheap wig of yours." Fabiola dug back at her.

"Oh bitch, you want to go there? Don't fuck with me—I'm from the Bronx."

"And?"

"And bitch, you don't want to fuck with me, I will—"

"Don't talk about it, be about it," Fabiola cut her off.

Charming had no idea that Royce was going to call in, but she loved every minute of it. This show was going to send the ratings off the Richter scale, and that's what Charming lived for. This was what her show was about.

"You only got your break because of me. If I had sung the song your name would be Fabiola Who."

"If, if, if! The only sure thing on if is . . . if you snooze, you lose. And at the end of the day, they chose me and not you to do the song. Besides, I made it a hit. I'd be mad, too if I was you."

"Mad for what? I got a platinum *album*—do you? I'm signed to a *major*—are you?" Not allowing Fabiola to get a word in, Royce sneered, "What reason could I possibly have to be mad?"

"If you're not mad, then why are you calling the radio talking ignorant like some project chick? Pointing, accusing, whining, crying, kicking, and screaming, like a little girl. Answer that?" Fabiola laughed a bit. "Come on, sweets, the people of New York City want to hear your answer. Darling, inquiring minds all over the homes, streets, and offices of New York City want to know," Fabiola said in an exaggerated Southern drawl.

"Because I want the people to know that you stole my song," Royce snapped. "That you are an imposter."

"Is that really the reason why, or is it because nobody will give you an interview of your own? Are you mad at the entire world because you can't grow hair and you wear stocking caps with holes under your bootleg wigs? Chello, is that why?" Fabiola didn't give Royce a second to get in a word before she continued, "I kind of understand, I'd probably be upset, too, and like Lil' Kim would say, 'If I were you I'd hate me, too.' "

"Bitch, it's on. When I see you, it's gon be on and poppin'. Believe what I tell you: I am going to make your walk in this industry a living hell."

"Baby girl, I've been there. I'm a warrior built for this type of weather, so if you feel like this is how you want to carry it, then so be it."

"Yeah, you ain't seen war. You might have heard of hip-hop war but homegirl you ain't seen R & B war yet."

Charming was getting a little peeved that she couldn't get a word in to further flame the inferno.

"You know I really feel sorry for you now," Fabiola said. "It's sad that you should say that, because as a black woman you should know it's hard enough to make it as it is, and you want to spend your time trying to tear another black woman down. That's really sad."

"Whatever, bitch. Fuck a sisterhood. I'm trying to make sure I'm okay."

"I feel sorry for you, I really do," Fabiola said as sympathetically as she could.

"Wait a minute, Royce." Charming Ching-a-Ling finally got her chance. "Did you say 'fuck a sisterhood'?"

"That's what I said. At the end of the day it's about me." Royce held her ground.

"Well, not that I am taking sides, but you just contradicted yourself. All of your songs are about love, friends, and having fun."

"Listen, Charming, if you want me on your show you schedule a fucking interview. And as far as you are concerned, Fakeola," she mocked, "you better get out of NYC, because when I see you, it's on. You country thieving bitch." Royce exhaled.

"Don't let the accent fool you!"

"On that note, since this really isn't your interview and you don't care about being on the Ching-a-Ling show, see you and I wouldn't want to be you!" Charming disconnected the line on Royce and laughed.

"So, we understand that Royce is really angry because of the wig incident and because you are exceptionally talented. Not only do you do what it takes to go to the top, you have what's most important: the right attitude. I know your interview was scheduled to be up a while ago but I would love for you to stick around and hear what callers have to say about you and Royce's conversation."

"I would love to, because at the end of the day it's about the fans, the listeners, sisterhood, and having great friends and supporters."

They took a commercial break, and while they were off the air, Charming told Fabiola, "After this interview every single radio show is going to want you, so get ready for a ride and don't forget about little old me who gave you your first interview."

Touch Me

It was a little after nine in the morning. Fabiola was hugging the pillow in the presidential suite when the phone rang.

"Hello?"

"Hello, baby. You okay?" Casino had been concerned about Fabiola ever since the Charming Ching-a-Ling interview. He wanted to fly back to New York to be by her side, so she wouldn't have to go through the drama alone, but Fabiola was having none of it. She said she was a big girl and could take care of herself. He needed to take care of whatever it was that made him have to go back to Virginia in the first place.

"I told you yesterday that I was fine, Casino. The only problem I'm having is that I miss sleeping in your arms at night. This bed is so big without you."

"That crazy girl did threaten you," Casino reminded her. "You can't take that type of thing lightly, ya know?"

"Royce? She's all bark and no bite. But there is something you can do for me."

"Name it."

"Tell me what you're wearing." She wanted to change the subject to something more pleasurable.

"What I'm wearing?" For a second he was wondering what that had to do with anything, and then it hit him. "Okay, I got you." Casino looked down at his attire, as if he had to be reminded of what he had dressed himself in that day. "I got on those Gucci pajamas you persuaded me to buy when we went shopping the other day."

"Take them off and come play with me," she teased.

"It depends on what you have in mind." Casino was warming to the mood. "Tell me what *you're* wearing."

She was touching herself where it mattered. "Nothing . . . nothing but a smile."

"In that case how does my hand feel nestled between your legs?" he played along. "You feel so hot and tight."

"I love when you play with my little kitten like that," Fabiola cooed. "She misses you." Since they took their relationship to the next level Fabiola found herself wanting to be with Casino more and more. Every time she slept alone all she thought about was him touching her.

"Do she mind if I take a sip of her warm milk?" he asked, moistening his lips with his tongue.

"She wouldn't mind that at all. To be honest, she'd like that very much." Fabiola kicked the sheets off of her naked body, looking around the room for her suitcase; it was on the floor by the closet where she left it. She got up to retrieve what she needed to make the experience a little livelier. She laid back down, spread her legs wide-open, and began to put the vibration on her clit.

Casino could hear the slight hum of the rabbit vibrator through the phone and felt himself growing to the idea. "Ummm, this is good, baby. It's sweeter than before, have you been eating something to make it that way?"

The stimulation of the rabbit pulsating on her clit, combined with hearing Casino's deep voice, took her where she wanted to be, where she needed to be. "It's the same sweet young kitten as always. It just tastes like that because it's been a while since you visited her like this."

"Put your hand on this," he said into the phone. "You feel how hard it is, baby?"

"Oh, yeah, it's rock hard. Did it get that way just for me?" she panted, her face a mask of pure ecstasy.

"Do you want to take it for a swim?"

Eyes in the back of her head, she said, "Yes, please, take it for a swim with me."

"You don't have to beg," he told her, "I'm testing the water right now, but I'm only part way in."

"P-put"—her breath caught—"it all the way in. D-don't you want to get wet?"

Casino was hard as penitentiary steel for real, and he wished she were there with him. "I'm going a little deeper," he continued the role play. "Do you feel it?"

"Do I?" Fabiola had the vibrator on high, her legs stretched straight out, muscles taut, toes curled under the balls of her feet. "Please don't stop. Whatever you do, don't stop"—breathing hard—"Uh . . . Uh . . . Uh."

"I'm not going to stop, baby. You want me to put it in deeper . . . harder."

"Oh my God," Fabiola shouted her imagination into over-drive. "P-please d-don't s-stop, I'm almost th-there . . ."

Casino was happy one of them could get off that way. "Then enjoy the ride, baby, enjoy the ride." And she did.

Animal Planet

Casino, Tonk, and Spade were gathered in Casino's sitting room, when the telephone rang. Tonk picked it up, "Hello? It's for you." He handed the phone to Casino.

"Who is it?" Casino asked, phone in midair.

"Fabiola's mother?"

Casino answered with an amused look on his face. "How are you, Ms. Mays?"

"You can call me Viola just like everyone else, Mr. Casino."

"Okay. Then I must insist that you leave the 'Mr.' off of my name—Casino will do just fine."

"Fair enough," Viola agreed.

"Now that we have what we should call one another out

of the way, to what may I ask do I owe the honor of this call?" Casino asked.

"Well, it's about Fabiola."

"I figured that much. What about Fabiola?"

"I want to start a record label for her, and I want you to be partners with me." Viola just put her cards on the table, not knowing how Casino would react. She was willing to throw long shots—that's how bad she wanted to make this happen.

"I think that's a wonderful idea—I even have a name for it." Ever since Casino had had the talk with Tonk he had been thinking about the exact same thing. "How about we call it Ghetto Superstar? That is, if that's all right with you?"

"I'm not sure about that name, Mr. Casino—why 'Ghetto Superstar'?"

"So now we're back to the 'Mr.' stuff?" Casino teased.

"I'm sorry, M—I mean, Casino. It's just such an odd name for a record company. Why that?"

"Because Fabiola will be a superstar, and she was born and raised in the ghetto. What could be better fitting?"

"Now that you put it like that, I think I like it. It has a sort of ring to it."

"Then all we have to do is talk to the lawyers to draw all the paperwork up. How about I get back to you tomorrow with all the formalities?"

"That'll be wonderful," Viola agreed and hung up the phone.

Casino placed his phone back on the hook as well. Now he looked to Tonk and Spade. "Where were we?"

"I've been keeping my ear to the streets. I heard a pair of twins may have been responsible for the attempt on yo life, Pops. Word is they up-and-coming killers-for-hire; teenage wanna-bes dat go by the names Li'l Ali and Baby Hova."

Casino was quiet for a second, and Spade continued, "The information I got is pretty reliable, Pop. Better than anything else we've come up with," Spade said.

"But," Casino questioned, "is it enough to have them killed in retaliation for something they may or may not have anything to do with?" He looked at both Tonk and Spade.

"I think it is," Spade said. "If for nothing else then to send a message to the next son-of-a-bitch that might have some'en stupid on his mind."

"What about you, Tonk?" Casino asked his longtime friend and employee.

"I want the coward bitches that done this shit to you dead as much as anybody else in this room, but I'm not sure if killing two kids that we *think* may have committed this unthinkable and unacceptable violation against you is the way to go." He shrugged. "I mean, we need to know who they are working for and why this was even done. This shit is bigger than those twins, but then on the other hand, I say shoot the fucking messengers."

No one spoke for several minutes. "The answers we are searching for could be as simple as watching the Wildlife Channel," Casino said.

"Pops, with all due respect." Spade looked at Casino like he was still under the influence of medications. "What the hell does National Geographic have to do with us returning the favor by putting some well-placed bullets in the head of a couple of clowns that probably tried to kill you for a few pennies?"

"If you take the time to pay attention, nature can be a blueprint not only for most of man's problems, but for most situations in life." Casino intertwined the fingers of both of his hands in the form of a steeple. "Take the lioness for instance: The lioness sits on the hill for hours watching every move of the entire herd until she is sure of her prey. She's not trying to set an example to the gazelles that her team runs the jungle. She has a purpose for her fatal tendencies—usually hunger. But even on the brink of hunger, and the burden of feeding not only herself, but her mate and offspring, she waits until she is sure, and when she moves she is unstoppable."

"Okay, Dad. I understand what you're saying. I'll keep my eyes open and my ear a little closer to the street. But if and when I find out them punks' hands are dirty, will you let me teach the next lesson?"

"Deal." Casino patted Spade on the back. "This meeting is adjourned. Anybody hungry?"

Before he could chow down, the phone rang again. It was Fabiola excited about the news her mother had just called to give her. "Thank you, thank you, thank you, Casino."

"Don't thank me. Your mother is basically the brains, I'm just bringing the necessary funds that you all need so that the world will know your name and talent."

"That's a big part of it."

"I am excited about the venture though, I will admit."

And indeed he was, but before he could focus on his future, he had to close a door to the past.

Big Things

Over the next six months, not only did Casino and Fabiola grow closer as a couple, but their business soared. With the influence of radio play and the take-off of "Boss Chick," there wasn't a shortage of majors wanting to join forces with Fabiola and the independently owned Ghetto Superstar Entertainment.

Viola's dream was finally coming true. Fabiola was a major player and well on her way to becoming a mega-superstar. All of Viola's hard work and studying the industry was finally paying off. She took an early retirement from her factory job to help run the fledgling record label for Casino.

Casino loved the idea of being the CEO and face of the

label. Fabiola sold more than a million copies of her début single, and they owned the entire pie, distributing the slices to their proper places. Casino was finally totally legitimized, or so it seemed—but he knew he still had to be careful of the FBI and IRS. It was a known fact that they didn't think a black man, with or without a formal education, deserved to have real paper in their world—not legally anyway. But this was a damn good start, and Casino took full advantage of it. Flossing!

Viola didn't take her job lightly. With the help of some pit bull attorneys and some advisors and consultants, she worked out one of the most lucrative first-time deals for Fabiola and Ghetto Superstar Entertainment in the history of Def Jam, or any other major for that matter. The deal was sealed two weeks before Fabiola's twenty-third birthday, but to let them tell it, her industry age was twenty-one. Her birthday, in conjunction with her new deal, was cause for a celebration; something befitting a star.

Wanting to keep his money circulating in his hometown whenever possible, Casino informed Viola of the plan and Viola did what she knew best. She called in Bambi, the best party planner on the East Coast, who just happened to live in Richmond and was known for her extravagant and flawless parties all over the country.

"So, what exactly are your expectations of me?" Bambi asked both Casino and Viola.

"I just want her to know how special she is to me and I want her to feel like the queen of the night." Casino stopped the sentimental spill and thought for a second. "Just the biggest damn party Richmond, Virginia, has seen in this conservative-ass muthafuckin' state since Ulysses S. Grant stormed this bitch. And money is not a factor. You think you can handle something like that?"

"Not a problem, Mr. Winn. What would you like the dress code to be?"

"Nothing less than fabulous," Viola blurted out, and Casino beamed.

Bambi consulted with everyone close to Fabiola and Casino for input on what direction to go with the event, ultimately choosing to go with a white-carpet extravaganza. On the night of the party, just as Bambi had planned, the event took on a life of its own, and Bambi was loving every minute of what she had created. Before anyone knew it, the party turned into paparazzi heaven. They loved her. Fabiola was quickly becoming a media darling. Everyone showed up at Fabiola's party: Johnny Wiz, Teflon-the-Don, Taz, Death Wish, Ching-a-Ling, Ricky and the band, various heavy hitters and industry players, plus other singers and entertainers who wanted to either show their support or just plain old be nosy and freeload on good food and champagne.

The locals that were lucky enough to receive an invite didn't miss their once-in-a-lifetime opportunity to party with the people they normally saw only on television. It was the first time that Richmond's underworld hustlers, players, and ballers attended an event with the city's black high society. It excluded none—even the mayor was there celebrating with a glass of champagne. No one wanted to miss it. The locals that couldn't get in stood outside. Richmond's police department was on hand to help the licensed security guards tackle crowd control.

"Damn, it's so good to see the hometown showing love like this," Fabiola said to Shug from the backseat of the white Phantom that Casino had rented for her birthday.

"Ain't it? And you can say what you want to say, but the city has surely represented for you," Shug said, holding a glass of champagne in her hand and enjoying every second and perk of being a part of Fabiola's entourage.

Casino was already inside. He thought Fabiola should make her grand entrance a little late, and she did. The white Phantom pulled up and they sat in the car for a while, just watching the crowd admire their ride. After sitting there about five minutes, Fabiola told the driver it was showtime. He went around and opened the door, and all the people could see was her blinged-out Giuseppi Zanotti shoes hit the pavement and next came her hand. Then there she was. Dressed to kill in a backless white short dress completely rhinestoned out—the bystanders were in awe and they began screaming, "Fa-bu-lous!" The reflections of the diamond bracelets that were on her long white gloves played tricks with the special-effect lights when she did the Princess Diana wave to the crowd as she stood for a few seconds letting the paparazzi and fans alike take pictures of her. She did a step in repeat with several reporters as she made her way down the white carpet and into the lavishly decorated club.

As Fabiola was being escorted by the people that were fortunate enough to have an invite, but not prestigious enough for VIP, Toy ran up to her.

"Girl, how come you haven't returned my calls?" Toy grabbed Fabiola's hand as she walked past. "I forgive you though. I know you be really busy with all this music business. Girl, I knew you could do it. I knew you could. You said you were going to do it and you did. Congrats!" She blew it all out in one long hot breath.

"Thank you, Toy. That was nice of you." Fabiola smiled as she kept it moving.

"Why is she in here?" Shug asked Fabiola once they were out of Toy's earshot.

"Because you always need some haters to bear witness to your successes, don't you?"

Both girls laughed.

When Fabiola stepped through the door, she had to admit that everything was magnificent. Everywhere Fabiola looked there were white flowers of all kinds: orchids, roses, carnations, catalillies, and one or two she didn't recognize. The entire place smelled like a florist's shop. And Fabiola, of course, was the center of attention. Everyone took the time to seek her out, wishing her a happy birthday and congratulating her on her success. Not wanting to crowd Fabiola or look like the overzealous boyfriend, Casino played the cut and kept a low profile while never letting her out of his sight. Whenever any one person took up too much of her space or time, he would send Tonk, Adora, or Shug to bail her out.

After making her rounds on the first floor, Fabiola ascended to the second tier of the four-level building. Upstairs, K-Slay was spinning the records, doing what he did best: turning the party out.

"I'm glad you could make it," she said to K-Slay after walking over to the booth that he was set up in. She had to shout over the loud music. He embraced her with a hug and a kiss on the cheek.

"You know it ain't nothing for you."

"It would have been blasphemy to ask anyone other than you. You were one of the first to spin my single in New York—even at the expense of pissing off the mighty Johnny Wiz."

It was too loud in the booth for conversation, so he just nodded and smiled to let her know that he was proud of her.

One thing about Fabiola, the girl knew how to spread the love and show her thanks.

A few moments later, Casino and Johnny Wiz bumped into

each another. It was almost reminiscent of the first time they met at Nathan's party.

"Nice party, Casino." Johnny Wiz gave Casino dap and a firm handshake, puffing on the cigar clamped between his teeth. "I've gotta give it to you, you did it up . . . Wizard Style."

"As I told you before, Fabiola's my heart, and I will do whatever I have to, to keep my heart beating." Casino noticed an odd look in Johnny's eyes, but whatever it was, Johnny quickly shook it off.

"You gon marry her?" he asked.

"Eventually." Casino smiled on the outside but he wondered what Johnny was up to.

"She's a pretty special woman."

"I concur." There was a long pause, and then Casino asked, "Are you satisfied with the hotel and other arrangements?" Casino had booked Johnny Wiz in the Jefferson Hotel in return for the first-class accommodations his company reserved for Fabiola and himself in New York.

"Wonderful," Johnny gushed in approval, using his thumb and index finger to form a circle. "And the champagne selection was superb."

"That's the way we do it over at Ghetto Superstar Entertainment. Glad you like it."

Johnny seemed a little distracted. Casino turned and discovered the newfound source of Johnny's attention. The woman was meticulous about her looks. At five foot eleven with almond-shaped eyes and high cheekbones, she could have been a high-fashion model if she had chosen to pursue the profession, but she hadn't. Instead, the curling irons were her calling. There was no denying that she was looking delectable. She always sported a polished look even when she was just kicking around in one of her cute little sweatsuits, making sure that every single one of Fabiola's hairs were always in place. However, this night Sheena was dressed to the nines for the occasion, with thin penciled-in eyebrows and a long thirty-inch Asian mink straight weave resting on her white halter dress. She looked like a million bucks.

"You like what you see?" Casino asked Johnny.

"Aw, man, she's gorgeous!" Johnny practically had his tongue hanging out his mouth.

"I could introduce you to her and see if maybe she can show you a nice time in my city."

"This is something you can arrange?" Johnny Wiz was practically salivating.

"My present to you, friend." Casino smiled and winked.

"That simple, huh?"

"When you're a man with power, everything is simple. You should know that firsthand."

Johnny Wiz watched Casino walk over and whisper something in Sheena's ear. Sheena then shook her head up and down, apparently in agreement to whatever it was he had said to her.

Sheena glided across the floor, stopping next to Johnny. "I'm ready whenever you are." The words blew from her mouth like soft wind.

"This is a wonderful party, but I would rather have a personal celebration with just you and me," Johnny stated, not taking his eyes off Sheena.

Both Sheena and Johnny went over to say their good-byes and give their best wishes to Fabiola. Before Sheena and Johnny were out and en route to the hotel, Fabiola knew what time it was and looked at Johnny. "Make sure you take care of my girl." Sheena just smiled.

"Don't worry; I am sure she will fill you in on all the details."

He winked at Fabiola. "Again, congrats! You deserve it, I really mean it," Johnny tried to say as sincerely as he could.

"Thanks so much."

He then placed a small peck on Fabiola's cheek. He grabbed Sheena's hand and walked away.

Fabiola watched Sheena and Johnny exit the club. Shug asked, "She's gonna really take one for the team, huh?"

"Yup. She's a warrior for real."

"She is that." Shug looked around and stopped. "Girl, I wonder how in the hell did G.P. get in here?"

"I have no clue, girl, but as long as his ass don't bother me, I'm good."

"Do you want me to make him leave? You know if you are uncomfortable, I can go get security to get him out."

"Naw, it isn't worth the hassle." Fabiola waved her hand, brushing the situation off.

Fabiola looked up and somehow made eye contact with G.P. from across the room. He waved, and she waved back to be cordial. Casino walked up and put his arm around Fabiola, and G.P. shook his head, acting as if he weren't bothered that Fabiola was in the arms of another man.

Later that night, there was an all-access, totally exclusive VIP meet-and-greet in a separate secure room in the club. A few fans were given the chance to mingle with all the celebs on hand. There were light hip-hop jazz instrumentals being played while the guests nibbled on a lavish seafood buffet. Fabiola mingled, working the crowd, when all of a sudden a loud ruckus erupted from the other side of the door.

"I can't get in?" G.P. was in one of the bouncer's faces. "What the fuck you mean, I can't get in?" He was loud and causing a scene.

"Sir, you don't have a VIP card to swipe at the door," the bouncer explained, not wanting to rough the much smaller G.P. up.

"Call Fabiola. Ask her. She'll let me in," G.P. insisted.

"If you were VIP, you'd be in there already."

"Fabiola . . . oh, Fabiola, you don't know me no more, huh?" G.P. banged the tinted, glass window on the side of the room. Fabiola could see out of it, but G.P. couldn't see in. He knew she was in there though, and he wanted in.

"You don't know me no more, huh? Why you gon play me? I knew you when nobody believed in you! Who listened to your pipe dreams? *Me!*" He patted his chest. "That's right, *me*. When niggas was trying to kill you, I saved yo ass."

Adora got up and went outside of the room to try to calm G.P. down before Casino noticed his behavior and ordered someone to take care of him.

"G.P." Adora put her arm around him, trying to walk him away from the room.

"You know that shit's fucked up, Adora." Security was on his ass like flies on shit. She tried to convince them that she had him calmed down, but the big burly bodyguards were still on both of their heels prepared to enforce pain to shut G.P. up.

"That shit is real fucked up and that's why I should've just fucked with you." G.P. would not let up on the verbal rant.

Adora was trying to hush him up, but it was apparent G.P. was drunk. "Please," she said to the bouncers, "he's drunk, I'm going to drive him home."

"Don't worry; I am going to make you a star just like I did her. I am. Your pussy better than hers anyway."

Everyone partied until well into the next morning. Once Casino and Fabiola finally exited the club, Casino took her hand and walked over to a beautiful candy-apple-red Mercedes Benz convertible fresh off the showroom floor that was parked smack dead in front of the club and handed her the keys. "Happy birthday," Casino said.

"Thank you, baby. Thank you so much. I love it. This was the best birthday ever." She gave him a big hug and a kiss.

"You are welcome and you deserve it. But listen up, it's rules to this here shit." He gave her a stern look.

She got behind the wheel practically bouncing up and down as Casino joined her in the passenger seat. She put the key in the ignition and the engine's purr nearly gave her an orgasm. Fabiola was so excited and high off of the events of the night and having a brand-new car that she didn't really want to hear any rules. As she put the car in drive, she glanced at Casino, taking her eyes off the road for only a split second.

"It's for your own safety. Nothing too excruciating, I promise." He looked at her.

"First and foremost, this is the first and last time that you will ride with the top down after dark. No exceptions. Secondly, never, under any circumstances, do you ride through the hood with the top down."

"Damn, baby," Fabiola said, shaking her head, "it's like my mother always says. Nothing in life is ever free and everything from a man comes with strings attached."

The After-party

That morning Bambi brought over some of the remaining flowers from the party to Casino's house and handed over a package that had come earlier the day before to Fabiola. "I almost forgot about this. This came yesterday to the club. It was a special delivery," Bambi added.

"Thank you," Fabiola said, admiring the big beautiful box with red hearts on the wrapping paper. For a second she hoped it was from Casino but prayed it wasn't from G.P. "Thank you for everything! Last night was beyond my wildest dreams."

Bambi smiled. "We aim to please, Fabiola. And we do weddings, too," she said with a grin. "In fact, I planned my sister Yarni's wedding and it made all the papers. I'm off to have lunch with her after I leave here."

"Well, that's not in my immediate future," Fabiola said, laughing, "but if last night was any indication, you are definitely hired."

Bambi and Fabiola chatted a few more minutes before Bambi had to leave.

"Hey, sweets?" Casino called out to Fabiola as she was walking back to the great room to join him.

"Yeah, baby?"

"Look and see if Tonk got the grill going."

Just then Tonk came back in the house. "The steaks still got a few more minutes," he said. "And it's hot as hell out there."

"Baby, I am glad that you suggested we barbeque. I can't wait to eat me a rib," Fabiola said. She had been dieting for a week to get into the skintight dress that Adora practically had to sew onto her last night.

"You ain't lying," Shug agreed, then told Casino, "You know Fab can eat food off the grill every day."

"I know she can," Casino said. "The last time we cooked out I barely got any food," he joked. Just then he noticed Fabiola carrying a box. "What's in the box, sweets?"

"I don't know yet." Fabiola looked at Casino. "It's one of the gifts from the party last night. Bambi brought it over, but this one doesn't have a gift tag on it." Fabiola turned the box over in her hands, examing it from all sides.

"Perhaps your little boyfriend left you a birthday gift?" Casino teased, making note that the gift was wrapped in fire-red paper with silhouettes of hearts all around it.

"Maybe it's that Rolex that the radio stations keep saying Teflon got for you?" Spade joked, raising one eyebrow. He had joined in on the conversation as he sat down next to the couple after fixing himself a plate of food. He exited the room as fast as he entered to take a phone call in another room.

"Y'all stop messing with that girl. It's probably from some shy fan," Viola suggested, joining them as she took a bite of corn on the cob.

"Or a stalker," added Adora, who was sitting next to Casino and Fabiola.

"Oh, stop it." Viola cut her eyes at Adora. "Just open the thing, chile."

Fabiola sat down and peeled the beautiful wrapping paper off the package and lifted the top. The foul odor of spoiled raw chicken hit her in the face, almost causing her to gag.

Fabiola screamed and dropped the box. "Oh my God!" She was shaking.

Casino put his arm around her to calm her down while Tonk ran over and scooped up the package. He looked inside and turned his nose up in disgust. "I'm getting this shit out of here." He walked outside with the package in hand.

They were just getting Fabiola calmed down when Tonk returned holding a pair of plastic handcuffs attached to a set of plastic hands. "I spotted these when I was throwing the package out. And there's a note."

"Read it," Casino ordered.

Tonk read, " 'In some countries they cut the hands off of thieves. You better act like a chicken and be scared, bitch!' "

"That damn Royce don't know who she playing with," Adora said.

"Now, baby, sometimes you have to take the higher road," Viola suggested. "She's just jealous."

"That bitch Royce just doesn't know when to let well enough alone. It's fucking on and popping now. Sho as my name is Fabifucking-ol-a, I swear to God I'm going to beat the breaks off this bitch," Fabiola promised.

"Don't worry about it, sweets, I'll take care of it," Casino assured Fabiola as he kissed her on the forehead.

"No, baby." Fabiola was shaking her head. "I have to do this myself."

"Don't be ridiculous," Casino said to her. "Baby, the only thing that you have to do is stay beautiful and keep making hit songs. No need to worry about the small things or people, like Royce."

The fact that she had just thrown the biggest party of the year and was scheduled to make her rounds on all the television music networks did nothing to alter Fabiola's decision. "I can't let you take care of everything for me, Casino. This bitch has crossed the line one time too many and I have to show her that I'm not some weak little Southern girl. Please respect that." Fabiola looked into her man's eyes with conviction.

"Let me do the honors, li'l sis. That's what big sisters are for." Adora took a sip of her Corona and relaxed herself.

"Nope, this one is on me." Fabiola was adamant.

"That's crazy!" Adora shot back. "Let someone else set the bitch straight."

"I need to handle this on my own, sis. But you can come with me though."

"Let's ride then."

"Let's ride?" Viola asked her daughters. "Have both of you gone mad?"

"Mama, this bitch ain't gon ever get it if I don't show her. You have to stand up to bitches like her to make them understand."

"Watch your mouth, before I wash it out with soap."

"Enough of this type of talk. Right now we should be enjoying each other's company. We'll talk about what we need to do about this other stuff later," Casino said.

After the box incident, everyone ate, had a few drinks, then watched a movie in Casino's theater room. It had gotten late in the evening and Shug had to leave. Fabiola offered to walk Shug out.

"That Benz that Casino got for you is crazy, girl. I felt like Beyoncé in that thing, and I can't even hold a note in the shower." Shug and Fabiola laughed, partly because it was true: Shug's singing skills were nonexistent.

"And I like yours, too," Fabiola complimented as they got to Shug's new Lincoln LS. "You know you going to have to give me a ride in it."

"We'll do lunch later this week, or better, I can drive it when we roll out to go beat Royce's ass."

"I like the second idea."

Girl Fight

"**A**re you sure that you want to do this, Fab?" Spade asked from the backseat of Shug's car. Earlier that morning he had discovered Fabiola and Shug's plans to confront Royce, so he forced them to let him tag along or he threatened to tell Casino what they were up to. "We're almost there."

They had gotten Royce's Inglewood Cliffs, N.J., address from Taz, and before leaving the house they programmed it into the car's navigation system. The bottom left corner of the device now showed that they had traveled six hours and their ETA was less than five minutes.

Fabiola kept her head straight forward. "Yeah, I'm sure."

A few minutes later, Shug was guiding the car up the driveway and parking at Royce's front door. "Let's get this over with." Shug got out of the car, leaving her keys in the ignition.

"Let's," Fabiola agreed after finishing off the rest of her bottled water. The girls walked up on the porch.

Spade got out of the car and grabbed the baseball bat he always carried with him for ass-kickings. He did a quick scan of the house; at least there were no cameras. He grinned devilishly when he checked out the place and saw the girls in motion. Why was he kidding himself? He knew he was going to be in big trouble. Casino was going to kill him when he heard about this shit. Shug was at the front door while Fabiola stood off to the side and out of sight.

They were in luck—too bad the same thing couldn't be said for Royce. She pulled the door right open with a telephone stuck in her ear. "Yeah, girl, I'm going to rock that mother—"

When Fabiola stepped into her sight, Royce's eyes grew twice their normal size. Before Royce could do anything, Fabiola caught her with a looping overhand right that knocked Royce off her feet and sent her phone flying across the yard. "Pull that bitch back out here," Fabiola yelled to Shug, not wanting to add breaking-and-entering to the charge of assault if it went down like that.

"My girl ain't finished with you yet." Shug grabbed Royce by the foot and dragged her out the door. Royce was too stunned and dazed to protest, especially when she saw that her freshly done lace-front wig was on the ground.

Petey heard the commotion and ran toward the ruckus. When he came around the corner of the foyer he saw two women wailing on his client and lover. When he rushed out the door to help out, he was held up by a man holding a baseball bat.

"Slow down there, chief. This here is between the ladies!"

Spade said, moving his jacket to the side so that Petey could see the gun on his waist. "Don't make it any more than that."

Fabiola put it on Royce's ass like there was no tomorrow, screaming at her in between each blow. "Don't! Fuck! With! Me! Bitch! Ya hear me?" She wanted Royce to get it once and for all that she wasn't the one to be playing games with. "You were the stuck-up bitch that didn't want to sing the song," she yelled as she kicked her. Then Fabiola heard a voice besides her own and Royce's screaming for Fabiola to get off her.

"That's enough, Fabiola," Spade advised. "Don't kill the bitch. You don't want to go to jail for this bald-headed bitch. You got a career to worry about."

If Fabiola wasn't in her right frame of mind before Spade spoke of prison, she was now. The possibility of losing everything for a nothing-ass bitch brought her back to reality. Casino and her mother were right. Why was she even there? She had nothing to prove, nothing to gain, yet everything to lose. Fabiola stopped hitting Royce and brushed the dirt off of her clothes. "Damn, that bitch made me break a fucking nail."

The three left Petey to tend to Royce's bruises to her body and ego as they got back in the car and drove back to Richmond. There was no need to speed away before Petey or Royce called the police—they both were famous singers. If any warrants were taken out, Fabiola knew she would have to take responsibility for her actions.

After they were safely back, for now, at Viola's house, Fab and Shug told Viola all the details of the beat-down. Viola was livid.

"Child, are you crazy? You know this isn't going to be good for press, nor is it ladylike."

"I think we might be okay, Ma. Everybody heard her threatening me on the radio. I don't think she's going to want what's left of her fans to know how I whupped that ass and dragged her through the dirt. Besides, we have a great p.r. team," Fabiola assured her mother, but Viola rolled her eyes.

"I know we do," her mother reminded her, "and you're looking at that great p.r. team. If this gets out it's not going to be that easy to spin. You could go from being viewed as the sweet underdog media darling to the aggressor."

Fabiola was about to address her mother's concern when she was interrupted by the ringing of her cell phone. "Excuse me, Mother, I want to take this." She hit the talk button. "How are you, Taz? . . . You gotta be kidding me? . . . On the radio right now? . . . Oh my God. Thanks for the news, Taz, but I'll get back with you later. I have to go."

Thug Politics

"Go right in, Mr. Winn," the secretary said after hanging up the intercom. "He's waiting for you." Casino strolled into Johnny's lavish office with Tonk by his side. Once inside he removed his coat, placing it on one of the designer sofas, and took a seat across from Johnny's desk and crossed his legs. Tonk stood in the corner.

"Well, to what do I owe the visit of such a good friend?" Johnny greeted them. "How are things going over at Ghetto Superstar?"

Ignoring Johnny Wiz's question for one of his own, Casino asked, "How's your mother's heart nowadays?" The two men's eyes locked.

"It's fine. Thanks for asking." Johnny smiled as he wondered why in the hell Casino was in his office. He would find out soon enough.

"Good, because I expect that it's going to have to be once she finds out that her only son—the great Johnny Wiz—is engaging in sexual relations with men. I don't think it's going to matter much that the man was very attractive."

"You can't prove any such thing, and she would never believe a street thug like you anyway."

"Well, she'll believe it when she sees this." Casino fished a disc and portable DVD player from his briefcase. "I knew you were not a person that could be trusted, so I provided myself with a little insurance policy—well, in this case a rather lucrative one."

The screen on the DVD player lit up with Johnny Wiz parading around a hotel room in nothing but a thong and black dress socks. A few seconds later what appeared to be a beautiful woman disrobed, showcasing one of the biggest dicks in the history of cocks. Johnny didn't look surprised at all. He grabbed the enormous swinging piece of meat and shoved it in his mouth like he hadn't eaten in a month of Sundays. Casino hit the button to stop the recording.

"I told you that I didn't play when it came to things dear to me. And what did you do? You tried to sabotage my woman in any way you could." Now he was in Johnny's face. "No need to piss your pants. I'm not going to kill you. This is only business. Certainly you didn't think that I would hand Ms. Sheena"—clearing his throat—"or should I say *Mr.* Sheena to you on a platter because you were my friend?"

Johnny didn't know what to say.

"No. It was business and I knew you'd bite. I always study the people that I do business with. By following you I learned your moves, your habits. I found out what had been rumored was not a rumor at all; men are your preference, and I was sure that Sheena would be your downfall."

Johnny's eyes teared up.

"There's no need to cry now—man up. It's time to pay the piper. You have to sacrifice something big to save something larger. This industry is full of sacrifice."

"What is it that you want?"

"It's simple. You are going to sign over forty-nine percent of Wizard Entertainment." Casino slid the papers describing the transaction across the desk.

"I can't do that," Johnny attempted to protest. "My mother will kill me."

"Do you want to kill her first? And how many business deals do you think you can close after the world sees you with your mouth full of another man's business?"

Johnny knew he didn't have much of a choice. It wasn't really his mother that he was worried about. But if that tape ever got out, he wouldn't be worth warm spit in this homophobic industry. Fifty-one percent of something was worth a whole lot more than one hundred percent of nothing. "Where do I sign?"

"Mr. Wiz, your mother is on line one."

"Give your mother my best." Casino smiled as he exited the offices of The Wizard Entertainment Group.

News Flash

Viola was bright eyed and bushy tailed, fully dressed, and having her morning coffee in the morning room of her new 5,000-square-foot house, when she got the call of an opportunity of a lifetime. She called out to Adora, "Are you on the phone with your sister? If so I need to talk to her."

"Good morning, Mother, and how are your doing today?"

"You can save that proper shit for the interviews and your fans, Fabiola. Girl, I gave birth to you, remember? I's knows you's ghetto."

All Fabiola could do was laugh. "Whatever, Mom. What's going on though? You never call me this early unless there's something going on with the family or business." Fabiola knew her mother like a Nikki Turner reader knew their favorite author's novels.

Now it was Viola's turn to laugh. "You know me like a book, child." She chuckled a bit. "It's business all right, and it's great news. You're not going to believe it when I tell you."

From the excitement in her mother's voice, Fabiola knew it was something big. "Try me," she said, holding her breath for whatever it was her mother had in store for her.

"Are you sitting down?"

This must really be big news. Fabiola took a seat on the edge of the bed. "Okay, I'm sitting. Now, what's going on. Please fill me in!"

"What have you been dreaming about ever since you were a little girl?"

"To be a singer," Fabiola answered without a second thought, "and thanks to hard work"—Fabiola got sentimental—"and those who love me—like you, Casino, and Adora—that dream has come true, and I love you all for what you've done for me."

Hearing her daughter say those words made Viola a little misty-eyed. God only knows she and Fabiola had gone through their share of mother-daughter spats getting here. "Thank you, baby, but what else have you always dreamt about doing? Think a little harder."

"Mother," Fabiola said, not having the time or patience for playing guessing games, "just tell me whatever it is that you want me to know."

Viola couldn't hold it in any longer, so she blurted out, "They want you to perform at the Grammys Sunday night."

She couldn't have heard right. "What did you say, Mother?"

"They want you to perform at the Grammys as a surprise performer. It's in two days and they know it's short notice, but it seems that one of the scheduled artists had to back out due to an unfortunate accident."

"Oh my God, Mother! The Grammys! I've wanted to perform at the Grammys ever since I was able to sing. Hell, before I was even able to carry a note." Then suddenly her tone changed. "What song am I going to sing? What am I going to wear? What about my hair? What about my—"

"Calm down, baby," Viola cut in. "No need to panic. Everything is going to be fine. Let us take care of all the particulars. All you need to do is sing your heart out on that stage come this Sunday night. Just promise me that?"

"I will. Oh yeah. When do I leave?"

"First thing tomorrow morning."

"Good"—she let out a sigh of relief—"because I gave Keys my word that I would come see him play tonight."

"That's fine, but make sure you don't stay out too late because you must be on that plane."

"I will. Nothing and I mean nothing is going to make me miss that plane. I can promise you that."

"Well, okay then, my darling superstar. I am going to start making all my calls to get everything in order. I will call you back."

"Okay, Mother, but can I ask you one question before you go?"

"If that'll make you feel better, go ahead."

It didn't really matter, but Fabiola just wanted to know out of curiosity. "Whose place did I take?"

Viola smiled. "Royce's."

That was all the inspiration, revenge, and drive that she needed. That alone would make her sing the roof off the building.

★ ★ ★

"Guurrrl, that nigga Keys did the damn thang up in that piece tonight," Adora gave praise to the piano player from Ricky's dysfunctional band. Keys had been wanting to do a solo jazz gig and finally he took the plunge.

Fabiola was so proud of Keys. "That ain't no lie." She took a quick peek over at her sister before putting her attention back on the road. Adora was definitely a few ounces of Grey Goose over her limit. They had been together since the morning running errands—shopping and paying bills—and Keys's performance at the Infantry Blues Café was a great way to cap off the evening, or start the night. The strongest thing Fabiola had drunk was Pepsi Zero—she never drank and drove. Besides, Casino would never let her hear the end of it if he found out that she did. She was already breaking one of the conditions he had handed her along with the keys to the convertible Mercedes by driving with the top down after dark.

It was a quarter after one and the wind was blowing through her hair as she glided down the black asphalt streets—joyriding—listening to her own CD playing one of the hottest songs in the country. The repeat button was glued to the *on* position and she couldn't stop thinking about how in less than twelve hours she would be on a flight to Los Angeles, and less than twenty-four after that onstage performing at the Grammys. *Dreams do come true.* Her thoughts were interrupted by a beeping sound, and the fuel light came on. "I'm pulling over at that Shell; we a hot second away from pushing this bad boy."

"That wouldn't be a good look for neither of us, gurl," Adora admitted. "I need to stop anyway; my mouth is dryer than week-old refrigerated cornbread."

"Okay"—they pulled into the station—"then I pump and you pay." Fabiola handed Adora a hundred-dollar bill.

"Bet"—she took the folded Franklin—"but we gonna have to cut this party short. If you don't get home in time to get at least a couple of hours of sleep before your flight, you know good and well that Mom and Casino is gonna blame me for keeping you out. It don't even matter that I ain't the one driving a damn thing."

"Chile, I ain't worried about no sleep. That's the last thing on my mind. Nothing is going to make me miss that flight. And push come to shove, I'll sleep on the plane tomorrow morning."

Fabiola got out and stood between Pump 4 and her car watching her sister sashay toward the Shell station, which doubled as a convenience store, to pay the cashier and get something to drink. She expected Adora to stagger, but surprisingly, Adora glided across the parking lot in four-inch heels, as graceful as a ballerina. She smiled as she thought about her sister being tipsy as hell but still on point as she listened to herself coming through the speaker.

"Since when did superstars start pumping they own gas?" someone voiced.

Fabiola looked up to find the owner of the voice. *Damn,* she thought, *Toy.* Not letting a hating bitch steal her joy, she said, "Hey, girl, how you doing?"

"I'm good," Toy said with a crooked smile. "You look cute."

"Thanks, girl, you do, too."

Toy swallowed the hollow compliment whole. "What you doing in these neck of the woods by yourself?"

"Oh, girl, I'm not by myself," Fabiola corrected. "My sister's in the store standing in that long-ass line. I had the honor of pumping while she stands on her feet in that small-ass cramped store to pay." She smiled as if she was getting the better end of the stick.

"Adora?"

"Yeah, girl, who else? That's the only sister that I have."

"Right," Toy said, ignoring the sarcasm, shooting her next question. "Are you and Casino still together?"

"Sure are," Fabiola reluctantly answered. "Why do you ask?" She knew Toy was fixing her lips to say something twisted, but there wasn't anything a no-good hating broad like Toy could say or do to deflate the bubble of good fortune she was riding on. She had a man who adored her and had her back, her song was at the top of the charts, and it wouldn't be long before the entire world would know her name.

Bluntly Toy shot from the hip. "Do you and Adora share him, too?" Caught off guard, Fabiola was momentarily speechless, and Toy knew it. "I mean, since you had no problem sharing G.P. with your sister and all."

"Girl, please" was all Fabiola could come up with. "You crazy as shit."

"Oh, you didn't know, huh?" Toy cracked a disturbing chuckle. "That's how it always goes: The main girl is always the last to know. Well, it's true: Your adorable sister, Adora, is fucking G.P. They tried to keep it on the down-low, but honey it's the talk of the town. Sorry I had to be the one to break the mind-blowing news."

"You a sad bitch." Fabiola shook her head and cut loose. "You have nothing better to do than fabricate lies about people." She replaced the gas pump handle in its proper place.

"I may be a sad bitch, but it's true—yo sister been fucking yo man from day one."

Truly caught up in the conversation, Fabiola didn't even see the two guys were beside her until she heard, "Give me everything out your pockets, your pocketbook, the keys to this fly-ass whip, and those Gucci boots you're wearing, too," the shorter of the two jackers said. The deep voice sounded cartoonish coming from such a small body; he couldn't have been much taller than five foot three. If he hadn't been holding a foot-and-a-half-long machete, Fabiola probably would have tried to take him out with a swift kick to the nuts.

"Bitch, this ain't no joke," the second carjacker barked. "Give us yo shit."

Fabiola begin to slowly take off her jacket and then her boots. The short one looked at Toy and she took off her rings and necklace.

"Y'all bitches ain't acting like hoes that wanna live. Hurry the fuck up."

Fabiola and Toy moved as fast as they could.

"What the fuck?" Adora screamed when she walked out of the service station and peeped what was going down.

No one paid her any mind.

She dropped her bag containing bottled water and plain M&M's, then shoved her hand inside the imitation designer pocketbook.

"Don't make me have to tell you again," the cartoon character said, talking to Fabiola.

Pop! Pop! Pop!

"Oh, shit," one of the jackers screamed. "I'm hit!" He was so shocked that he had been shot that he started dropping things to focus on his wound.

His partner had already taken off running. Before Adora could get off another shot, the knife-wielding jacker was in the wind, too, limping, while Adora rushed to her sister's side.

"Oh my goodness." Fabiola was in shock but managed to grab her stuff off the ground.

"Give me the keys! Come on, we gotta get the fuck out of here."

"They took my keys."

Adora ran over a few feet and grabbed some of the stuff that they had taken—Fabiola's jacket, boots, the keys, and her purse.

Adora hopped behind the wheel while Fabiola jumped in the passenger seat.

"Hand me your cell phone so we can call the police."

"Ain't no need. You know dem niggas ain't pressing charges. They were trying to jack you. And we don't need that kind of press anyway. We need to get you home, and get ready for your flight." Adora pulled off and took another look around and noticed Toy for the first time, hiding under a blue '92 Taurus. There was no time to bond with Toy now, they had to get the hell out of there.

"You all right, girl?" Adora asked her sister as she stuffed the gun back in her bag and turned out of the parking lot.

"I'm a'ight. I just can't believe that happened to me."

"It's my fault. You shouldn't have been pumping gas."

"No, it's not your fault at all. It's mine. I should have listened to Casino and not disobeyed his rules. I gotta call him." Fabiola didn't know what to do next. She was scared. She was shaking as she dialed his number.

"Hang up. We will tell him when we get there."

Fabiola noticed how calm Adora was. "Where did you get a gun? I didn't know you had a gun."

Looking a little anxious, Adora said, "I got it from G.P."

"G.P.?" she questioned. Then her phone rang. It was Casino calling back.

"Don't tell him or anyone what happened," Adora whispered. Fabiola wasn't ready to share the details of the night with Casino right away, so she only told him she was on her way home to him.

Once she was done talking to Casino, the conversation

picked up where it left off. "Sister, it's not what you think. Please, let's not talk about this now."

"Why not? It seems like everybody else is."

"It's not what you think. It's just not," Adora said to her sister. "Mommy cannot know about what happened tonight."

"But what about G.P.?"

"He can't know either," Adora responded.

"I didn't mean that. I meant, what's going on with you and him?"

"Nothing, we are just cool."

"Toy said y'all are fucking with each other."

"That's not true. I swear it's not true."

Fabiola could tell her sister was lying through her teeth. She was hurt but she couldn't bring herself to hate her sister, the same sister who had been living in her shadow all her life and had just saved her life.

The ride to Casino's was quiet.

★ ★ ★

Fabiola entered the house, and as she headed to the master suite to try to wind down from the drama, she overheard Spade and Casino talking.

"Pop, I am sorry that of all the people it had to be her."

"Yeah, me, too."

Spade was silent a moment before speaking again. "I mean, I always thought she would be your ride-or-die, bottom bitch."

"I guess she got tired of waiting for me to commit to her." Casino shook his head. "Maybe she felt that if I had to lean on her and if I was fucked up, then maybe I would be able to appreciate her more."

"But then Fab fucked that up, because she came into the picture. But still that shit is crazy. Because I thought that bitch really cared about you."

"You know, son, one thing you will learn is that women are complicated creatures."

"But one thing that you taught me is that a snake is a snake, a rat is a rat. And we deal with them all in the same way."

Casino took a deep breath and said, "She will be dealt with, son."

★ ★ ★

Fabiola quietly tiptoed halfway back down the steps and then called out, "Honey, I'm home."

"I'm in here," Spade called out to be funny and break up the tension.

With all that she had heard, she knew that Casino had a lot on his mind and decisions to make and didn't want to add to his problems with her stresses. The carjacking was one of those things that would just be her and her sister's little secret. Especially since she had only an hour or so left to spend with Casino, she wanted to enjoy those last minutes in his arms as if they were their last.

In a Blink of an Eye

Fabiola looked absolutely magnificent as she walked down the red carpet toward the performers' entrance of the Kodak Theater in LA preceded by Kanye West, Akon, and Lil Wayne. She wore a beautiful ocean-blue gown—made especially for her—by none other than Adora.

"Fabiola." A correspondent from Entertainment Tonight walked up to her, putting a mic in her face. "May I ask you a few questions?"

"Sure," Fabiola said, smiling.

"First of all, I want to tell you how marvelous you look in that dress. Did your sister make it? I heard that she makes most of your clothes."

"Yes, my sister, Adora, created this as well as the outfit that I'm performing in tonight."

"I can't wait to see it. You've become somewhat of a fashionista these days."

"That's so sweet. Thank you."

"I'm happy that you were able to make it. I've heard that you were asked at the last minute to perform due to a cancellation."

"Well"—Fabiola gave the cameras a smile that lit up half the block—"I'm just happy to be here. Performing at the Grammys has always been a dream of mine since I was a little girl. I also want to thank Royce for recommending that I take her place, and I wish her well." Fabiola blew a big kiss at the cameras. "Ciao."

The reporter looked back into the camerea. "Fabiola Mays is really turning into America's Sweetheart."

Fabiola was a little nervous as she sat backstage waiting to go on. To calm her nerves, she and Casino sent text messages to each other.

—I'm sitting backstage waiting to go on, nervous, I just keep thinking about you . . . my superstar.

—I'm sure all superstars get nervous but you have nothing to worry about. You are the best at what you do plus you my wifey.

What? Wifey! Fabiola smiled and was taken by the thought of being Casino's wifey. She needed clarity. What exactly did that mean?

—Wifey? Sounds like music to my ears. Are you sure about that?

She had to know.

She'd just pushed the send button and was waiting for Casino to reply, when she got her cue indicating that it was time to set up. She was next. *Damn it!* She didn't want to leave her phone, because she was eager to know Casino's response. Fabiola took a deep breath and handed her phone to Adora.

"Hold this, Adora, until I come back."

"No problem! Break a leg."

"I certainly hope not," Fabiola shot back with a smile.

"You know what I mean, sis. Give 'em all they lookin' for and then some. I'll be right here when you finish," she said excitedly.

Fabiola nodded. She met the stage director at the door and followed him to the prop she would use to make her grand entrance.

Fabiola's heart was beating a million miles a minute until the lights came on and she heard the orchestra playing her music and the people screaming. She rocked the stage and when she finished singing everybody in the theater was on their feet screaming for more.

Right after her best performance yet, she went backstage and everyone congratulated her. Shug gave her a big hug but sported an even bigger smile as she handed her friend her purse and BlackBerry. "Girl, this thing has been going off like crazy." As they began to leave the area, Fabiola redirected her attention back to her phone to see if Casino had responded to her.

Her phone was flooded with over sixty new text messages from people congratulating her. She scrolled through the names and numbers trying to find Casino's message and noticed a strange area code, 609, that she didn't recognize right away. She decided to open it.

—Always remember what goes up must come down.

At that moment she knew it was from Johnny Wiz, because she remembered something he had said months ago, not to mention the strange area code.

Hater! She smiled because she knew she had made it. This was indeed the happiest day of her life. She finally found Casino's text, the text she had been looking for, and was high off all the energy going on around her. She had just rocked the Grammys and the crowd was still going crazy over her and now the love of her life, her knight in shining armor, the man of her dreams, was about to make the ultimate commitment to her. Talk about flying on cloud nine. She was high. She clicked on the text message to open it and was about to read it, when someone came up to her and said, "Fabiola Mays?"

"Yes." She smiled, never looking up.

"You have been charged with aggravated assault in the shooting of Victor Lewis."

"What?" She looked up. "What are you talking about?"

"You have the right to remain silent. Anything you say can and will be used against you . . ." Fabiola didn't hear the rest. She was in a daze as six police officers almost swept her off her feet and cuffed her. Before she knew it, she was being whisked through a crowd and into a squad car. Although she wanted to break down and cry, she held it in, because she didn't want the world to see her sweat. Paparazzi clicked pictures and the crowd went bananas.

What had been the best night of her life had turned into her worst. And as she sat in the back of the police car, she saw all that she had worked for slipping away. She glanced back and caught her sister's eye.

Was Adora smiling?

Acknowledgments

First and foremost, I HAVE to thank my God above who watches over me around the clock and allows me the great opportunity to touch so many lives, through a gift that HE gave me.

Next, I would like to thank my children, Kennisha and Timmond. Though you've both grown up so much you will always be my babies. The love of my life, I have to thank you for your patience with me, whether I lose, win, or draw, you always got my back.

My little sister, Chunuchi! I will never forget that day when it was pouring down rain and I was so sad because I thought my day was going to be ruined, and you told me that the rain was just the haters crying. That's when I knew you were my little sister. My dear friend, Yvette Caslin, I thank you for the vacation to Mexico, it was the perfect gift after I finished my edits. I am still laughing at all the fun we had. Kenya Howard, thank you for always telling me to push on and for being ready to pitch in wherever I needed you to.

My dear friend, big brother, and life coach, Damon "Dee Swagger" Williams, you navigate me through this crazy world all while keeping me laughing, so uplifted.

Marc, my agent, I thank you for always thinking outside the box when it comes to my career. I love you and wish you the very best in all aspects of your life. Melody, I thank you so much for all the time you spent molding this book into such a fabulous book. Jane, Sarina, Dreu, Porscha, and the entire Random House family, for your undying support, hard work, and for making this all possible for me and Nikki Turner Presents.

The authors of Nikki Turner Presents, Seven, Freeze, and Dana, I am wishing you all the best of luck in all your endeavors.

Styles P, thank you so much for my dog; you were right, she has touched my life.

To my loyal Nikki Turner readers, I would never be able to do any of this without you. I thank you from the bottom of my heart.

About the Author

NIKKI TURNER is a gutsy, gifted, courageous new voice taking the urban literary community by storm. Having ascended from the "Princess" of Hip-Hop Lit to "Queen," she is the bestselling author of the novels *Black Widow, Forever a Hustler's Wife, Riding Dirty on I-95, The Glamorous Life, A Project Chick,* and *A Hustler's Wife,* and is the editor of and a contributing author to her Street Chronicles series. She is also the editor of the "Nikki Turner Presents" line, featuring novels from fresh voices in the urban literary scene. Visit her Website at nikkiturner.com, or write her at P.O. Box 28694, Richmond, VA 23228.